River of Light

River of Light

Wendy Schultz

Cover design: Mike Karpa

Cover image: Peter Barreda

Author photo © Robert Payne

Published by Mumblers Press LLC, San Francisco CA USA

ISBN 978-1-963221-00-8 (paperback) | 978-1-963-221-01-05 (e-book)

LCCN: 2023923183

This book is for my Aunt Ria, who opened her expansive library to me without restriction and who talked with me, as an equal, about philosophy, metaphysics, and good books. Thank you, Auntie.

Contents

Part One

Chapter One

June 1996

The courthouse steps under her butt were as hard as rocks. She looked at them—they *were* rock. Some kind of white stone, maybe marble. Marble came from limestone, a metamorphic rock. She knew stuff like that: igneous, sedimentary, and metamorphic rock; all fifty states and their capitals; the names of the kings and queens of England. She wished she knew how to drive a car instead. She wished she was old enough to drive a car.

The click of high heels sounded behind her, coming from the courthouse. Not the right heels—it was a judge's solid shoes she was listening for. Stealthily, she wiped a trickle of sweat from her temple and rubbed it on her denim cutoffs. Her sockless feet in red high top Converse felt like they'd been greased. Ninety-five degrees according to the display on the side of the bank along with the time, 12:58.

Heavy footsteps sounded on her right side. She looked up as a pair of blue pin-striped legs stumped past her. The legs belonged to a tall, white-haired man wearing a gray long-sleeved shirt. He carried a briefcase in his right hand. From the back, he kind of looked like the picture of the judge in the newspaper. He looked solid, anyway. She sprinted down the steps after her quarry.

"Sir?" She planted herself on the sidewalk in front of him.

He stopped, peered down at her and said, "Yes?"

"Sir, are you Judge Potts?"

He was wearing sunglasses with mirrored lenses and he slid them down his nose as he said, "Yes, I am. If you have an upcoming court case, I can't talk to you."

She shook her head and pushed her sweat-soaked curls off her forehead. "I don't think so."

Wrinkles radiated out from the sides of his blue eyes making her think of Santa Claus. He waited politely, although she could see impatience in the way he shifted his briefcase from one hand to the other.

She blurted out, "What do I have to do to get my name changed?"

He slid the sunglasses back up. "Well, if you're at least eighteen . . ." Bushy gray eyebrows rose inquiringly above the mirrored lenses.

She shook her head, "I'm ten—but I'll be eleven in three months."

"Well, then, you'll need your parents' permission for the change. Do you have that permission?"

"She's the one that gave me the name."

"Hmm, I see. Just what is your name, might I ask?" The judge slid his sunglasses down again. His eyes twinkled at her.

"Fresno Bakersfield Ingersoll." She waited for him to

laugh. He didn't, but his eyes widened slightly. Then he said, "What would you like your name to be?"

"Clare, C-L-A-R-E, Elizabeth Ingersoll." The name, with its particular spelling, unrolled from her tongue as smoothly as if she had been an anteater feasting on insects. She'd been practicing for the past two years.

"Well, that's a fine name," he said, smiling at her. "Do you think you could get your mother's permission?"

She shook her head glumly, staring at the sidewalk, feeling the heat through the bottoms of her Converse. "My mom likes weird names. My brother is Barton Tahoe Ingersoll because that's where he was born. Miggie, that's my mom, said she named me after where I was conceived." Fresno delivered this information as if she had said it a million times, which, by her count, she had. "She said she didn't know which place she made me, so I got both."

Judge Potts slid his sunglasses back up. His mouth firmed in a straight line and Fresno could tell he was trying not to laugh. She tried not to mind.

"If you don't think you can get your mother's permission, may I suggest a work-around? That's a lawyer's term for getting something done in a different way when you can't do it the regular way." His mirrored lenses pointed at her.

Fresno's eyes lit up as she looked up into the judge's face, her disappointment morphing into hope.

"You don't have to make a legal change to change your name," said Potts, "but you'll have to be patient and determined. Can you do that?"

Fresno nodded her head so hard it felt like it was still bouncing after she stopped.

"All right, then. All you have to do is to tell everyone that your name is now Clare Elizabeth Ingersoll and that you won't answer to any other name. Then, you have to make sure that you only answer to Clare, and you only write Clare as your name—that's the determined part."

"What about the patient part?" Sweat trickled down her temples under her hair.

"It's going to take a while for people who know you to remember to call you by your new name. They might not like it; they might not remember it. So, you will have to be very patient with them and very determined to answer only to your new name. You have to remember it all the time, even at school with your friends."

That was the most important place to remember it as far as Fresno was concerned. She straightened her shoulders. "I can do that."

"I can see how determined you are," said the judge. "May I be the first to congratulate you on your new name, Clare Elizabeth Ingersoll?" He switched the briefcase to his left hand and held out his right to her, sealing her new name into existence.

As she shook Judge Potts's hand, the newly named Clare Elizabeth Ingersoll felt a tidal wave of hope wash over her. Her first step toward being a normal person—if only she could make Miggie accept it.

Chapter Two

Clare Elizabeth Ingersoll floated the six blocks home from the courthouse, her red Converse barely touching the ground. Instead of the police station, the fire station and the paint store on the corner, Clare saw herself in front of her grandmother and brother, saw the smiles on their faces, heard their voices repeating "Clare Elizabeth Ingersoll" back to her. Grammie Ellen had always said what a crime it was to saddle a little girl with a name like Fresno Bakersfield and tried to avoid using it, calling Fresno "little girl" or "sweetheart," instead. Only when she was really angry did Grammie roll out *Fresno Bakersfield Ingersoll* in ringing tones.

Clare decided she would tell Barty and Grammie Ellen first. She wasn't sure how or when to tell her mother—no matter how she did it, it would be a battle. Well, Miggie would just have to deal with it, since Clare was going to make sure that everyone knew her new name.

School would be starting in a few weeks. Now that they

were living with Grammie Ellen, Clare would be going to a new school. With a new name, she could finally make friends. She'd go early on the first day to talk with her teacher before class began, and then the kids in her class would only know her as Clare. Judge Potts was right, it would work.

Clare flew up the steps sloping up the tiny front yard and onto the porch of her grandmother's house. Through the sheer, avocado-green curtain panel in the living room window, she could see the television. Some sort of game show was playing.

Crapadoodie. Her mom was home.

She slid the chain with her house key on it back under her T-shirt and eased through the front door. If she were quick and quiet, her mom might not notice her as she sneaked past the living room and down the hall.

Miggie was sitting at the table in the L-shaped junction of the kitchen and living room, surrounded by her jewelry making supplies—clear plastic boxes of small gemstones, a coil of silver wire, silver fastenings, a bottle of flux. She held a soldering iron in one hand, poised above a wire-wrapped pendant. Looking up as Clare sidled into the living room she said, "Where you been? Come check out my newest pendant."

Clare inched closer to the table, praying that Miggie wouldn't have one of her psychic moments and be able to read her mind. If she stood too close to her mother, it could happen.

Miggie looked up from her work. "You can't see from across the room. Come here."

Feeling like a mouse about to be swallowed by a cobra, Clare stretched her neck out, a placating look of interest plastered on her face, her eyes fixed on the pendant on the table. The rest of her stayed put.

"It's cool. I like the dragon. Is that jade?" She retracted her neck, prepared to complete the flight to the room she shared with Barty.

"Dragon vein agate." A tiny silver dragon wrapped around one side of a circular, translucent green and brown stone. "I thought it would be interesting to have a dragon on a dragon vein."

Eyes focused on the little dragon, Miggie's hand slid over to a box of tiny jewels in a variety of colors. Her fingers picked up two bright green jewels. Clare was always amazed that Miggie could pick out the colors she wanted without looking. She turned toward the hallway only to hear Miggie's voice.

"Hey, where are you going so fast?"

Most of the time, Miggie didn't notice whether Clare was in the room or not; most of the time she did her jewelry making at her friend Jenapher's studio. Most of the time—just not today.

"Sit down and talk to me."

Crapadoodie.

Sitting down and talking with Miggie meant answering questions. Questions about school, about what Clare was doing, about her non-existent friends, while Clare passed Miggie tools and boxes of beads. Miggie never seemed to pay attention to the answers, but Clare worried that the closer she was to her mother, the greater the possibility that she would spill her new name. And she wasn't yet ready to face Miggie's sure-fire opposition.

Clare edged toward the hallway, trying to formulate an acceptable excuse. Miggie turned toward her, frowning, "What's up with you? You look like you're about pee your pants."

Perfect. "Yup, too much Gatorade, gotta pee." Clare sped

toward the bathroom, knowing that Miggie, absorbed in her work, wouldn't even notice when Clare didn't return.

Chapter Three

Clare Elizabeth Ingersoll. Clare Ingersoll. Clare, Clare, Clare! My mind ran variations of my new name around and around as we ate dinner. Together. All four of us. Miggie almost never joined us for dinner, preferring to drift in and pick up a little of this or that and drift back out. But tonight, amazingly, we were all gathered around Grammie's not- from- a- box macaroni and cheese with its chewy edges and crusty top. It was my favorite meal, but I couldn't wait to finish eating so I could tell Grammie my new name while she and I washed the dishes.

"I have a van. I'll be taking it on the road for the next three months with my jewelry." Miggie's casual announcement dropped like a load of wet laundry onto my happy thoughts. The forkful of noodles and cheese stopped on its way to my mouth as I tried to focus on her words.

She hadn't said "I bought a van," which I knew she couldn't have done because Miggie was broke. That's why we'd been living with Grammie Ellen ever since school let out for the summer, even though Miggie and Grammie didn't get along.

Where would Miggie get a van? Where was "on the road?" For three months? Did Barty and I have to go? Would we have to live in a van? What about school?

Grammie Ellen, her fork clutched like a dagger in her hand, peppered Miggie with the questions I wanted to ask: Where did you get a van? . . . Do you even know how to drive a van? . . . For three months? . . . You're not taking the children?" The last question sounded more like a statement than a question. Or maybe it was an exclamation since Grammie's voice scaled up. "And just where are you planning to go on the road? . . . By yourself? . . . Where will you live? . . . Three months, how will you pay for this?"

Go Grammie. I concentrated on finishing my mac and cheese and waited for the answers. Barty, silently splashing ketchup on parts of his mac and cheese that didn't yet look like a traffic accident, kept his head down. I'd have to hunt up the heating pad—he'd need it for the stomachache he would surely have before bed, one that would have nothing to do with mac and cheese.

I saw my mother take a big breath as she flipped her long golden hair back over her shoulders and pushed her chair back from the table—putting some distance between herself and Grammie. Distance and nonchalance (my most recent new word) were Miggie's style, not direct battle.

I put my napkin on the table and asked my grandmother if Barty and I could be excused. Miggie didn't care about manners, but Grammie did.

Grammie turned to me, fire sparking in her blue eyes, but the fire wasn't for me. I could see her throttle back her anger when she started to answer me, but Miggie spoke up.

"Fresno, you might as well stay so I don't have to say

everything twice," she said, looking up at the ceiling. "Dan gave me a van to use so I can go to the craft fairs to sell my art. I'll be gone three months and, since I'll be living in the van, there isn't room to take you and Barton."

First, I heard "Fresno." How much longer would I have to hear that horrible name? Then I heard "I'll be gone three months." Three months was more than enough time to teach everyone to call me Clare instead of Fresno without Miggie messing it up. It was enough time to start in a new school with that new name and to make some friends who would know me only as Clare. Barty would probably be sad without Miggie, but his stomachaches might stop.

Grammie Ellen launched into attack mode. "Leaving the children here is the only sensible thing you've said," she said from lips so tightly pressed together I couldn't see how the words got out. "Since you've told your children your *plan*, maybe they could be excused so that you and I can discuss it."

Miggie shrugged as I scooted my chair back from the table and grabbed Barty's hand. Neither of us was finished with dinner, but being absent from the fireworks was way more important.

As we walked through the screen door, I could hear Grammie's voice begin to escalate as if saying things louder would make my mother pay more attention to them. It was always this way: as soon as Grammie's voice rose, Miggie would turn turtle and refuse to talk at all. She'd pretend not to listen, which would make Grammie mad. And, no matter what Grammie said, Miggie would get into a van and drive around for the next three months, anyway. Grammie was like a battering ram and Miggie just went underground. You'd think one of them would notice how it always happened, but no, it was always the same.

·   ·   ·

"Let's go for a night ride." I made my voice sound happy and excited. Barty's round hazel eyes looked at me doubtfully.

"We're not supposed to ride our bikes at night," he said.

"It's summer. There's still plenty of light. Grammie and Miggie will be talking for a while. We'll be back before it gets really dark. C'mon."

I pulled my battered bike off the porch and down the steps and then laid it in the grass before going back to help Barty with his. According to Miggie's friend, Dan, my blue bike was a "stand-in" for a nicer bike as soon as he could find one. Dan had given Barty the Stingray bike that had been his own when he was a kid. Dan said it was a classic, which I figured was another word for old, but the bike was pretty cool with its copper frame, white banana seat, and something Dan called a sissy bar on the back. My bike wasn't cool or classic; it was just huge and old. But, as hard as it was for me to maneuver the thing, it gave me a sense of freedom that I loved.

I led the way, keeping to the sidewalk, just in case Grammie happened to look outside. We'd be in enough trouble if she found out we were riding our bikes at night, no sense in making it worse by riding in the street. I stood up on the pedals to ride, not being able reach them if I sat on the seat. Barty cruised behind me, the cards in the spokes of his Stingray making a clacking sound with each revolution of the wheel. When he put them in for Barty, Dan said all the cool kids had cards in their spokes when he was a kid.

I hadn't gotten around to putting cards in my spokes, but now I was glad of my bike's silent movement. It was like gliding, with my short curls flying back from my face in the quiet summer air. There weren't any other kids on our block, just old people like Grammie, sitting on their porches with a cigarette or watching the eerie blueish light of their televisions filtering through lace curtains out into the night.

The sidewalk went on and on and the evening grew dimmer and quieter. I was a silent moth flying through the secret night. The clacking behind me stopped and Barty's voice wailed, "Where are we going?"

Barty was eight, but he scared easily. I had known him since before he was born, before Miggie even knew she was going to have a baby, I'd known Barty—his feelings, his needs. Miggie always told the story about how, at two and a half, I chattered away about the baby in her tummy, the baby who was sleepy, had hiccups, didn't like something in the food she had eaten. Barty still didn't like garlic. When he was ready to be born, I'd dragged Miggie's baby bag over to the front door. I'd felt my brother's panic when he got stuck coming out, even though he was in Barton Hospital with Miggie and I was staying with Grammie in a motel. When Miggie brought him home from the hospital, I was full of joy at finally getting to hold my best friend.

I turned my bike around. As we began to head back to the house, I stopped. "Hey Barty, I talked to Judge Potts today."

Barty's eyebrows raised. "Yeah? Who's he?"

"The judge at the courthouse. You know—where bad guys go and the judge decides if they go to jail or not—like Judge Wapner." At his blank look, I continued with, "He told me I could change my name." I skipped the part where the judge said that I wasn't old enough to make it a legal change. "So now you have to call me Clare. Or Clare Elizabeth. And you have to remember it and never call me Frezzie again."

Barty called me Frezzie instead of Fresno because he knew how much I hated my name. His own name was almost as awful, but he didn't seem to care about it. Maybe it was because he was a boy; maybe it was because Bart sounded like a real name—not a crazy, made-up name. Maybe it was because he was named after only one city. Barton came from the name of the hospital where he was born. Even Miggie had recognized that South Lake Tahoe was too much and had shortened his middle name to Tahoe.

Barty looked at me and shrugged. "OK, cool. *Clare.*" He hesitated before saying, "Did you tell Grammie and Mama yet?"

"Nope, you're the first." I knew he would like that, and suddenly, I was glad that he was the first to know.

Barty grinned and mounted his banana seat. As he rode back toward the house he shouted, "OK, CLARE! Hurry up, CLARE!"

I laughed all the way home, wind in my hair, trying to catch up.

By the time we reached Grammie's house, the sun had set and the sky was streaked with purple and charcoal. We dumped the bikes on the front porch. The house was dark except for the light in the kitchen. Grammie and Miggie were nowhere to be seen—probably in their own bedrooms, which was where they usually went after an argument.

Barty and I slipped silently into the living room. My feeling of freedom from the ride and joy in my new name evaporated when I felt the tension that seemed to linger. Barty turned on the TV and flung himself down on the floor in front of it. I tiptoed down the hall and got the heating pad out of the linen closet for him before climbing into the high-backed swivel rocker—my favorite chair in the world. I felt safe with its arms wrapping around me. When I felt lonely, it was like a friend that hugged me. And it was the best place I could think of to wait out a storm.

Chapter Four

The next morning, I got up as soon as I heard Grammie stirring about. Barty and Miggie were still asleep, but Grammie left the house at seven-thirty sharp every morning, stopping for coffee with friends before going to work at her job at the bank.

"Can I help you make your lunch, Grammie?" I loved doing that. If Grammie was still mad at Miggie, it didn't show –she smiled at me and gave me a morning hug.

She made herself a tuna sandwich while I put baby carrots and apple slices in sandwich bags and told her about my talk with Judge Potts. I revealed my new name and spelled it for her, hoping she would like it.

"Clare Elizabeth Ingersoll," Grammie repeated slowly. "What an elegant name, sweetie. I love it! And you talked to Judge Potts, too." She hugged me again. "I'm so impressed with your initiative."

Initiative. I filed that word away in my mental word bank. It seemed like a good thing, the way Grammie was smiling at me. It made me feel strong and smart.

Grammie added her sandwich to the bag of carrots and apples I had already put in her bright pink lunch tote. She smoothed back my hair and asked, "How did you come up with it?"

"There was this book of names in the library in Pollock Pines, where we used to live." One of the many places we used to live, I thought. In the past two years, Miggie had moved us all over Northern California—from Lake Tahoe to Pollock Pines to Murphys to Cameron Park to Placerville and then again across town to Grammie's house. A lot of moves, a lot of boyfriends and too much craziness.

"There were a bunch of good names, but I finally decided on Clare because it means 'bright.' It was really shady where we lived, so bright seemed like a good thing. And there are a lot of people named Elizabeth—two of them were queens." I liked the thought of shining brightly and, of course, being a queen so I could be in charge of things.

"Well, you are a queen to me, Clare Elizabeth Ingersoll," Grammie said. "And very creative too."

As we grinned at each other, I slipped the note I'd written while we were talking into Grammie's lunch tote. Grammie loved her notes.

So far, I had told two people about my new name and they had both liked it. It was like opening a really great present on Christmas. Thinking about how this new name would change my life filled me with excitement. All I had to do now was to tell my new teacher about my name change so everyone in my class would know. And inform Miggie.

Miggie was part of the reason I'd been up so early. I'd worried all night about how to tell her and what she would do. I hadn't gotten much sleep. I had decided to make double sure that Miggie really was leaving and that Barty and I didn't have to go with her before telling her. "Grammie, will we be staying here if Miggie goes in the van? I don't want to miss the start of school."

We turned at a noise behind us to see Miggie walking into the kitchen wearing the tank top and boxer shorts she slept in, her long hair tousled. Grammie turned toward the sink and began rinsing our lunch prep tools, leaving me to face my mother. Maybe Grammie thought I wanted to tell Miggie on my own, but I sure would have appreciated it if she had waited on washing up.

"You might be the only kid on the planet who doesn't want to miss school," drawled Miggie, helping herself to a mug from the cabinet. "Well, you'll be happy. You and Barton will be staying here."

She didn't seem to care that she was leaving us for three whole months. And even though I *was* happy that we wouldn't have to live in a van and we could stay with Grammie, her lack of concern bothered me. I wanted to bother back.

I blurted out, "I changed my name. Judge Potts said I could. So now I'm Clare Elizabeth Ingersoll instead of Fresno Bakersfield Ingersoll. I won't answer to any other name." The last sentence came out in a sort of whisper as Miggie turned her green eyes directly upon me.

"Fresno Bakersfield is a name that *means* something." Distorting her mouth, as if the name had a sour taste, she said, "*Clare Elizabeth* could be anybody."

"It's *normal* . . . and that's what I want." Defiantly, I stared right back at my never normal mother.

Miggie shrugged. "Why would anyone want that?"

Grammie turned to face us and feeling her at my back, solid and safe, I put my head up and my chin out. "I do."

Miggie looked at the two of us, firmly in alliance. She shrugged again and said, "Whatever. Just don't expect me to call you that, *Fresno*." Then she sauntered out of the kitchen with her empty mug.

Chapter Five

"Little pitchers have big ears."

Aunt Nita slid a look in my direction over the top of her coffee cup. She and Grammie were sitting at Grammie's kitchen table. I could see them from my nest in the living room armchair if I swiveled it in their direction, but today I was practicing invisibility and had my back to them. I knew they were going to talk about something interesting—something I wasn't supposed to know about.

I loved this game. Grown-ups laughed and shushed each other, whispered sentences for me to piece together and puzzle over. How long could I stay in the room listening before someone kicked me out? When they started whispering, could I figure out what they were talking about without giving myself away?

I almost always knew when the adults were lying, even if I didn't understand what they were talking about. I just knew. Part of my knowing was probably because I spent so much time watching them. Another part was certainly the listening I was always doing, but the rest of it was just. . . knowing.

Until I learned to be invisible, I used to say things that startled the grown-ups or I asked questions about things I wasn't supposed to know—like the time when I'd asked Aunt Nita's friend, Audrey, if I could be a flower girl in the wedding. Audrey had looked at me with surprise on her face. I was surprised at her surprise. Maybe she didn't know which wedding I was talking about. So I told her I meant when she and John got married outdoors next June. Audrey gave me a strange look and made a fake laugh. No, no wedding was planned, she said. She and John were just dating.

I was so confused. Was Audrey just trying to keep a secret? It couldn't be a secret if I knew about it. I dropped the subject and three days later, on Audrey's birthday, John asked her to marry him and they decided to get married in June—in Audrey's mom's backyard. And I wasn't asked to be the flower girl.

For a few days after John's proposal, all the adults seemed to tiptoe around me. They looked at me out of the sides of their eyes like I was dangerous and they had to keep an eye on me.

Knowing things I wasn't supposed to know and saying something about it happened a few more times, including when I told Aunt Nita that her baby didn't like cigarettes. No one had even known Aunt Nita was pregnant. She stopped smoking after the miscarriage—and avoided me like the plague for six months. Aunt Nita had been like my other mother, but now there was always a distance between us. I still missed her warm, effortless love, something I only had now with Grammie and Barty.

Sometimes knowing things ahead of time was good, like knowing long before everyone else when the ice cream man was coming, but it wasn't helpful in school. It made me seem too smart and the other kids weren't comfortable around me. More than anything I wanted to fit in and have friends. I didn't want to be the weird kid who was always alone.

It was hard to disguise all the ways I was different from other kids. Miggie wasn't a parent like other parents and we didn't live like other families. I *knew* things, especially about babies, things that no one else seemed to know. It made me feel different. . . and lonely. I just wanted to be like everyone else. Some of the ways I was different were obvious to me, like knowing things I wasn't supposed to and having a horrible name, but other things, like my height, had never occurred to me until the kids in my class began calling me "shrimp."

"Just ignore them," said Miggie when I told her why I was crying. I knew I shouldn't have told her. Miggie didn't know how hard it was to be teased about things you couldn't fix. I went to Grammie with my problem, but she said kids only called me names because they were jealous. It was the first time I'd thought that Grammie was really old and possibly crazy. There was no way anyone on the planet could be jealous of a shrimp with warts on her knees and a stupid name.

Since I didn't have any friends, I taught myself to be invisible around grown-ups, melting into the background, quiet as a mouse and carrying a book around so I could pretend to be reading. Using books and new words to block my "knowing" and to shut out the needs and songs of babies kept me out of trouble. Grown-ups thought I was a book-worm which was fine by me, just as long as they didn't think of me as scary.

My invisibility trick backfired because, after months of opening books and pretending to read, I became so interested in the stories on the pages that whole conversations happened around me without me being aware that anyone was speaking. But not today.

Grammie said, "I don't know why she's with that man. Is he a sugar daddy?"

Aunt Nita snorted. "Well, he gave her a van, didn't he? And bikes for the kids. And he's so much older than Miggie."

They were talking about Daddy Dan. He wasn't anyone's daddy, but ever since we'd moved in with Grammie Ellen, he had been in our lives. I wondered what a sugar daddy might be. Candy? Dan wasn't that.

Miggie met him when she took Grammie's car to his auto body repair shop to have a dent in the door fixed. He was so tall that he had to duck every time he went through a door. That always made me laugh. I liked his calm, quiet voice. He and Miggie went line-dancing together, but even though he showed up on weekends and took all of us, even Grammie, on picnics or fishing, Miggie said he wasn't her idea of a dream guy.

Barty started calling him "Daddy Dan" and since nobody told me not to, I called him that too. He called me "darlin'."

Daddy Dan was teaching Barty how to play catch. Even now, with Miggie on the road in his old van, he still dropped by Grammie's house occasionally to have a glass of iced tea with her, play catch with Barty, and tease me about the new words I'd picked up. Sometimes Barty and I walked the four blocks to his shop, but the paint fumes made me sneeze. I loved watching Daddy Dan painting pictures or flames on the cars, but he said that was only for fun. I thought they were beautiful.

Grammie said, "He's only eight years older. And he has his own business. He seems stable."

"Since when did Miggie want stable ? Mom, she doesn't

even want normal." Nita's voice was scornful. "If he's a sugar daddy, then I'm a walrus. He's hardly Miggie's type. She'll dump him soon enough."

The two of them, with their heads close together, looked so much alike: round bright blue eyes, heart-shaped faces with small straight noses and pointy chins. They were both shorter than Miggie. Only their hair was different—Grammie's hair was straight like Miggie's and cut into a streaky blond bob, while Nita had wavy shoulder-length golden - brown hair. Grammie and Nita were round; Miggie was tall and full of angles, the kind that supermodels had. The only round things about Miggie were her large green eyes. I figured she must look like her father, the one that no one ever talked about. Miggie and Nita said they didn't even remember him. I had those same green eyes, so I hoped I might get some of Miggie's height as well, but that didn't look promising.

Grammie's voice dropped even lower. "How are the treatments going? Are you pregnant yet?"

Nita dropped her voice too. I had to strain to hear her say, "Not yet, but we'll keep trying."

The conversation switched to what was happening on "General Hospital." I stopped listening. Besides, Nita would find out soon enough—despite my best efforts at ignoring, I could hear her little girl.

Chapter Six

September 1996

Every day for a week, I had ridden my bike to school to see if the class lists had been posted. Finally, the Friday before school started, I saw it—"Fresno Bakersfield Ingersoll"— typed on the list taped to the window of B-4, the classroom that housed Mrs. McNealy's sixth grade class. I was in a sweat all weekend, hoping that no one else would notice that horrible name. Grammie saw my jitteriness and told me to calm down. She took Barty and me shopping for school clothes. Maybe she thought new clothes would help.

School didn't start until Wednesday because of Labor Day and Teacher Prep Day, but on Tuesday morning, I rode my bike to the school again. I had to get that name changed before too many people saw it.

There were a lot of cars in the parking lot, but the school seemed as deserted as it had been the week before. I put my bike in the bike rack and rounded the corner of the office building toward B-4, feeling like an intruder.

I double-checked the list on Mrs. McNealy's window. Still Fresno. With Grammie's note rustling in my pocket, I took a breath and opened the door.

The room was pristine. Pristine was another new word picked up during my summer reading, and this room with its thirty clean desks arranged into five neat rows of six, fit the definition perfectly. The whiteboard was pure as snow with only the teacher's name and the date on the upper right corner. Bulletin boards covered two walls, one with science facts, another with a huge map of the United States, the individual states made of foam board. In front of a window was a large metal desk with a pile of packets on one end. A small woman with dark curly hair, wearing jeans and a green and white striped T-shirt, was putting a packet on each of the student desks. She looked up when I slipped inside.

A wave of nervousness overcame me. Would she be mad at me for coming in during Prep Day while she was getting ready? What if she wouldn't change the name? Worse—what if she thought it was cute? I patted the pocket of my cutoffs which held Grammie's note about my name change. I thought about how I had waited on the courthouse steps and the judge said I needed to be patient and determined. I squared my shoulders and took a step toward my fate.

"Are you Mrs. McNealy?"

"Yes, I am," smiled the woman, continuing to put packets on the desks. "And who are you?"

"Well, that's the thing," I said, twisting the bottom of my pink sparkle T-shirt. I turned to the window where Barty's face could be seen peering in. He'd followed me. I frowned at him and motioned him down. "On the class list, my name is

Fresno Bakersfield Ingersoll, but I changed my name to Clare, C-L-A-R-E, Elizabeth Ingersoll this summer. Judge Potts said I could do that." I added Judge Potts's name to make it sound more official.

"Oh. I wondered who Fresno Bakersfield Ingersoll would be," said Mrs. McNealy. "Nice to meet you." She balanced the packets in one hand and held out the other to me. I'd never touched a teacher before, but I took her hand and gave it an awkward shake.

"I came in early so you'd know," I told her. "And maybe you could scratch it off the list before . . ."

"Before the other students see it?" Her voice was kind as she nodded. Then she gave me a straight look. "Does your family know that you've changed your name?"

I nodded vigorously.

She laughed. "Well, that's good—I wouldn't want to call you by a different name when we have conferences."

Putting down the packets on her desk, Mrs. McNealy added, "I can call you whatever you wish in our classroom, but we'll have to change it with the office too."

I pulled the note out of my pocket and smoothed its crease before handing it to her. "My grammie said you would need this."

After reading the note, Mrs. McNealy peeled back the tape adhering the class list to the window and lined out "Fresno Bakersfield Ingersoll" with a Sharpie. Then she neatly printed "Clare Elizabeth Ingersoll" next to it and said, "This makes it almost official. I can take your grandmother's note over to the office right now to make it a formal change." She smiled again. "Could you finish putting packets on the desks, Clare?"

It was the best start to a new school year I had ever had—

Mrs. McNealy had accepted my name. She had even used it. And she let me help. Already, changing my name was changing my life.

Chapter Seven

Miggie returned from the craft fairs in late September, tanned and full of energy. The jewelry cases in the van were almost empty and Miggie had made enough profit to tide her little family over till the end of the year. She spoke of new orders, new design ideas, and wanting to get started in a voice that seemed more enthusiastic than Clare had ever heard.

Clare surprised herself by being glad to see her mother and was surprised again when the usually undemonstrative Miggie grabbed her up in a bear hug. After hugging Barty and Grammie, Miggie produced presents—a set of arrowheads for Barty, a hand-painted scarf for Grammie, and for Clare, a notebook with handmade paper and a decoupage cover of stars and sunflowers. Clare was delighted with her gift, especially after Miggie said, "I figured you might need something for your stories and all those words you're forever collecting."

In spite of the general joy surrounding Miggie and her return, Clare couldn't help worrying that the quiet peace of the past three months would dissolve with Miggie's chaotic presence. At school, everyone called her Clare, not Fresno. She had two good friends—Alanna and Megan. She loved sixth grade and her teacher, Mrs. McNealy, who encouraged her writing and had even chosen one of Clare's stories to put up on the Excellence bulletin board.

Barty still didn't like school, but he hadn't had a stomachache in the months during Miggie's absence. Grammie had seemed more relaxed while Miggie was gone, too. During the summer, she'd taken Barty and Clare swimming in Lake Tahoe, hiking, and to the county fair.

Dan showed up on the second day Miggie was home, bringing a new bike for Clare as a late birthday present. Clare was thrilled with the beautiful green color and the way the bike fit her. Her opinion of Dan, already good, jumped up a notch, since adults in her experience, except for Grammie, hardly ever kept their promises.

Dan also brought flowers for Miggie. If asked, Clare would have told him that Miggie wasn't the cut flower type— she liked picking wildflowers better. But Miggie hugged him too and then the two of them went out to check out the van. Clare challenged Barty to a race on her beautiful new bike.

Despite Clare's misgivings, life with Miggie flowed along smoothly with only an occasional spat between Miggie and Grammie. Soon after Miggie returned, Nita announced that she was pregnant, and the New Year of 1997 began with everyone in the family eagerly waiting the baby's birth in February. Clare went on sleepovers at Alanna's and Megan's houses, loving the spa treatments they tried on each other and the giggling. She filled her new notebook with big words and stories, doing her best to pretend she didn't hear Nita's baby.

When the baby was hungry or had the hiccups, this was especially hard to do. And the song—it seemed that all babies had their own wordless song which got louder as they grew. Nita's little girl had a particularly lovely song and ignoring it was a challenge. For the first time, Clare was glad they only saw Nita once or twice a week.

It wasn't just Nita that Clare felt she had to be careful around, but her beloved Grammie as well. When Clare told her that Barty was stuck being born, Grammie had told her she was just dreaming and should go back to sleep; when she told Nita about the cigarettes, Nita had told Grammie. Clare still remembered Grammie sitting her down for a "talk."

"You shouldn't make up things about people, sweetie."

"But Grammie," Clare had protested. "I *heard* him! Aunt Nita's cigarettes made him feel bad."

Grammie had shaken her head. "No—we don't talk about things like that." Her voice was firm, her eyes stern. Grammie had never talked to her like that before and Clare felt ashamed that she had done something to make Grammie mad. Now, even though she clearly remembered Barty's panic and Nita's first baby's anguish, she said nothing about Nita's new baby. Still, she brought her aunt bottles of water when the baby was thirsty, tried not to giggle when she heard the baby hiccup and stopped herself from humming along with the baby's song.

Miggie was the only person who still called Clare "Fresno," but Clare was using Judge Potts's "workaround" idea: bringing her friends over when she knew her mother wasn't home, going through Grammie for permission to do things instead of Miggie—easy to do because Miggie spent most of her time at Jenapher's studio making jewelry and plans for going on the road again.

Next summer, Miggie was taking the van to the county

fairs and craft festivals. She was leaving in May for the Calaveras County fair and returning in October after the Renaissance Faire. Dan mapped out a route and created an itinerary for her to follow. Clare wondered if she would.

Dan courted Miggie with festivals, concerts, and line dancing as well as picnics and hikes with Clare and Barty. Clare watched him with sharp eyes, noticing his every thoughtful gesture, his continual and consistent way of treating Miggie like an adored princess. She wasn't sure how Miggie felt about Dan since she appeared to keep him at a distance. Clare liked Dan very much, but she didn't want Miggie to marry him. She hoped Dan would stick around because he was fun and Barty really liked him, but her experience with Miggie's boyfriends, especially those who had lived with them, made her wary.

When Nita went into labor on February 28, Clare went into the room she shared with Barty and stayed there, even though Grammie and Miggie had asked her if she wanted to go to the hospital with them. She told them she had to finish making a present for Barty's birthday which was coming up in a week. Grammie cocked an eyebrow at her but said nothing.

While Barty was off riding bikes with his friends, the quiet bedroom they shared provided a comforting space for Clare to stop blocking Nita's baby and try to tune into her as she emerged into the world. At first, as Clare relaxed, lying on her bed, she could hear nothing from the baby. She worried that, because she had ignored the baby for so long, she might not be able to hear her now. If she could no longer hear babies, life could be a lot easier than it was now with having to push their voices into the far back of her mind and pretend that she didn't hear them. It might make her less weird and she wouldn't be in trouble with Grammie. Still, it felt that losing her connection with babies would be missing something important, something that was a part of herself. And she wanted to help her new little cousin if she could.

Gradually, Clare became aware of a low monotone. The droning filled her ears, staying at just the same pitch and intensity no matter where she moved and coming, not from the room or outside, but from inside her head. It sounded busy, as if machinery had been turned on. Then, the droning picked up speed and the pitch sounded higher as if whatever had been turned on was now actively working. The feeling of busyness increased.

She realized the droning was coming from Nita's baby—a change in the baby's usual song to a getting-down-to-business song. It wasn't the same feeling as when Barty had been born —there was no panic, no feeling of being pulled, no pressure of metal squeezing a head. This felt like moving, sliding with ease on a purposeful path. And, even though the droning became higher-pitched and louder, it was steady, as if the baby knew exactly what she was doing.

Clare lay back against the pillows on her bed and allowed herself to be carried along with the baby's song. It felt a little like the Lazy River ride at the waterpark, slow and quiet. Then the Lazy River picked up speed and Clare felt her heart begin to pound. There was a brief pause in the droning, a startling burst of light and then the droning continued, fast and loud. Clare began to feel anxious as the droning took another pause. There was another burst of light and then silence.

Clare realized that the baby was no longer in a place that she could hear with her inner self. As the anxiety she had felt began to subside, and her heart resumed its usual rhythm, Clare decided the baby girl must have been born. Now, she was going to have to wait, like everyone else, to find out how Nita and the baby were doing.

Twenty minutes later, as she was making decorations for Barty's birthday, the phone rang.

"You have a cousin!" Grammie's voice was full of joy as she added, "Her name is Taylor Christine and she weighs seven pounds, five ounces. And she's twenty-one inches long."

"Is Aunt Nita OK?" As she waited for the answer, Clare used her ruler to measure out twelve inches against her body, and then another nine. Taylor was already almost half Clare's height. She sighed—another person who was going to be taller than her in no time.

"Juanita is fine," Grammie said, "and Jeff is over the moon! We'll be home in a little while so they can have some time together."

The final bit of anxiety in Clare's stomach released and she ran outside to find Barty. It hadn't been that scary. The baby was fine and so was Aunt Nita and even though Clare didn't want to be different, she was glad that she could still hear babies.

Chapter Eight

In April, when Mrs. McNealy assigned us an end-of-year project to make a family tree, I was excited. With this legitimate assignment to complete, I might be able to get Miggie and Grammie to talk about the missing fathers in our family. I had asked Miggie about our father, Ravi, before—lots of times—but she was always too preoccupied or too busy to answer questions. Besides, Miggie hardly ever answered a direct question directly.

While Grammie was in the kitchen making potato salad for dinner, I positioned myself at one end of the kitchen table with the family tree worksheet and my sharpest pencils. Miggie sat at the other end, fingers sorting beads into like colors while she read a book on past life regressions. It drove Grammie crazy that Miggie could tell colors just by touching them—probably why Miggie chose to do her sorting and reading in the kitchen instead of in her bedroom.

"I have to make a family tree for school," I announced as I carefully printed my chosen name in the bottom box. Not even for this important project would I use Fresno

Bakersfield Ingersoll. Then, I printed "Marjorie Ellen Blomquist Ingersoll" in one of the boxes above my name. Aunt Nita couldn't say "Marjorie" when she was a baby, so Marjorie became Miggie. Grammie and the government were the only ones who called her Marjorie now.

"I don't remember our dad—Barty's and mine, I mean." I looked at Miggie hopefully.

Miggie picked up a red bead from a pile of multi-colored beads without looking and threaded it on the earring wire next to the other red beads. "I don't remember mine either."

Grammie's chef's knife clattered onto the cutting board. The way Miggie said it, it sounded as if it were no big deal. Maybe it wasn't, to her. Miggie's dad had died when she was four and Aunt Nita was two. Grammie never talked about him; no one did. I didn't even know his name.

"But your dad is dead. Our dad is still alive, isn't he?"

"Probably," Miggie muttered under her breath, her face bent over the earring in her fingers.

"Is Ravi his real name?"

She snorted. "Byron Macy Ingersoll. And that is all I'm going to say about that." She swept the beads into a box, picked up her equipment, and went down the hall toward her bedroom.

As little as she said, this was the most information Miggie had ever given me about my father. I printed Byron Macy Ingersoll in the box next to Miggie's.

Grammie had her back to me. She swept the mound of cubed potatoes, chopped onion and dill pickle relish from the cutting board into a big crockery bowl. With my pencil tip hovering over the box above my mother's name, I asked, "Grammie, what are your middle and maiden names?"

She looked over her shoulder at me and said, "Ellen *is* my

middle name." She smiled at me as she said, "My given name is Mavis Ellen Lewis."

Mavis? At my upraised eyebrows, Grammie's smile became a wide grin and a shrug. "I know, it's horrible. So I just always have used my middle name."

I wrote Mavis Ellen Lewis in the box. "So, what is . . ." I didn't know exactly how to ask about Miggie and Nita's father. I'd never thought of him as my grandfather. It didn't seem proper to call him her husband and calling him "Miggie and Nita's dad" seemed as if something was missing.

Grammie added mayonnaise to the bowl and began mixing it in before answering the question I hadn't figured out how to ask. "John Franklin Blomquist." She kept her back to me as she said, "And Ravi's parents are Richard and Carolyn; I don't know their middle names."

She stopped her mixing and said, "I forgot to get Dijon mustard at the store. Can't have potato salad without Dijon. Be back in a few minutes." She grabbed her purse and keys from the table in the entryway and was out the door before I finished writing John Franklin Blomquist.

I knew, assignment or not, I wouldn't be getting any more from either Grammie or Miggie. It was more than I had ever gotten before, and yet less than I hoped for. I'd found out that name changing was apparently a family tradition and now I knew the names of all four grandparents and my father. I just didn't know anything else about them.

As I peered into the refrigerator, looking for a cold drink, I noticed something on the door shelf—a half-filled jar of Dijon mustard.

Chapter Nine

May 1997

"But I don't want to go." My voice whined in my own ears. Miggie had just told me that she wanted to pull me out of the last few weeks of school so that I could go with her on her planned circuit of fairs and festivals. If she'd been like other mothers, I might have thought she just wanted to spend a little time with me. But Miggie wasn't like other mothers, as far as I could tell. Not like Megan's mom, who took Megan shopping and out to lunch, just the two of them, every month. Not like Alanna's mom, who yelled and cheered so loudly every time Alanna scored a soccer goal or her brother got a hit playing baseball. Not like them at all.

Grammie, busily rearranging the spice cupboard, flicked a look over her shoulder at me. What? I knew Grammie didn't think highly of missing school, but her over- the - shoulder look at me seemed to indicate that I should do it.

"I don't want to miss the class picnic."

"We'll have lots of picnics along the way," my mother said. "This is going to be one big picnic."

I doubted it. Going to county fairs and festivals might have sounded like fun to a lot of kids, but I was sure that Miggie only wanted me along so that she'd have someone to pack and unpack the stuff and man the jewelry booth while she drifted off somewhere. As far back as I could remember, I had been the one to remind Miggie that we were out of food or needed to go to the laundromat. I'd learned to change Barty's diapers by the time I was four. Miggie's brain didn't think about practical things like groceries, childcare, housecleaning or laundry. It was as if she were a big, older kid that I had to take care of, along with Barty and myself.

Now, living with Grammie, there was someone else with whom to share the practical stuff that Miggie didn't do. I had been looking forward to spending the summer swimming and hanging out with my friends, not living in a van with my mother for the next three months and packing and unpacking like a slave. I wanted to start seventh grade in September like everyone else.

I was about to register another protest when Grammie turned around and said, "Why don't you think about it? Your mom really wants you to come with her." At my look of disbelief, she said, "If you don't like it, you can call me and I'll pick you up. But you might be surprised at how much fun you'll have."

Miggie shot her a smile, while I threw her a frown of shock. Grammie looked back at me and winked. I didn't trust Miggie, but I did trust Grammie. For some reason, she thought I should go.

"OK," I said, "I'll go."

Even to my ears, the reluctance in my voice sounded like

I was being dragged toward certain doom, but Miggie said, "Great! We'll have fun."

The International Frog Jumping contest at the first fair we went to in Calaveras County was fun, but hanging out with Miggie wasn't. We didn't talk—not even on the scenic two-hour drive from Placerville to Angel's Camp in Calaveras. I tried, "So where are we staying?"

"Hmm, I'm not sure. Probably there's some parking for the vendors."

"Are you going to put everything out or hold some stuff back for the other fairs?"

"Don't know yet."

She turned the radio on. Some country song about being a little too late, a little too gone. Whatever. I picked up my book and pulled out a granola bar from my backpack. From previous road trips, I already knew there was no point in asking to stop for a bathroom break or food. Miggie was like a camel: she never needed to pee and food was something she only ate when she thought about it—like once a day.

When we got to the vendor parking area, we pulled into a vacant spot and it was downhill from there. I made peanut butter sandwiches and unpacked chairs to put outside. Miggie found some guys to flirt with. One of them, Fred Pyne, was pretty cute. He said he was a frog wrangler and his frog, Lipstick Lily, was going to win the championship.

I spent the four days of the fair doing exactly what I thought I'd be doing: unpacking the jewelry and setting up the booth, manning the booth and exploring the fair. I dogged Fred Pyne's every move, but he was only interested in Miggie.

Wrapped up in my sleeping bag outside, I could see the

stars, but mosquitos and the rowdy talking and laughing of the other vendors kept me awake. I missed my friends, I missed Grammie and Barty, and I missed real food. By day three, I had read all the books I'd brought.

We'd be doing this until September—driving, packing, unpacking, eating peanut butter sandwiches, getting no sleep, and not talking. At the end of the Calaveras fair, when we'd finished packing up and were getting ready to drive to Dixon for the next one, I told Miggie I wanted to go home.

There was a silence and then she said, "Whatever."

We drove to a nearby store and Miggie called Grammie from a phone booth. I waited inside the van, biting my nails, wondering if Miggie was mad at me. She hadn't argued or tried to convince me to stay, so maybe she didn't care. I never really knew what my mother was thinking.

Later that day, Grammie and Barty picked me up at the McDonald's in Sacramento just off the Highway 50 exit. Miggie had shuddered in horror when Grammie offered to buy her a burger, and then she drove off in the Greenbrier van, on her way to Dixon. Except for Grammie's offer of a burger, no one had said anything, not even goodbye.

As we rolled down Highway 50 toward Placerville, Grammie asked me, "Why did you decide to come home?"

I finished chewing my french fry before answering, "Sleeping in the van was too crowded."

Grammie's question made me feel that maybe I hadn't given it enough time, that maybe Miggie and I would have found something to talk about eventually. Maybe we would have found a way to work together. But maybe not. If Grammie was disappointed in me, she didn't say so. Still, I handed my french fries to Barty in the back seat. I didn't have room for both fries and guilt.

Chapter Ten

September 1997

"I thought your name was Fresno," sneered the girl. She was taller than Clare— as was everyone—and lanky, with long arms and legs. She swept lifeless-looking brown hair behind her ears and put her hands on her hips.

Crapadoodie. Clare swept a glance around to see who might have heard. The first day of middle school and Marva Doyle had to show up. Clare remembered her from the elementary school she'd attended the last semester of fifth grade, before they moved in with Grammie Ellen.

Kids were walking all around them, but no one seemed to be paying attention. Should she pretend that she'd never seen Marva before or tell her the truth that she had a different name now? This was what Daddy Dan called a no-win situation—when no matter what you did, it wasn't going to change the way things turned out. She remembered something else about Marva—she got into fights all the time, and since she was big and strong, she usually won. Even against boys.

Taking a breath, Clare shifted her backpack straps more securely on her shoulder and said in a brusque voice, "That was before. I changed my name and now you can call me Clare." She strode confidently past Marva—at least she hoped it looked confident.

For a moment, her no-nonsense approach seemed to have worked. But then, two confident steps past Marva, Clare felt a heavy hand smack down on her shoulder, yanking her back.

"Fresno Bakersfield," Marva hissed. "The little shrimp with the big, stupid name."

Clare could see that her mother's advice to ignore was not going to work. She shrugged off Marva's hand and turned around to face her. "Good memory, Marva, the completely unmarvelous beanpole. I hope your memory helps you out in seventh grade." Marva, as she remembered, had been at the bottom of their class. At the other girl's puzzled frown, Clare smiled and said, "See you around."

Even though her knees were shaking and she fully expected Marva to deck her, Clare held her head up and walked at an unhurried pace to her homeroom. Her shoulders were tense, but the expected blow didn't come.

In the doorway of her homeroom, Clare sneaked a look back over her shoulder. Marva was standing still, looking uncertainly around herself. Clare found an empty seat in one of the middle rows and as she slung her backpack across the back of the chair, she felt an unfamiliar bubble of triumph rising in her chest. She'd stood up to a bully and she wasn't dead or even maimed. She didn't feel humiliated or like she should hide in the girls' bathroom to cry. This was new. This was good.

Alanna and Megan came into the room, giggling. They spied Clare and hurried over to sit on either side of her.

"Hey Clare!" they chorused.

Clare felt a glow of belonging. After exchanging compliments on each other's new clothes, Alanna started to tell her about how Megan's mother's car had died right at the crosswalk in front of the school and how embarrassing it was, with Megan chiming in about her mom using a bunch of words they weren't allowed to say. The homeroom teacher, Mr. Smits, walked in and rapped on his big metal desk for silence.

As Mr. Smits began to pass out the forms that were to be taken home for parent signatures, Clare reviewed her triumph over Marva, which, of course, she couldn't share with her friends. She'd been Clare for more than a year, now. All the kids in sixth grade had called her Clare; she had friends, two of whom were now sitting next to her, and she'd been invited to birthday parties. Mrs. McNealy had turned out to be a great teacher, her favorite so far, and now that Miggie was spending most of her time at Daddy Dan's, she didn't seem to want to move again. Clare didn't have to worry so much that her mother would call her by her old name in front of anyone. Changing her name had changed her life.

Megan whispered that she'd seen some friends from their old school already. Alanna, on her other side, whispered back that she hoped her friends from the other two elementary schools would be in some of their classes. Clare nodded, smiling, until a horrible thought occurred to her. Sixth graders from three elementary schools became seventh graders at George S. Peabody Middle School. What if Marva wasn't the only one who remembered Clare as Fresno Bakersfield Ingersoll?

Chapter Eleven

"She's going to marry that guy? And move to Utah? Utah, of all places," Nita rolled her eyes. She shifted in the kitchen chair to better accommodate Taylor, who had fallen asleep against her shoulder.

Clare's eavesdropping ears pricked up; her eyes widened over the top of her book.

"He's a good guy, Nita," protested Grammie Ellen. "He owns his own business, he's a Christian and he loves the kids. And what's wrong with Utah?"

"Don't tell me this guy is a Mormon. And since when do you care about someone being a Christian?" Nita transferred the baby gently into the Pack and Play and picked up her Coke from the kitchen table.

Grammie Ellen sighed and gave Nita a one-shouldered shrug while looking down at the table. "Marjorie has changed since she got back from the fairs this summer. I think something happened to her on the road. She's—different."

"No one could be *that* different!" Nita's low tones had become a whispered shout. "She's been stringing him along for a year and now they're getting married? Can you see Miggie living in the land of Mormons, going to Temple, and becoming a sister wife?"

"Juanita, you really need to pay attention to the world," Grammie Ellen said. Her dry tone told Clare that she was irritated. "Not everyone who lives in Utah is Mormon and they haven't practiced polygamy for a hundred years."

Clare's book fell out of her nerveless hands. Polygamy— what the heck was that? How would you even spell it? Hastily, she reached down for the book when both Grammie Ellen and Nita looked over at her. Keeping her eyes on the book, not taking her eyes off the pages as she picked it up, she pretended to be so absorbed in the story that she was oblivious to all else.

Settling back into the recesses of her chair, Clare turned a page. After a moment, her grandmother and aunt began talking again, but their voices were even lower than before and Clare couldn't make out what they were saying. Then they got up and moved away from the table further into the kitchen where Clare couldn't see them anymore.

Ignoring the pages in her lap, Clare reviewed the conversation. Miggie was marrying Daddy Dan? And moving to Utah? What about Barty and her? And what were Mormons like, anyway? An eighth-grade boy had made a presentation in her homeroom about joining the Mormon troop of Boy Scouts. He'd made it sound like a special thing. But Aunt Nita sounded so scornful. If Miggie married Daddy Dan and became a Mormon, would she and Barty have to be Mormons too? And what was a sister-wife?

Miggie *was* different since she'd come back from the county fairs at the end of August—two months earlier than expected. She was quiet, slower to react to things that Clare and Barty did. She spent most of her time over at Daddy

Dan's house. She even held hands with Daddy Dan, something Clare had never seen her do with any boyfriend. Her mother had always been what Grammie Ellen called a "dreamer, " but now it seemed as if her mind was always somewhere else, thinking about things that had nothing to do with the people around her. She was never really present with Barty and Clare, even when she was home and they were right in front of her.

Of all of her mother's boyfriends, Dan was the nicest and best. But Clare finally had her own friends; she liked her school and this little town. She didn't even mind sharing a room with Barty because it was the same room in the same house where she had been living for sixteen whole months—the longest she remembered living anywhere.

She also liked the order and routines in Grammie's house: Grammie was up by six every weekday morning. Clare got up at six-thirty and they had breakfast with Barty at seven. Then, they went to work and school. On Wednesdays after the newspaper ads came out, Grammie did the grocery shopping after work. On Saturday mornings, she and Clare cleaned the house and did the laundry. Saturday night was rent-a-movie night and Sunday was for yardwork and playing. It was so normal that Clare felt normal, despite Miggie's unpredictability and Clare's own secret baby sensing.

She needed to know more about Mormons and Utah. And sister wives. The library would have information. The reference librarian, Miss Lydia, knew everything. Clare flew into the kitchen.

"Grammie, can you drive me to the library? Please, I 've got homework," she begged.

Grammie frowned, interrupted in her conversation with Nita, but Nita said, "I've got to go home—Taylor needs a nap in her own crib. I'll drop Clare off." Clare threw her grandmother a pleading look, knowing that she was a sucker for getting homework done. Sure enough, Grammie told her that she would pick her up in two hours.

On the short drive to the library, after Clare had to wait forever for Nita to bundle Taylor and all her baby paraphernalia into the car, she asked her aunt about Mormons. As soon as the words were out of her mouth, Clare wished she could suck them back. Nita would know that she'd been listening. Again.

Nita looked uncomfortable. "I'm sorry you heard that." Cutting her eyes over to Clare, she said sharply, "Eavesdropping is a bad habit to get into."

Clare looked down at her lap. Busted, and by her own question. Before she could think of what to say, Nita slowed and turned into the library parking lot. "It's one-thirty. Make sure you're out here for Grammie around three."

Clare nodded as she slid out of the car. "Thanks."

Nita waved goodbye and her aunt drove out of the lot, Clare realized that Nita hadn't answered her question.

Miss Lydia was a font of information. She helped Clare find some special reference books that you could only look at in the library and some books that she could check out. She told Clare about the Mormons that had come through El Dorado County looking for gold and now the road they had taken was called Mormon Immigrant Trail. They camped in a place only a few miles from Placerville and named it Pleasant Valley. And then they went home to Utah.

From her research, Mormons sounded OK except for the polygamy part. Would Daddy Dan have other wives? That would be weird. But Grammie said Mormons didn't do that anymore. According to Clare's research, Mormons didn't drink alcohol or caffeinated drinks. Miggie was allergic to alcohol and she only drank herbal tea. But the articles Clare had read said that young Mormons had to become missionaries and that was not anything she thought she wanted to do.

She waited for Grammie in front of the library, balancing one book about Mormons and another about Utah in her arms. Nita was sure to have told Grammie about Clare's eavesdropping, so no point in trying to hide them; she'd just have to suffer Grammie's lecture.

Clare peeked through the book about Utah. It had some great pictures and Utah looked like it might be an OK place. But it didn't matter whether Utah was OK or not—there was no way she was going to move to Utah and become a Mormon, no matter what Miggie did.

Chapter Twelve

Daddy Dan sat in Barty's little desk chair, his long legs coming up to his chin. I would have laughed at how uncomfortable he looked except that I was too miserable. I lay on my stomach on my bed, head buried under a pillow, my tear-swollen eyes peeking out at Dan.

"Darlin'," he began. "Could you help me out here?"

From inside my pillow cave, I threw him a suspicious glance. He wasn't going to talk me into moving. No way, no matter how nice he sounded.

Daddy Dan took a breath. "You see, I don't want you to be unhappy, but I don't know which thing is making you so sad. Is it that your mama and I are getting married or that we want to move our family to Utah? Can you tell me?" Dan's toes in their scuffed cowboy boots pointed awkwardly toward each other, making a wide V on the carpeted floor.

His voice was so gentle and sad sounding that I took the pillow off my head. Talking to my pillow, I said all in one breath, "I don't want to move to Utah; I don't want to have to become a Mormon and I don't want to be a missionary. I don't want Miggie to be a sister-wife."

There was a smothered sound. I lifted my head to stare at him. Dan was looking down at the floor, his hand hiding his mouth. Was he laughing at me?

After a moment he looked up, his brown eyes soft. "You don't have to be a Mormon if you don't want to. And if you're not Mormon, you won't have to go on a mission, either." He paused and chuckled. Shaking his head he said, "As for me, one wife is all I'm prepared to handle. And two kids. No extra wives—just the one. Is that OK?"

Despite his chuckle, I could feel the anxiety beneath it. I didn't want him to worry so I said, "I'm OK with you and Miggie getting married. I think you'd be a good daddy."

I felt a little shy as I said it, because when Miggie had told Barty and me that they were getting married, she hadn't said that Dan would be our daddy. Still, it felt obvious to me. Barty definitely thought of Dan as "Daddy." Dan smiled at me and I smiled back. Then, I focused on the real problem. "But I finally have friends and I want to stay here."

Dan sighed and said, "I've already sold my business. My uncle Jack is sick and needs help, so we're going to live on my family's farm with him."

It was a done deal, then. My shoulders slumped.

After a long moment, Dan said, "When my parents moved us to California, I was only four. I cried almost the whole way here."

I peered at him, trying to imagine the gangly man in front of me as a little boy who could cry, a boy like Barty.

"See, I didn't want to leave my grandparents and our farm. I had a pet pig too, but my daddy had a good job opportunity and the farm wasn't doing well. So we came here. It took me a long time to make friends. I always felt like I didn't fit."

Exactly. I'd had that feeling all my life until coming to live at Grammie's and I didn't want it to come back. Even though I still had lonely moments when it felt like something was missing, this was where I fit.

After a minute or two of silence, Dan added, "Let's see what we can do. How would you feel if your mom and Barty moved to Utah with me? Would you still want to stay?"

That was a new idea for me and I kicked it around for a minute. Miggie probably wouldn't care whether I went or not, but Barty would. Still, Barty followed Dan around like a puppy; he wanted to do everything Dan did. He even ate the same food in the same way as Dan which included putting mustard, which Barty hated, on his hot dogs. Barty would love living on a farm and riding his bike everywhere. He would miss me and I would miss him like crazy, but he would have Daddy Dan. I looked over at Dan, saw the worry in his eyes. Barty would be OK with Dan.

"Do you think Grammie would let me stay here?"

"I think she would be happy to have you, darlin,'" Dan said as he stood up. "But you can always change your mind."

I jumped off the bed and wrapped my arms around his waist. As his arms came around me in a brief hug, I thought, "I'll never change my mind." Because the second step of my plan to be normal—to live in a stable home—was finally becoming a possibility.

Chapter Thirteen

October 1997

"You'll be coming to visit when school is out," Daddy Dan reminded me. His forehead furrowed as he bent down to look in my face. "And, if you ever change your mind about moving to Utah, we'll be happy to come get you. Anytime."

He put a gentle hand on my shoulder. I took his hand, the one with the shiny gold wedding ring on it. "I'll see you when school's out," I told him. Reaching up, I gave him a quick hug as he leaned down toward me. Now that it was really happening, I just wanted the leave-taking to be over. I didn't want to cry.

Dan turned away to hug Grammie. I looked over at my mother who was leaning up against Dan's custom-painted turquoise pickup, watching me. Dan had sold the Greenbrier and Miggie was driving the pickup to Utah while Dan and Barty drove the huge U-Haul. They were going to stay in motels along the way. Barty couldn't wait to go swimming in the motel pools. He had already hugged everyone and packed himself inside the U-Haul cab as if afraid of being left behind.

It was strange—Miggie, Barty and I were used to moving, used to packing up and heading somewhere new. Grammie had grown to expect a move every year—that's why she always used a pencil to record our new addresses in her address book. But Dan had only moved once in all his thirty-eight years. He was stable, according to Aunt Nita. Now, he was married with two kids and he was moving his whole life to Utah. And for the first time in twelve years, I was staying put. Weird.

The wedding had been at the county government center, with the Recording Clerk officiating. Officiating, another new word. I liked the sound of it. The clerk had been funny and nice, placing Barty and me on either side of Miggie and Daddy Dan. Miggie wore a long blue sundress that laced up the back and a big floppy hat. Daddy Dan wore a navy blue suit with a white daisy that Miggie had taken from her bouquet of white and yellow daisies and pinned in his lapel. She looked like a mermaid; Daddy Dan looked like a judge— a really nervous judge.

Afterwards, we all went out to dinner at The Independent on Main Street—Grammie's treat. Then Miggie and Dan walked down the street to the Honeymoon Suite at the Cary House Hotel while Barty, Grammie and I went home and had ice cream.

It wasn't a big deal like Aunt Nita and Uncle Jeff's wedding where I'd had to wear a scratchy pink dress and throw fake flower petals on the carpet. The bridesmaids and I had to stand still for ages, next to Aunt Nita who was wearing a huge poufy white dress. There had been organ music and a singer and there was dancing later and a tall white cake with flowers on it. A much bigger deal than with the Recording Clerk.

Next to the pickup, Miggie jingled the keys she held and shifted her weight from one hip to another. She was staring at me, like she wanted me to do something. I stared back at her —I wanted Miggie to hug me hard. I wanted her to be sad, maybe even cry a little bit. I wanted. . . something. She'd taken the news that I was going to stay with Grammie with her usual nonchalance, shrugging as she said, "Suit yourself."

I waited for Miggie to beg me to go with them, even as my mind told me how great it was going to be with Grammie— going to the same school as my friends, being able to have them come over to my house, not worrying about whether we had food or clean clothing or that Miggie wasn't wearing underwear. But Miggie didn't move from her position next to the pickup and the keys kept jingling, so, feeling her eyes on my back, I walked over to the passenger side of the U-Haul. The door was open and Barty was perched on top of a pile of pillows and blankets, already wearing his seatbelt. He looked down at me from his high perch, excitement sparking in his eyes. I pulled a bag of Skittles out of my jeans pocket and held them up. Tropical, Barty's favorite. He smiled and held out his hands as I threw them up to him. He caught the bag with one hand and a grin.

"Be good, Barty." It was a stupid thing to say, but nothing else would come out. My little brother, my best friend. My heart gave a little hiccup.

He gave the bag of candy a triumphant shake and looked down. I saw the excitement leaving his eyes, changing to dismay like when you mix red and blue and get purple. "Why can't you come too, Fre. . . Clare?"

"You know. I told you. I don't want to move; I want to stay with Grammie, but—I'll miss you, Barty." My eyes filled despite my resolve not to cry. We were used to saying good-bye, but not to each other. Barty's bottom lip quivered and I said. "It's OK, you'll have fun on the farm and I'll have fun here, and we'll talk on the phone and tell each other our stories."

He nodded, slowly. Daddy Dan came up behind me and closed the door as I moved out of the way, waving to Barty. Dan gave me another hug and went around to the driver's side of the U-Haul, climbing up inside. He said something to Barty, who pulled on his seatbelt, showing Dan it was fastened. Dan started the truck and the excitement came back into Barty's eyes. Dan blew the horn long and loud and the truck rolled away, Barty craning his neck around and waving back at Grammie and me.

Grammie had come to stand next to me, resting her hand lightly on my shoulder. I touched her hand and looked over my other shoulder at Miggie, waiting. Our eyes met. Miggie jingled the keys. Grammie took her hand off my shoulder as if releasing me. But I didn't move.

Miggie opened the pickup door and climbed inside. Grammie walked over and leaned through the driver's side window to give Miggie a kiss. Then she stood back and looked over at me where I was standing, still waiting for Miggie to come to me.

The engine started.

The pickup drove past me. My mother drove with her eyes staring straight ahead. The truck turned left at the stop sign at the end of the block and disappeared. I stood on the sidewalk and waited for her to come back, but the turquoise pickup was gone.

Chapter Fourteen

Marva Doyle might be a little slow, but she was definitely dogged. I gazed back at the kids forming a semi-circle in front of me. Dogged as in not giving up, as in persistent beyond all belief.

After the first six weeks of school had passed without anyone but Marva taunting me with my old name, I had hoped I was home free. But no. Marva the Dogged (the new word courtesy of Charles Dickens) had been rounding up every kid from the elementary school we had both gone to in fifth grade. Every kid who would talk to her, that is. Fifth grade, the last year I had been Fresno Bakersfield Ingersoll.

There were seven kids facing me—five girls, including Marva, and two boys—blocking the path to the multi-purpose room and chanting "Fresno Bakersfield Ingersoll" with great glee. I remembered their faces from that semester in fifth grade, but I didn't remember all their names. Miggie's advice to ignore them was not going to work yet again—I was going to have to tell her what a bad idea that was someday. Walking confidently through them wasn't going to happen either, since they were standing with their hands on hips, elbows bent out and touching, forming an uneven wall of pointy elbows and solid bodies.

I looked down at my lucky red high tops and prayed for a yard-duty person to appear. The world's longest thirty seconds crawled by with no help in sight. Finally, I looked up from my shoes, took a breath and yelled, "Don't any of you have mothers?"

There was a hitch in the chanting, as if the mob were trying to figure out if I'd insulted them. Then, just as the chanting started up again, I raised my voice once more and said, "I mean mothers who have embarrassed you? Said something or done something right in front of everybody that was so lame that you could just die?"

The chanting broke down like a wrecking ball going through a building—not all at once, but bit by bit, with one straggling voice disappearing into, "Fres-no, Bake-rs-field, Ing-er-solllllllll."

I fixed my eyes on Marva, the one whose dogged nature had done this, and spoke directly to her. "Well, I have one of *those* mothers. She gave me that name and I *hate* it." I glared at them all, my chin stuck out, daring them to remember their own embarrassing moments. I raised my palms and eyebrows in disbelief. "Can you believe a mother would do something like that?"

I stared at my tormentors; they stared back. An endless moment passed, and then a girl with long red hair, Jennifer somebody, said, "My mom makes me kiss her when I get out of the car at the bus stop. It's so embarrassing." Her face flushed pink. Faces, startled or confused or both, looked around at her. More silence.

Finally, one of the boys, a skinny dark-haired kid, said, "Once, my mom whacked me on the butt in front of all the neighbors because I was playing in the street. That was pretty lame." He looked at me and shrugged.

I nodded at both of them. "I'm not the only one then."

Feet shuffled; kids stared off into space as if remembering something. A couple of kids looked at me, twisted smiles of commiseration on their faces as their elbows dropped. Then I said, "But. . . I did something about it." All seven pairs of eyes flew toward me as I continued, "I went to the judge at the courthouse and changed my name."

"By yourself—you went to the judge by yourself?" The note of awe in the red-haired girl's voice filled me with pride.

"Yes, I talked to Judge Potts. He said I could change it, so I did."

"Didn't your mom get mad?" The dark-haired boy spoke up.

"I handled it." I tossed my head, acting tough, with my hands on my hips. I looked each of them in the eyes. I felt their angry energy moving away from me toward a common enemy—embarrassing parents. Swelled with triumph, I swaggered—there is no other word for it—through an opening in the semi-circle, between Marva and the boy whose mother had whacked him. I strode into the multi-purpose room. My Lunchables had a special tang of victory that day, especially when two of the girls from the circle outside asked if they could join Alanna, Megan and me at our table.

Walking home from school that afternoon, I was so filled with the euphoric replay of The Chanting Incident that the last three periods of the school day were a complete blank.

The next day, Marva Doyle caught me at the lockers, her tall shadow falling over me like doom. Leaning down, crowding me against the metal boxes, she rasped, "You can really change your name?"

Her breath smelled like sausage and she was way too

close, but when I looked into Marva's face, I could tell that she really wanted to know—she wasn't trying to scare me, even though she did. I repeated what Judge Potts had told me, "Yes, you can, but you have to be patient and determined." Then, I pushed her back from me gently and asked, "What would you like to be called?"

The rest of the school year was awesome. I had a little group of friends, including the red-haired Jennifer and Marva. We all called each other by the names we would have chosen if things had been left up to us. I was the only one who insisted that my true name be used in all situations, but Marva confided that she had told her father she wanted to be called by her middle name, Amanda. Her father told her mother and they had finally agreed that Marva could be Amanda, at least at home, and maybe full-time when she went to high school. Marva/Amanda wasn't my best friend, but she was part of our group and no longer a threat.

My classes were going well, too—especially Language Arts. My teacher, Mrs. Rhodes, read my essays and stories out loud in class and asked me if I would like to write for the school newspaper. Grammie said she was so proud of me. Reading my stories to her made each one of them better.

At home, we settled into a routine. Grammie and I took turns making breakfast and packing each other's lunches. I practiced my gourmet concoctions on Grammie and she almost always ate them, including a peanut butter, celery and honey sandwich with curry powder. Once a week, after school, I walked down to the bank where Grammie worked. I did my homework in her office and then we'd walk to one of the downtown restaurants near the bank for dinner after the workday was done.

On Wednesday nights, we took a yoga class at Town Hall and later, we watched *Friends* and *ER*. Grammie's wry comments about Joey's lack of intelligence, Phoebe's flakiness and Dr. Doug Ross's hotness revealed a wicked sense of humor that cracked me up. We went to the movies, something I had only done once or twice in my life, but Grammie loved the movies and we often checked out the newest offerings in town or rented a video.

Grammie said I was very mature for my age. I had always thought that Grammie, at fifty-three, was old, but now she didn't seem so old, and she could be a lot of fun. She was different than when she was around Miggie, but then, so was I.

My baby sensing ability had gone underground. I didn't know anyone who was pregnant and only felt an occasional blip when I saw a lady with a baby bump on the street. Easy to ignore; easy to pretend to be normal. Sometimes, it felt as if a part of me was missing, but I was OK with that. My three part plan to become a normal person—changing my name, having a real home and not hearing babies—was working.

Even though I enjoyed living with Grammie, I still missed Barty. I was used to making sure he ate breakfast, had a lunch for school and was wearing clean clothes or at least, not super dirty ones. Used to looking out for him. On the days when I didn't meet Grammie downtown, the house was too quiet. I did my best writing on those days, fueled by missing Barty, Dan and even my mother.

During one of our weekly phone conversations, I asked Barty what he was doing and if he had made any friends. It felt weird to be asking; I'd always known exactly what Barty was doing and I'd known all his friends.

"Daddy's teaching me how to take care of the sheep and we have a bunch of kittens and a cow and maybe we're going to get a horse." He sounded excited. There was a slurping sound in my ear as he drank something. "There's a kid my age who lives down the road and we ride bikes together. He goes to my school."

Barty was almost always succinct. Another of my new words that year. Then his voice changed, became a little quavery. "Are you coming out here pretty soon?"

"When school's out. Are you OK?"

"Yeah."

I could hear in his voice that he missed me, but I knew he would never say so. I said it instead.

"I miss you, Barty."

"Yeah."

There was no point in asking about Miggie or Daddy Dan. Mr. Succinct would just tell me they were OK and leave it at that. Daddy Dan gave me more information when we talked: telling me about his job in town at a body shop, what a great helper Barty was, that his Uncle Jack wasn't doing very well, that they missed me and loved me. Miggie's conversations were almost as succinct as Barty's—she asked whether Grammie Ellen and I were getting along, how was school and if I had friends. Always questions, but no real information about what she was doing or if she liked Utah. When I asked, Miggie said only that the mountains were beautiful and Utah had an interesting vibe.

I worried about Barty and sometimes I felt sad and left out after I talked to him and Miggie and Dan. But I'd often felt that kind of loneliness before, even when they were around—as if I was missing something or someone. Now, at least, I could remind myself that it was my choice to be where I was, that it was even better than I'd hoped it would be and in only a few months, I'd be summering in Utah with them all, just like a normal family.

Chapter Fifteen

June 1998

The air through the open farmhouse window was already warm. It smelled of grass and growing things. Clare stretched luxuriously and rolled out of the small bed. The furniture was old and sparse: a chest of drawers, a wooden rocker with a cross-stitch cushion, a leather-bound trunk and, of all things, a dressmaker's dummy. If she hadn't been so tired last night from the flight and the excitement of seeing her family again, the dummy would have given her the creeps. Daddy Dan said it had been his grandmother's room and that she had loved sitting near the window and looking out at the mountains. Clare checked out the view, surprised that the mountains still had bits of snow clinging to the peaks in mid-June. She heard a car. Turning from the mountains to peer at the road in front of the house, Clare saw her mother in the little green Camry that she drove, speeding toward town.

It was only 7:30 in the morning. Where could Miggie be

going? Clare threw on shorts and a T-shirt and walked barefoot into the kitchen. The old wooden floors were slightly uneven and creaked when she stepped on certain boards, but she loved the way they looked—sturdy and solid as if they would be there for a thousand years.

The kitchen appliances were old—a refrigerator with rounded corners, like a little old man with hunched shoulders, a stove with chips out of its white enamel surface and shadowed black gas burners, wooden counters, and a huge stone sink. Yesterday, when they had returned from the airport, Dan proudly told her how hard Miggie had worked to spruce up the kitchen: painting the cabinets and window trim with a bright white paint and hanging pale yellow curtains at the big window that looked out over the front yard and the road. Clare had been too surprised at the thought of her mother doing domestic decorating to say anything.

Sunlight filled the room. Daddy Dan was pouring coffee from the coffeemaker into a Thermos. He was already dressed for work in jeans and a long-sleeved work-shirt. He moved around the kitchen quickly as if he had been up for hours.

"Mornin' darlin'. You sleep OK?"

"Yeah. Was that Miggie leaving?"

Dan nodded as he turned to the refrigerator and pulled a couple of frozen burritos out of the freezer compartment. He put them in his lunchbox along with an apple. "You want some cereal?"

"Yes, thank you. Where did she go?" Clare said. "I just got here and she's already gone." Even to her own ears, she sounded whiny.

Dan sighed and said, "She'll be back around nine-thirty. She studies with some Mormon elders four mornings a week."

"Miggie wants to be a Mormon?" Clare couldn't imagine her New Age mother wanting to be part of a traditional religion. Druid worship maybe, but not anything with a Sunday school.

"Well, I don't know about that," Dan said as he set both granola and Froot-Loops in front of her. Clare grinned at the choice: Miggie believed in healthy food, but she didn't like grocery shopping. It was obvious to Clare that Dan had taken over that chore. Good thing too—Clare remembered plenty of days when she and Barty had had to forage for whatever they could find to eat. A lot of ramen soup days.

"She started out just wanting to know about Mormons because almost everyone in town and all our neighbors are Mormon. If she set up a craft show, she thought people might not buy her jewelry if she wasn't a Mormon. Then, she got interested in it." He sighed again, "Now she's getting ready to be baptized."

Baptized? "What about you and Barty? Are you going to be Mormons too?" Clare's stomach tightened. In the eight months since she'd seen them, her family had changed, leaving her feeling off balance and left out. Maybe she was the one who was different, although the only change in her life was that she had just gotten her first period and was hoping that Grammie was correct when she said it would make her boobs grow. Thinking about the changes, she fidgeted with the bag of granola and eyed the Froot Loops.

"I'm already baptized Mormon, but I haven't been to church since my family moved to California. Don't have much interest in it," he shrugged. "Barty can make his own decision about it, but he doesn't have to be Mormon if he doesn't want to." He said this with a touch of defiance in his voice, as if he'd had an earlier argument about this with someone.

"Is Barty still asleep?" Clare decided to forego the cereal and have toast instead. Toast sounded easier, somehow. Easier on her still tight stomach. As she rummaged in the cabinets looking for bread, she noticed how well-stocked they were. And last night, Miggie had made dinner. A real dinner with Clare's favorite mac and cheese as well as roast chicken and asparagus. Clare had been touched that Miggie had made such an effort—an apple and a peanut butter sandwich was Miggie's usual two course dinner.

Now Dan said, "Barty's been up for hours, tending the lambs and helping me with the sheep. He'll be inside in a moment."

That was another unexpected change—her slug-a-bed brother up early during summer vacation. He'd given her a tour of the farm yesterday, starting with the barn where he showed her the three baby lambs that were his special charge, explaining to her how often they had to be fed and how he had to keep them safe. Then he'd taken Clare to all of his favorite places on the ranch—the pond where he fished, the creek where he proudly showed her the narrow stretch over which he jumped his bike, the willow trees where he and Dan were building a tree fort, the pastures where sheep grazed. They played with a border collie Barty had named Einstein.

"He's really, really smart," said Barty, stroking Einstein's black velvet ears. "He rounds up the sheep. There's only a few left, but he's really good at getting them."

When Dan called them in, Barty said, "Mom made a special dinner because you're here." He added, "She cooks almost all the time now, with meat and vegetables and everything."

It wasn't just changes like food preparation and Mormonism that made Miggie different, Clare thought as she buttered her toast. At the airport, Miggie had given her a long hug as soon as she had come through the gate. She hadn't said much on the ride to the ranch, but she had seemed glad to see Clare, giving her daughter's arm a gentle squeeze when she showed her into the downstairs bedroom.

Dan's Uncle Jack, who owned the farm, was sick and unable to join them for Clare's welcome home dinner. Miggie disappeared after they ate, leaving Dan, Barty and Clare to clean up. Clare tried not to mind that her mother left the welcome home dinner so soon and wondered why she had.

Dan and Barty swung into action as if this was a well-practiced routine. When Clare picked up her plate and silverware, Dan told her to put them down. "You just got here —we'll take care of this, tonight," Dan said. "Why don't you check out the house and get familiar with the layout?"

She had wandered into the living room with its ancient leather recliner, lumpy fabric-covered couch and collection of armchairs, end tables and rag rugs. There was a console television directly in front of the recliner. A huge black and silver woodstove sat on a stone hearth. It felt comfy and homey, in an old-fashioned way.

Leaving the living room, Clare walked down a hallway covered in yellowing wallpaper with little beribboned bouquets of flowers. She peeked into the first room on the right—Uncle Jack's room. Clare had met him earlier that day. He looked old and sick as he lay in the hospital bed, but he'd smiled at her and said he was glad to meet her.

Now, she saw Miggie, her back to Clare spooning something into Uncle Jack's mouth. Then she gently wiped away the excess. The tenderness in her mother's movements flashed a pang of jealousy through Clare.

Miggie had never been the huggy-kissy kind of mother that Clare wanted her to be. When her children were ill,

Miggie treated them with herbs and tinctures, instead of kisses and children's Tylenol. Either they got well or they didn't, according to their karma. Fortunately for Barty and Clare, they always got better. Eventually.

Miggie looked up to see Clare hovering in the doorway. Jack's eyes followed the direction of her gaze. "Well, hello little lady," he rasped out. "Come to watch an old man slurp his soup?"

Embarrassed to have been caught staring, Clare looked to Miggie, who nodded at her. Clare sidled up next to the side of Jack's hospital bed as Miggie spooned another mouthful into Jack's mouth. His blue eyes twinkled at Clare over the top of the spoon.

Miggie wiped soup from the side of Jack's mouth. Then she placed the bowl and spoon into Clare's hands and said, "I need to use the bathroom. Can you finish up for me?" Without waiting for a reply, she slipped quickly out of the room, leaving Clare staring after her.

I tried to keep the dismay I felt off my face. What did I know about feeding an adult human? As I looked into Uncle Jack's face, he grinned and reached for the bowl and spoon, plucking them from my unresisting fingers. "Don't worry," he rasped as he began feeding himself. "I'm not that feeble." He chuckled before swallowing and then said by way of explanation, "Just never had a beautiful woman feed me before."

His grin widened. When his eyebrows quirked up in a conspiratorial lift, I started laughing. When Miggie reappeared, I was peeling an orange for Uncle Jack as we chatted companionably about the places on the ranch he thought I would enjoy.

"Well, I see I wasn't missed." Miggie's words were spoken

lightly, but her eyes flicked over to the nightstand where the empty bowl and spoon lay. A tiny frown crinkled between her eyebrows, but she said only, "I'm impressed. Maybe you should feed Jack all the time."

She didn't sound impressed at all. As she plumped up the pillows behind Jack and took the orange from me, Uncle Jack and I exchanged winks behind her back. Then I left the two of them to continue my explorations.

Miggie's care of Uncle Jack surprised me, but her chilliness at finding that I had supposedly fed Jack successfully did not. Miggie liked to be the center of attention, even if it was bad attention like when Grammie got on her case. In a way, it was reassuring. She hadn't changed completely.

Later, Barty found me coming down from the furniture-stuffed attic and pulled me into his second-floor bedroom. He showed off the Hot Wheels track he had built by himself and the twin beds for sleep-overs. He told me there was a basement in the house, but he would show me that later. "Come help me feed the lambs and then I want to show you something, "he said.

We bottle-fed the lambs, which was fun, and then played with them for a while before Barty shut them up in the barn. Then, as the night sky was turning indigo, but there was still enough light to see by, Barty grabbed a flashlight from the porch and we walked down toward the pond.

There were two beat-up lawn chairs that I hadn't paid attention to on the first tour of the pond. The ground was marshy at the edges and cattails flourished along one curved side. The chairs were near the marshy area. Barty sat in one chair and retrieved a bottle of bug repellant from under the chair. "You'll need this," he said as he rubbed the lemony-scented stuff on his arms and face. "Don't get it in your eyes."

I covered myself in the sticky goo, wondering why we

were out in mosquito country at nine-thirty at night, but I decided to let Barty do his thing. The plastic straps on the chair were sticky and the bottom was sprung. I settled in, scooching my butt around until I was reasonably comfortable. The mountains were almost invisible in the darkening sky. Close by, I could hear the singing of frogs and, further away, the steady chirp of crickets. Something splashed in the pond, but it was too dark to see what it might be. I couldn't even see Barty very clearly. I was about to ask him to turn on the flashlight, when he touched my arm and said, "Look!" as he pointed into the night.

At first, I thought he was pointing at the stars which were appearing in amazing numbers, popping out in all their brilliance like a huge rash in the sky. Then, he said, "See, there, in the cattails."

Small yellowish lights appeared, blinking, between the reeds. Individually, they vanished and then reappeared above, below or to the side of their previous appearance. Frogs sang in choruses; crickets chirped in tandem with the light show among the reeds and the sky bloomed above us—mesmerizing, mind-expanding—it felt like a very private showing, arranged just for me.

"Dad and I come out here most nights," Barty whispered. "Fireflies aren't supposed to live in Utah because it's too dry, but Uncle Jack told us they come by the pond for a few weeks in May and June every year. Always about this time of night."

I saw the gleam of his eyes in the starlight, the shine of his grin as he looked at me. "I knew you'd like it."

I felt it then, for the first time, that Barty knew things that I didn't know. That he was confident in his knowing and not afraid anymore. He *was* different. I felt sad and proud at the same time. My baby brother was gone, but my brother was growing up.

Chapter Sixteen

Clare, sitting on the fence, saw the rooster tail of dust chasing the car flying down the unpaved road toward the house. The dust cleared for a second and she could see that it was Miggie's Camry. She sat up straight, straining to see, worried that Miggie's erratic speeding meant that something was wrong. Usually Miggie drove like she walked—slow and drifty.

Inside the Camry, Miggie was steaming. This was the last straw, she told herself. Screw redemption! Her mind threw out every curse word she'd bitten back in the past year. She'd done everything: married Dan, taken care of Jack, moved out to a lonely ranch in Utah, planted a garden—everything! She made sure Barty went to school, most of the time, and she cooked. She drove to the rec room basement of the church four days a week (in a Camry, no less) to learn how to be a Mormon. She'd listened to the Bible Babes expound and made the decision to get baptized. When the head Bible Babe, Mrs. Earlene Miller, called her aside last week to whisper that it would be respectful of the Lord and the

Church if she wore more appropriate clothing to their daily Bible studies, Miggie had looked down at her tank top and denim shorts and nodded demurely.

But today was the last time she was ever going into that church again—even if no one ever bought any of her handcrafted jewelry. She'd worn a long-sleeved muslin peasant blouse and ankle-length cotton skirt. Everything was covered up. But the head Bible Babe—Bible Bitch—Miggie grimly corrected herself, had sidled up to her after class and said, "Mrs. Allred, when we spoke about wearing clothing appropriate for the Lord and the Church, we thought that would include underwear."

Like she could help it if the air-conditioning in the basement was set to zero. She never wore underwear—it wasn't healthy to be confined. She needed freedom in order to think. If the Church needed underwear and "appropriate clothing," then fuck it.

She'd repented her wild ways; she'd served; she'd tried to do what everyone had been telling her she should do for years. But if God needed underwear, she was damned if He was going to get it from her.

She flew into the farmyard and saw her daughter sitting on the fence, dark curly hair shining in the sun. Now there was an underwear wearing kid. A kid who lived by every rule and who fit in because of it. Miggie had never fit in. Now she wasn't even going to try. God, she'd missed that kid!

Miggie got out of the car slowly, giving herself time to pull it together. Clare hopped off the fence and walked toward her, worry creasing her face. Three months from becoming a teenager, she still looked like a little girl in her shorts and T-shirt. Miggie wondered when she had become old enough to be the mother of a teenager. Teenagers and underwear, it was all part of getting old.

. . .

Clare watched as her mother slung her hobo bag purse over her shoulder. Miggie didn't carry a purse unless she was driving because the purse lived in her car, providing a home for Miggie's driver's license, a few granola bars and a bottle of water. Now, it bounced over Miggie's shoulder as she jerked the car door closed and walked stiffly, angrily toward the house. Was she mad because Clare was here, in Utah?

Clare took a breath and asked, "How was your Bible study?" She was completely unprepared for Miggie's look of fury just before she threw her hobo bag into the dirt of the yard.

"Those old biddies told me my clothing wasn't appropriate! That God wanted me to wear underwear!" Miggie's voice was ragged, as if she might be going to cry.

Clare took a step back. Miggie never cried—ever. She hardly ever got mad, either—it wasn't her style. Miggie's style was one of careless indifference. She didn't worry; she didn't yell; she didn't throw stuff. She didn't care, or at least she pretended not to care.

But Clare recognized anger and hurt when she saw it, having felt enough of it herself. She moved closer to her mother and ventured, "Wow, that was pretty rude."

Clare couldn't believe she was saying this since Miggie's lack of underwear had caused her daughter a ton of embarrassment. But those church ladies sounded like real wieners. "If God brought you into the world without underwear, probably He wouldn't care if you wore it or not. Even in church."

Miggie wished she had thought of saying that to the Bible Bitch. She looked into Clare's green eyes, filled with sympathy. Green eyes like her own. Green eyes that weren't, for once, judging her. She felt her anger beginning to drain away.

She picked her bag out of the dirt. "Let's go in and make some lemonade."

Clare's voice over her shoulder asked practically, "Do we have lemons?"

"Nope."

Chapter Seventeen

The rest of the summer was surprisingly pleasant. Miggie and I weren't exactly the best of friends — we were too different for that—but we worked around each other. Miggie still called me Fresno, but not often, and when she did, it was in a teasing way, so I teased her back by calling her Marjorie and both of us would wince and then laugh.

She worked hard taking care of Uncle Jack whose Chronic Obstructive Pulmonary Disease and congestive heart failure continued to progress. By the end of the summer, he could no longer feed himself and breathing was a constant struggle. Miggie was patient and caring with him. She even had a schedule for his meals and medication— my free-spirited mother who had always said that routines were for people with no imagination.

The change in Miggie struck a chord in me and I tried to do whatever I could to make things easier for her: fixing dinner sometimes, reading to Uncle Jack, doing laundry. In between my self-imposed chores, I roamed the ranch with

Barty, scouting out all the places Uncle Jack had told me about. We took care of the lambs and swam in the little pond which grew smaller every day.

Between ranch work and his job at the auto body shop in town, Dan was busy and tired. While he was making breakfast each morning, I would make his work lunch, which gave us a little time to talk. During these mornings and in the evenings when he joined Barty and me at the pond, I grew to know him better and I saw that he truly loved my mother and Barty.

The last night that the fireflies graced the pond, Barty, Dan and I went to watch the insect Morse code. I'd never seen fireflies in California, so they were an endless delight to me. While Barty flitted around the pond looking for bullfrogs with a flashlight, Dan relaxed in one of the beat-up lawn chairs next to me. I heard him sigh, as if he were blowing out all the tension in his body.

"This is the best part of my day," he said. Usually, he brought a beer to drink during our firefly nights unless he had already shared one with Uncle Jack. It was supposed to be a secret that Uncle Jack drank beer. He said it made him a bad Mormon and at this point in his life or death, he was trying to be a better one. Still, it was a lifelong habit, his single beer, and once every two weeks, Dan drove sixty miles to purchase two twelve-packs of Coors at the state-run liquor store. He could have bought beer at the grocery store in town five miles away, but Uncle Jack had always bought his beer out of the county to keep his secret. He hid it in a root cellar that wasn't used for anything else. Just in case, he told me with a twinkle, an elder should come calling.

"Do you like living on the ranch?" I asked Dan. "Better than in California?"

It was too dark to see his face, but I heard the tension in

his voice as he said, "It's not really whether I like it better or not that's important, although nights like this when it's so quiet that all you can hear are the mosquitos buzzing, are the best." The aluminum frame of the chair squeaked as he shifted position. "It's more that I need to be here right now, with Jack, with your mom and Barty, building a life together." He paused, "I wish you'd consider being here with us all the time."

I had thought about staying. I did like it here, being with my family, even though it was a little isolated. But I had friends in Placerville; I had Grammie and school and a place where I felt at home.

There was another reason I had considered staying. Dan treated Miggie like a precious and delicate being—making sure she wasn't doing too much and leaping up to carry anything for her that looked to weigh more than a pound. If my baby radar hadn't already clued me in that Miggie was pregnant, Dan's tender care of her would have been a big clue. It took my breath away to think of having a new little brother, but in a good way.

Miggie accepted Dan's attentions in her usual lackadaisical fashion, but I noticed that she seemed to touch him more often than I remembered her touching other guys—taking his hand when they went for walks around the property or squeezing his shoulder in passing. Whenever she did this, Dan lit up like a birthday candle. She had the same effect on Barty.

"Dan, I know about the baby," I said in low voice, not being sure if Barty knew yet. He hadn't said anything to me about it and I knew he would have—at least I used to know whether he would have told me or not.

I felt Dan go rigid beside me. "Did . . . your mom tell you?"

"No, I uh. . . figured it out."

I had never told him about my baby sensing. In my family, it was a taboo subject. I wasn't even sure that Barty knew precisely what I could do.

There was a silence, broken only by the sound of Barty's feet splashing around the pond's edge and the sight of his bobbing flashlight.

"Are you OK with it?" Dan's voice sounded worried.

I thought about my answer for a moment and then I said, "Dan, you're a great dad—Barty and I both love you. I guess you haven't told him yet, but I bet he'll be thrilled to have a baby brother." I paused. "I'm sorry that I can't live here and help out with the baby, but this truce between Miggie and me won't last. You and Barty are going to be great with the baby."

"We were waiting to tell him until you were here and then it got so busy with Jack and . . ." Dan's voice trailed off. Then he whispered, "You said 'baby brother.' What makes you think it's a boy?"

I didn't feel like it was the time to tell Dan of my special ability, while we were fighting off mosquitos in the darkness where I couldn't see his face. "Did I? I guess I'm just used to brothers."

Barty bounded up to us. "I'm getting out of here! There's not enough mosquito spray in the universe to keep these things away."

I heard Dan chuckle and his lawn chair creak as he stood up. "Lead the way, mighty mosquito fighter. It's time for pie."

The following afternoon, Miggie and I were in the kitchen—I was making chocolate chip cookies and Miggie was washing lettuce for a salad. As I measured and mixed, I thought about the baby and how Miggie was finally acting like a mom—

fixing meals, taking care of Uncle Jack, doing laundry. She still didn't make lunches for work or school, get up with Dan at breakfast, or grocery shop, but she was better about mom things than she used to be. Still, I worried about whether she would look after this baby more carefully than she had Barty and me.

I'd been the one who made sure Barty and I had something to eat, who took care of him when he had a cold or tummy ache, who nagged Miggie when we had to go to the laundromat, who reminded her when we were low on food and who tidied wherever we were living at the time. Now, I wanted to know how she felt about the baby to reassure myself that she would be there for him.

"Dan told me about the baby," I said as I dropped tablespoons full of cookie dough onto a baking sheet.

Miggie nodded as if Dan had told her that I knew. She gently shook the water from the lettuce.

"So, how do you feel about having another baby?" My directness and Miggie's elusiveness were often at loggerheads, but I couldn't figure out any other way to ask.

Sure enough, her answer wound around like a curl of hair on a finger. "Dan is a good man; he'll be a great father." She wrapped the lettuce in a clean dish towel and began patting it dry.

Duh, but that wasn't what I asked. I tried again. "I mean, how about you?"

"I'm feeling fine. No worries."

Was she trying to blow off my question? With Miggie, you never knew. I got out another baking sheet and tried a little misdirection of my own. "When are you going to tell Barty?"

"Barty is doing such a good job with the lambs, he'll probably be a good big brother." She drifted over to the window and peered out into the yard.

I plopped cookie dough on the baking sheet with enough force that the pan rattled and my drop cookie looked more like a big splat. Barty was going to be a great brother—he already was—but Miggie's evasiveness was, as always, annoying. Very annoying. I wanted clear answers; Miggie never seemed to be able to give one. I opened the preheated oven and tossed my cookie-splattered baking sheet inside. If she couldn't even talk to me about the baby, then what would happen once he was born?

As Miggie drifted toward the refrigerator and I began loading a second baking sheet with cookie dough, I thought about the usual way things went when Miggie and I bumped heads: I would ask more and more questions and she would become more and more elusive until I finally gave up and did whatever I felt needed to be done.

When we had lived our nomadic life, and Miggie wouldn't answer questions about whether we had food for dinner, money for the laundromat, or had signed the permission form for a field trip, my frustration would drive me to take action—I would cobble together whatever we had in the kitchen for dinner, pick through our clothes for the least dirty things I could find, or sign the field trip permission form myself. That last one had gotten me into trouble at school since my cursive at the time wasn't the best.

We had talked about me living in Utah with them. I did want to be with my family when the baby was born and I wanted to help out and bond with my new baby brother. Maybe if Miggie knew for sure that I was going back to stay with Grammie, I would get a real response to my questions.

"I think I'll stay with Grammie this school year," I said,

sliding my eyes towards her, waiting for her to say something real.

"Whatever you want to do." Typical Miggie response—elusively vague.

Home in Placerville with my always direct grandmother looked better every day, even if I would only see my baby brother from time to time. From what I could sense, he was content, singing his own baby song, the wordless one that all babies seem to have. Probably that meant that Miggie was content, too.

Chapter Eighteen

November 1998

My back hurt, my head hurt. The words on the white board at the front of the classroom looked fuzzy. Even Mr. Keller, my world history teacher, looked fuzzy. I was so tired I could barely hold my head up. Mr. Keller walked up and down the aisles between our desks, expounding on the ancient Sumerians or maybe it was the Black Death—who knew? I sure didn't. He walked past me, still talking and then stopped and backed up.

"Are you feeling well, Clare?"

Nope, not feeling well at all. The words didn't make it out of my mouth, though I did try. Faces turned to look at me. I felt a strong arm around me and Mr. Keller's voice said, "Candace, will you please walk Clare down to the nurse's office?"

A skinny arm replaced the strong one. Candace Muller, the class suck-up. Bright-eyed and perky like a chipmunk in class, but mean as a snake in the real world. She'd probably drag me if I didn't walk on my own. I stood up, my head spinning and feeling as if I were going to barf. I managed to reach for my backpack.

Candace wrested it away and made soothing sounds as she guided me out of class. Once outside, she frog-marched me all the way to the office. Someone opened the door for us and Candace pushed me inside the office and supported me as she told the school secretary that Mr. Keller had sent me to the office. She didn't say I was supposed to see the nurse. Then she was gone and Mrs. Shattuck, the secretary, told me to take a seat.

Minutes later the school nurse walked into the office on her way to her own office. I felt myself slither off the plastic chair, then saw her worried eyes looking down at me as everything went black.

Curled up like a fetus in the front seat of Grammie's car, I was still feeling dizzy and fuzzy as Grammie drove the few blocks to our house. Also, puffy and very, very cumbersome—almost as if I was an enormous balloon filled with water that was churning around inside me. It was the balloon feeling that made me realize who else was feeling this way. Urgency propelled me into a sitting position. My head pounding, I said, "Grammie, we've got to call Miggie. Something's wrong."

Grammie shot me a questioning look, but she said only, "Are you OK?"

"It's Miggie, not me." As soon as the car stopped in our driveway, I scrambled into the house and dialed the number in Utah on the phone in the kitchen. It was an hour later in Utah, a little after three o'clock. The phone rang and rang, like screaming into a void. After twenty rings, I hung up. Where was she? Barty got out of school at 3:30 and Miggie was almost always home at that time because Dan didn't get home from work until after five. I dialed the number again. The sound of the empty rings made me want to throw up. Where was she?

Grammie took a look at my panicked face and said, "Tell me what's going on."

I knew Grammie didn't want to listen to any claims of my being able to sense babies, but now, in addition to Miggie's condition, I could hear the frightened cries of my tiny brother, a trapped passenger. I felt his panic. They needed help and they needed it now. "We have to hurry! Miggie's not answering."

Grammie stared at me for an interminable second, as if weighing something in her mind. Then she reached into her purse and pulled out the little leather address book she always carried. She flipped a few pages and said, "I have Dan's work number."

She read the numbers off to me and I punched the buttons as fast as I could. I asked for Dan Allred when a voice answered and in a few minutes that felt like days, Dan's mellow voice said, "Hello?"

"Where's Miggie?" I blurted.

"Clare?" Dan sounded astonished. "Are you alright?"

"I called the house and Miggie didn't answer. Something's wrong, Dan. You have to go home."

Dark, blurry images and pain flooded into me, doubling me over. Grammie caught me and helped me into a kitchen chair. I gripped the phone tightly as Dan started to say something. Interrupting, I almost screamed the words. "She has to go to the hospital. Right now!"

Even as I said this, I realized how crazy it must sound. I

tried to calm down by asking questions. "Has she had a headache? Are her hands and feet swollen?"

Grammie's eyes widened and a look of shock filled her face.

The phone was silent and then I heard the doubt in Dan's voice as he said, "She woke up with a bad headache today and, yes, we've been joking about how she can't wear anything but slippers on her puffy feet. But she said that's normal at this stage of pregnancy."

"You need to get her to a doctor right now. I don't know what's wrong, but she and the baby need help and she's not answering the phone."

His voice sounded strained. "Clare, she's probably just taking a nap. She's been really tired lately."

How could I get him to realize this wasn't just a freaked out teenager crying wolf? That the lives of my mother and my little brother depended on his taking action? I started crying, but before I could say another word, Grammie took the phone from me.

"Dan, if Clare says Marjorie needs to see a doctor, you better go home and get her right now." Her voice was commanding—her don't-mess-with-me voice.

I looked at her in surprise; I had never heard her talk to Dan in that voice. Her use of it now made me straighten up in gratitude, realizing that she believed me.

I heard Dan's voice asking something, but Grammie said, "I'll explain later, but it sounds like Marjorie might have preeclampsia. She needs to see a doctor immediately."

There was another mumble from the phone and then Grammie hung up.

Preeclampsia? What was that?

Grammie reassured me that Dan was going to go home

and check on Miggie. Still feeling nauseous and dizzy, I leaned against the back of my chair and looked up at her.

"What's preeclampsia?" I could barely get the words out through the pounding in my head, but I had to know.

Grammie took a breath. "Look, honey, I'm no doctor and swollen hands and feet are pretty normal during a pregnancy. Even headaches are." She looked away from me, trying to act as if it were no big deal. I kept my eyes on her until she looked back at me. She gave in, saying, "Sometimes a mother's blood pressure shoots up and then there are . . . complications." She stopped. "It can be serious for both the mother and the baby."

"Can they fix it?"

"I don't know. Usually, they try to deliver the baby early." At my horrified face, Grammie said quickly, "Dan is on his way and he'll take her to the hospital. If she does have preeclampsia, the doctors will take care of her and if the baby has to come early, Miggie is already thirty-five weeks along. He'll be fine. They both will." She stood up and put her hand on my head, like a blessing. "You've done everything you could. Now we just wait until Dan calls." She felt my forehead, checking for a temperature, and then looked at me searchingly. "Will you be OK if I go back to work and close things up? I won't be gone more than an hour."

For a moment Grammie's practicality made me mad. How could she leave when we didn't know what would happen? The dizziness and headache I'd felt were finally lessening, as if I were feeling them at a distance, but I still felt swollen and puffy. I wanted her to stay. But Grammie needed to be Ellen, the responsible employee. I swallowed my anger, thinking that maybe it would be better to be alone, try to work through these feelings I was getting from Miggie and the baby. Reluctantly, I nodded. Grammie kissed me and then picked up her purse and left. I crawled into the high-backed rocker in the living room, wrapping myself in an afghan and anxiety to wait.

Chapter Nineteen

The hour until her grandmother's return lasted days. Clare tried to concentrate on the baby, breathing deeply to calm herself and sending reassuring thoughts to him. She could sense nothing from him. He'd been so clear and strong earlier. She didn't want to think about what his lack of presence in her mind meant, but thinking about him and Miggie was all she could do. She made herself get up and check the phone several times, picking it up and listening for the dial tone. Then she went back to sending reassuring thoughts.

Clare heard the car come up the driveway and had the door open before her grandmother could use her key. They looked at each other with question in their eyes, which dropped as soon as they saw that neither of them had an answer.

"How are you feeling?" Grammie asked as she came inside, dropping her keys and purse on the plant stand in the tiny entry.

"Still have the headache and I feel puffy, but it's not as

bad as it was." Clare followed her grandmother down the hall and into her bedroom, waiting anxiously as Grammie changed out of her suit into a pair of jeans and a sweatshirt.

"Should we call again?" Clare tried to keep the quaver out of her voice, but her grandmother heard it anyway. She put her arms around Clare and they stood, holding each other.

"Dan said that he would call and it's only been an hour." Grammie smoothed down Clare's curls. "Let's wait another hour and then we'll call."

They called the house in Utah at five-thirty and again at six, but there was no answer. A few minutes before seven, the kitchen phone rang. Both of them sprang to answer it, but Clare stepped back and let her grandmother pick it up.

Clare watched her face as she listened to half of the conversation.

"Dan, how is Miggie?"

Miggie, not Marjorie. Clare had never heard Grammie call Miggie anything other than Marjorie. She must be way more upset than she was showing. It made Clare shiver.

There was a lot of talking on the other end with Grammie nodding occasionally. "What about the baby?" More talking. "Where is Barty?" After still more talking, Grammie held the phone out to Clare.

"Dan wants to speak to you."

Clare took the phone eagerly, questions tumbling out before her mouth even got close to the mouthpiece. "Whoa, whoa," Dan said. He sounded tired. "Your mom is going to be OK. The baby will be born tomorrow. Grammie will fill you in with all the details and I'll call you after he is born." He paused and then said, "I just wanted to tell you that we love you and thank god you called."

Clare heard an unfamiliar voice asking if Mr. Allred

could sign some papers. Dan spoke into the phone. "Honey, I have to go, but I'll let you talk to Barty and we'll call you tomorrow."

"Hello?"

Clare felt a rush of joy at the sound of Barty's little voice. "Barty, are you OK?"

"Sure. The doctor said we got Mom to the hospital just in time and tomorrow they're going to make the baby come."

Just in time? "What happened?"

"Dad drove up as I was getting off the bus and we went in the house. He said we needed to find Mom. So I looked downstairs and Dad went upstairs and then he yelled down for me to call 9-1-1." His voice dropped. "I was so scared and then Dad carried Mom downstairs and put her on the couch. He told me to watch her while he talked to the 9-1-1- person."

"Was she unconscious?"

"She was sort of awake but she wasn't talking. She looked awful. Then, the ambulance came and the paramedics took Mom to the hospital. Me and Dad jumped in the truck and followed them."

Clare waited, but there was no more. Typical Barty. "But Mom is going to be OK?"

"Yeah, the doctor said that she has some kind of pre something, so they need to make the baby come early. They're keeping her here to make her pressure go down. Then, she can have the baby."

He sounded so matter of fact, but Clare still felt anxious. Her heart was beating as if she had run around the block. She looked at her grandmother who nodded at her. Grammie would tell her everything. She hoped.

"We gotta go home, now. Dad says we have to feed the animals and Mom is in good hands."

"OK, Barty. I love you. Give Daddy Dan a hug from me."

Barty made a non-committal grunt and then Clare heard the dial tone.

When Barty hung up, Clare turned to Grammie. "Grammie, tell me what's really happening. I want the whole truth and don't leave anything out."

Miggie did have preeclampsia, according to the doctors, and it was not severe, but it was dangerous. She was being taken care of, but the only cure for it was for the baby to be born. The doctors wanted to get her stabilized before they induced labor.

Clare had no idea what "induced labor" meant and said so.

"The doctors will give your mother a shot that will start the process of labor and then the baby will be born," Grammie informed her.

"But he's not due for a month. Will he be OK?" The anxious feeling in Clare's stomach wasn't going away—it was getting worse.

Grammie sat down at the kitchen table and then she looked up at Clare with worried eyes. "Look, honey, I am going to be honest with you. Miggie, (there it was again) is still in danger and that puts the baby in danger, too. But the doctors are prepared for him to be premature and we just have to pray that both of them come through this safely."

The baby wasn't born the next day. The doctors had to give Miggie steroids for forty-eight hours to strengthen his lungs. Calls flew back and forth from Utah to California. I got to talk to Miggie for a few minutes. She said she was feeling better and that she was wearing at least a thousand beeping things to monitor her every movement and the baby's as well.

Then she said, "Dan told me you called and told him he had to go home and get me."

"It was just a feeling I had." I didn't know if I should tell her about the blurry vision and the headache and tiredness. And the nausea and pain. She'd felt those things herself. I didn't know how Miggie, whose ability to tell colors by touch was never talked about, felt about my baby sensing. Grammie had long ago forbidden any talk about the subject.

"Something, someone, sent you a message," Miggie said softly. "You're my little baby channeler."

Tears welled up in my eyes. "Baby channeler" made what I did with babies sound official—like something real that could be talked about—something that Miggie accepted.

"Thank you, Clare. I love you."

I was too choked up to answer, but I didn't need to. Clare, not Fresno. And, maybe now, my secret baby thing was a secret no longer. Maybe now we could talk about it.

Neither Grammie nor I left the house for two days. I spent the whole time in my room talking to the baby, telling him to be strong, that everyone was waiting for him, that he was safe and loved. Something worked—prayers, love, medication, whatever—because Jacob Daniel Allred was born at 8:23 p.m. on November 12, 1998. The doctors had to keep monitoring Miggie for a few weeks in case she did develop eclampsia, but after Jacob spent a couple of weeks in the neo-natal ward, he emerged strong and loud, at least from what we could hear in our nightly phone calls after they brought him home.

. . .

The day after the drama of Jacob's birth, I brought up the subject of my baby channeling with Grammie while we were enjoying her delicious mac and cheese.

"Grammie, you told Daddy Dan that if I said Miggie needed help, he should believe me. Does that mean you believe me? Does that mean we can talk about things like that and about Miggie and her colors now?" I took a big bite of crusty cheese and noodles and stared at her, giving her time to answer as I chewed.

Grammie put down her fork and looked back at me. Eyebrows lifted, she said, "Clare, I knew something was wrong by the way you were acting. That doesn't make me psychic." I swallowed and opened my mouth to protest, but she continued, "It was an amazing coincidence that, thank god, helped your mother and Jacob, but we aren't going to indulge in fantasies because of a single incident."

Coincidence? What about Barty? And Aunt Nita's first baby? What about Miggie being able to sort beads and jelly-beans by color without looking? I opened my mouth again, but Grammie gave me the same stern look she had given me the only other time we'd talked about this, when I was seven. She held up one hand.

"We will not discuss this any further Clare."

Her gaze softened and she put her hand down. "I love you and I trust you. You are my shining star, but psychic abilities are not real and believing in them will only get you into trouble." She picked up her plate, which still had a little heap of macaroni and cheese and two spears of asparagus on it and carried it over to the sink.

This time I didn't feel ashamed to have angered Grammie—I was mad. She and I talked about everything—everything—and yet, she wouldn't talk about this. It was as if I was a crazy person for even trying. Of all the people in our family, Grammie had been through more of my baby sensing episodes than anyone else. She and I had been together when Barty got stuck and I told her about the silver things pinching his head; Aunt Nita had told her about the day I'd said that her baby didn't like cigarettes because they made him sick and no one even knew she was pregnant until she miscarried. Grammie had seen what I was going through with Miggie and Jacob and Dan had even corroborated the things I'd said were happening to Miggie. Why, why, why was this a closed door?

I needed to talk about the baby stuff with Grammie. I'd felt Miggie's pain and Jacob's fear—it was real, not a fantasy. I'd never talked about my baby sensing with Miggie and now, she was too far away and busy with Jacob, Barty, Dan and Uncle Jack for me to ask. My friends wouldn't understand. They would think I was weird, or maybe crazy. Barty was too young. How could I figure this out on my own?

I felt adrift and. . . wrong. Was this how Miggie felt since Grammie wouldn't talk about, or even acknowledge, Miggie's ability with sensing color, even when she was doing it right in front of Grammie? I thought of Aunt Nita being so upset with me about her first baby and the way she turned her head when Miggie was picking out all the red jellybeans of the candy jar without looking. I couldn't talk with Nita either.

Shut down and shut out. Was this thing I could do even something I should do?

Chapter Twenty

2001

Clare barely remembered her father. There were fuzzy pictures in her mind of living in a tent, of being picked up and almost being able to touch the tops of trees, of a dark-haired giant with a beard and white teeth who always wore bright colors and beaded necklaces. She hadn't seen him since Barty was born. Barty had never seen him. Now, Ravi wanted to see her.

Like her, like Miggie, even like Grammie, Byron Macy Ingersoll was a name changer. Grammie told her he'd changed his name to Ravi in high school. She said that people who met him for the first time saw his dark hair and olive skin and thought he must be from India.

Clare had been able to weasel bits of information about her father from Grammie, things she knew Miggie wouldn't tell her. Ravi, according to Grammie, was a year older than Miggie and they had gone to El Dorado High School together. He played the guitar and made things out of clay.

The day after Miggie graduated, the two drove to Lake Tahoe and got married.

"Without any of us, without any money and without a plan" was the way Grammie described it. "Then they kept on moving, being artists and living off the land." Her mouth had quirked up in a twist of sarcasm.

Two days ago, Ravi had called Grammie and asked if she had contact information for Miggie and Fresno. He said he wanted to see his daughter. Grammie said he hadn't even asked about Barty.

Why now, after all these years? Why not Barty too? Grammie hadn't given Ravi Miggie's phone number or address, but she had told him that Clare was living with her in Placerville. Ravi said that he was coming through Placerville on Saturday and would stop by, if that was OK. Grammie had called Miggie, who said it was up to Clare.

Now, as Clare changed her clothes for the third time, she wondered why Miggie had given her the choice. True, at fifteen, she felt she was old enough to decide for herself. Maybe her mother recognized that as well. In any case, with or without Miggie's permission, Clare would have chosen to satisfy her curiosity about Ravi.

The meeting had been set up at Grammie's house since Grammie wouldn't allow her to go anywhere with Ravi. "We don't know anything about what he has been doing all these years or who he has become," she said.

Clare put on mascara and lip gloss; she straightened her curly locks with a curling iron. She changed her clothes two more times, wondering what was appropriate to wear when meeting your father for the first time in twelve and a half years. Preppy, dressy, or casual? Should she try to look older or younger? Sexy was out—way, way out.

In the end, she opted for a pair of jeans and a lavender V-neck sweater that made her green eyes pop. Green eyes were the only feature she shared with her mother and somehow, she'd wanted her father to remember the woman he'd left before Barty was born.

Waiting for Ravi to arrive, anxiety gave way to anger—this man had left them; he'd never bothered to contact them; he'd never tried to support them. Why should she care what he thought of her? And he was still calling her Fresno. He should be grateful that Grammie was even allowing him into her home. By the time a lime-green pickup with a beige camper shell rumbled up to the curb in front of the house, Clare was ready to rip whoever showed up into shreds.

A man wearing pointy-toed cowboy boots and a purple tunic over ripped jeans stepped out of the pickup. A battered brown cowboy hat with tightly curled edges rested on his head. His curly black hair was caught back into a loose pony-tail. His eyes were hidden behind oversize sunglasses and he sported a bushy moustache over a carefully trimmed beard that outlined his jaw.

Clare shot away from her hidden vantage point behind the living room curtains as the doorbell rang. The unaccustomed sound burst into the quiet house like fanfare, propelling Grammie out of the kitchen where she was putting finishing touches on their planned lunch.

Clare positioned herself primly on the edge of the couch and then, as her grandmother glanced at her before opening the door, she bolted down the hall toward her bedroom. From behind the open door, she heard a baritone voice say, "Well, hello Ellen, it's been a long time."

"Really?" Grammie's acerbic voice. "Won't you come in?" So that's how she was playing this—very prim, very proper. Clare took her cue, waiting until Ravi had seated himself in the living room, before she sauntered down the hallway, as unconcernedly as if there was no one waiting for her but a Girl Scout selling Thin Mints.

She had planned to stop and look down her nose haughtily at the stranger before proceeding into the room, but walking close to the wall with her head held high brought her hip painfully into contact with a narrow table. Throttling back a gasp of agony, Clare just managed to catch the ceramic vase she'd toppled from the table before it could shatter on the floor. Red with embarrassment, she came to a halt. Ravi was sitting on the couch directly in front of her. He'd removed his sunglasses and his hazel eyes gazed at her like a bright-eyed bird.

So much for a classy entrance. He stood up and Clare noticed his wiry figure was only a few inches taller than her grandmother. She nodded up at him and then slid silently into the armchair kitty-corner from the couch. Ravi flipped the sunglasses he held in one hand up and down. There was a pause. The sunglasses flipped up and down again before he said, "Hi Pumpkin. You've really grown."

Pumpkin. The name thrummed a chord deep within her. She almost remembered being pumpkin. The comfort of being rocked in someone's arms. Ravi's?

Grammie broke into the silence and asked, "Would you like something to drink, Byron?"

"Wow, it's been awhile since anyone's called me *that*." His thick eyebrows quirked as his eyes bugged out comically.

Clare almost snickered, but she caught the frostiness on Grammie's face and decided otherwise.

"I'll take some tea if you have it. Or water if you don't," Ravi said. He flipped the sunglasses up and down once more as he returned to a sitting position. Clare noticed his action and saw him do it again when he began jiggling his knee. So, she wasn't the only one feeling nervous. It made her feel better, but still unbalanced. She remembered that she was the aggrieved party here and this stiffened her spine. She looked at him directly, challengingly.

Ravi had earrings in both ears—tiny gold hoops. He wore three beaded necklaces. She could see them through the V of his tunic, lying against the dark hair on his chest. Clare had thought men with lightly furred chests were sexy, but now that one of them was her father, she might have to rethink things. She moved her eyes up from his chest to his face. He was gazing at her with appraisal.

"You look like my mom—except for your eyes. They're like peridots."

Peridots? He didn't say her eyes were like Miggie's. Maybe he didn't remember. His eyes, on the other hand, were like Barty's, and when he grinned as he was doing now, Clare felt a shiver, seeing Barty's grin on a face with a mustache and beard. She wondered what Ravi would think of the new and improved Miggie—if he ever thought of her at all. And what would he think of Barty—if they ever met?

She saw her family more often now since they lived closer; they had moved to Nevada last year after Uncle Jack died and the Utah ranch was sold. Dan said California was too expensive, so they had purchased a house with five acres in Minden, only a few hours away from Placerville by car. The house had a view of the mountains from every window. Barty told her there were wild mustangs that sometimes ran through the property and Einstein, the dog loved to chase after them.

"I just couldn't keep up the ranch, darlin'. It wasn't me, after all," Dan told her when they had stopped at Grammie's house on their way to Nevada. Dan had looked so sad that Clare had hugged him gently.

Pulling from all fourteen years of her accumulated

wisdom she'd said, "It's OK, Daddy. You only get to live one life and isn't it better to live the way that works for you rather than try to live the life you think you should?"

Clare came to herself with a start. Ravi said she looked like his mother. Her other grandmother—the one she'd never seen. That she could remember. "I don't remember her," she said.

"Well, I'd be surprised if you did," said Ravi, knee still jiggling. "She only saw you once—when you were a baby." He looked away from her and jumped up to help Grammie bring in the tray of refreshments.

Clare noted that Grammie had put out a Diet Coke for her. Since her grandmother thought sugar-free soft drinks were poison, Clare wondered if this was Grammie's way of softening the blow of meeting her father. She watched as Ravi took a mug of tea and set it carefully on one of the stone coasters from the set on the end table.

"I remember these coasters," he said, holding one of them aloft, admiring it. "Tried making some out of wood, but they didn't sell."

Grammie's mouth tightened, but she said nothing.

Ravi flipped the sunglasses once more and took a sip of his tea. He looked down toward Clare's ever-present red Converse and a small smile came over his face. Clare reached over for her Diet Coke, wondering at the smile.

"Don't do sugar, huh? Me neither. Cancer loves sugar." His smile became a grin with uneven teeth gleaming whitely from within the curtains of his moustache. Then he looked at Clare directly. "But that aspartame stuff is bad too. You shouldn't drink it."

Clare fumed. How dare he presume to tell her what to do? Like he had any right to do so. She glanced at her grandmother, who gazed back impassively. Clare read that look as reminding her to watch her temper.

Deciding to forgo her fury, she asked, "So, what do you do?"

"A little of this, a little of that." At her look of impatience, he chuckled. "Right now I'm between projects. I just sold my ceramic shop and I'm starting a new venture."

"Where?" Her grandmother's dry voice broke in, the single word sounding as if she hoped it were far, far away.

Ravi took another sip of tea and smiled like a cat stretching in the sun. "I haven't decided just yet. Maybe I should move back here to my hometown."

Before the sparks shooting out of her grandmother's eyes could incinerate anything, Clare asked, "Do you still do ceramics?"

"I am a ceramic artist," Ravi announced, which did nothing to clarify anything. "Here, I brought you something." He reached into the side pocket of his tunic and pulled out a small, translucent pale green bowl and presented it to her. "It's a porcelain tea bowl—one of my best." Out of the other pocket, he produced another tiny bowl, brown with a burnt sienna colored glaze dribbled down the sides. "And this is for you, Ellen," he said, setting it down on the table between them.

Clare turned the tea bowl over and over. "Ravi" was etched in tiny letters on the bottom of the bowl. Light from the living room window glowed through the bowl and Clare could see the shadow of her fingers. It was a beautiful thing, warm to the touch. Clare tried not to like it.

"Thank you," Ellen said stiffly. She neither inspected the bowl on the table nor touched it.

"Thank you," echoed Clare. She set the bowl down on an end table and looked at her father.

He smiled at her and said, "So how old are you, now?"

There were a thousand questions crowding her mouth, but she wasn't sure if they would be answered. She wasn't sure whether some of them, like *Why did you leave us?* should even be asked in front of her grandmother. She wasn't sure who this stranger was or why he was here. So she answered simply, "Fifteen."

"Oh. Wow." This information seemed to rock him as evidenced by sunglasses flipping and knee jiggling.

It shouldn't be a surprise, since he was, after all, her father. "Barty is twelve," she added, watching his eyes. "We have a picture if you want to see him."

Ravi's eyes shot toward the front door. He set down his mug slowly, spending much time centering it on the coaster. Then he turned back to her and smiled. "Oh, that would be great."

Clare turned around and picked Barty's sixth grade school picture off a shelf full of family photos, including one of Miggie and Dan on their wedding day. Ravi's eyes followed her and stayed, gazing at the shelf, until she handed him Barty's picture. In it, Barty's dark hair was cut so short that his curls were extinct. His hazel eyes, exactly like Ravi's, stared out at his father, his grin a replica without a mustache.

Ravi stared down at the picture as if looking at a Wanted poster. He glanced away and Clare produced the picture of her mother and Dan. "Here's Miggie and Daddy Dan." She held it out in front of his eyes.

Ravi glanced for a nanosecond and then said as he stood up, "Very nice. Well, I've got to be going. I'm on the way to Nevada." He set Barty's photo down on the table and flicked his sunglasses. "It's good to see you both again." He moved toward the door.

Good to see you both again? After almost thirteen years,

her father finally came back into her life and all he could say was "Good to see you both again?" As if she and Grammie were the same age; as if they were former neighbors and he was just passing through the 'hood. Not even staying for lunch? And hadn't he just said he hadn't decided where he was going yet? Was Nevada big enough for both Ravi and Miggie?

Grammie walked Ravi to the door and ushered him through it. Out on the porch, Ravi touched his hat to them and then walked hurriedly down the sidewalk to his lime-green pickup. It started with a rumble and a snort of blue smoke from the tailpipe. As it rolled down the street, Ravi's hand waving over the top of the cab, Clare remembered that she hadn't told him about her name change.

Still clenching Miggie's picture in her hand, the frame cutting into her palm, she wondered why both her parents had left her in luridly colored pickups.

Chapter Twenty-One

April 2002

Dan came to pick me up for spring break during my junior year at El Dorado High School. I had gotten my driver's license six months earlier, but while Grammie let me tool around town in her Corolla, I wasn't yet allowed to drive the two hours from Placerville to Minden. Someone had to ferry me back and forth on vacations and holidays. Sometimes Dan did it; other times Grammie brought me to Minden and stayed for a few days.

It was Dan's turn to pick me up and, since he'd had to work that day, he didn't arrive at Grammie's until after seven in the evening. She tried to talk him into staying the night and leaving early in the morning, but Dan said he felt like driving. It was only an eighty mile drive, but we had just had a spring dumping of snow a few days earlier. Our route would take us up Highway 50 into the mountains over Echo Summit to Meyers near South Lake Tahoe, and from there to Highway 88, the old Mormon Emigrant Trail, and through

Luther Pass and more mountains. Dan said there was a lot of snow, but the roads were clear and the passes were open, with no restrictions.

Grammie made us eat dinner but allowed us to leave despite her concern about going over the snow-covered passes late at night. As we tucked Jacob's huge Easter basket and a bunch of mysterious Easter gifts into Dan's pickup, Grammie handed me ten dollars and made us promise to stop by the gas station to pick up a couple of extra-caffeinated coffees. I made a face—coffee tasted like burnt sunflower seeds to me— but we promised. We exchanged quick goodbye hugs as it was already too cold outside to linger on this April night.

At the gas station, Dan told me to keep the ten and he disappeared into the mini-mart. He returned with a large coffee for him and a Mountain Dew for me, along with two packages of mini doughnuts—powdered sugar for him and my favorite crumb cakes.

Fueled with sugar and caffeine, we drove up Highway 50 which was almost deserted. With the road mostly to ourselves, we talked about school and my work on the school newspaper, about what Barty and Jacob were doing and the new jewelry Miggie was making. Dan told me a little about his job at the auto body shop and some new paint designs he wanted to try out when he found the right vehicle.

The Mountain Dew was disgusting, but it was better than coffee. I didn't want to hurt Dan's feelings, so I drank the whole thing and ate all six of my doughnuts. I wasn't used to caffeine and could already feel a buzzing in my ears. My heart was racing. During one marathon monologue from me, Dan grinned and said, "Slow down, ladybug. That Dew is messing with you. If you talk any faster, the words are gonna smoke on the way out of your mouth."

I blushed and tried to modulate my speech, but Dew and

doughnuts were a deadly combination. Grammie wouldn't have to worry about me falling asleep—it felt like a jolt of lightning had passed through me.

The snow on the sides of the road slowly increased as we approached Echo Summit. Moonlight boosted the whiteness like a super-power. The pines were black silhouettes with silver, gray and charcoal shadows beneath them. Dan turned the heater up.

"Hasn't been any snow for two days, but there's been some melt and it's cold enough to freeze it into black ice," Dan said.

I knew about black ice, but I hadn't driven in it yet. "Why do they call it 'black ice' again?"

"It's ice on the road that you can't really see against the black of the asphalt, except that it gleams in the headlights like the road is wet. It's dangerous because people don't notice it and they drive the way they always do. If you hit the edge of the ice or you're going too fast, you'll spin and skid."

Grammie hadn't let me do much driving at night, especially when it was snowing, but I knew that you were supposed to steer in the direction of the skid and not use your brakes. I peered at the road. It looked shiny to me. "If you're supposed to steer in the direction of the skid, is that the way the front of the car is going or the back?"

Dan's eyebrows quirked up as if he couldn't believe the question, but he said, "The back, darlin', the back."

The piles of plowed snow grew higher. Dan slowed and I could see the sheen of ice on the highway. Headlights bloomed behind us, growing brighter and bigger as a vehicle grew closer. As a blinding light filled our rear view mirror, causing both of us to wince, I heard the rumbling roar of an engine. Then, a huge yellow pickup truck charged past us in the passing lane, the word "Dodge" emblazoned on the tailgate. The truck accelerated in front of us and then, shockingly, it was whirling, spinning across both lanes of the highway before catching the berm of hard-packed snow with a tire. The truck flipped over in the air and landed on its side before gliding to a stop.

In the seconds it had taken for the truck to go from four tires on the ground to no tires on the ground, Dan had reacted by taking his foot off the gas and gently touching the brake, steering us away from the flying vehicle. Our back end began to slide, making both my hands and stomach clench, but Dan steered us out of the skid and brought us to a stop in the opposite lane.

Silence filled my ears like a ball of cotton. Then I began to hear the ticking of our cooling engine. The highway, lighted only by our headlights and those of the truck lying on its side, was an eerie meshing of dark and light. Dan unbuckled his seat belt and turned to me. "Are you all right?" His voice was anxious, one of his hands patted my arm, my side, my face as he leaned toward me.

Moving as if I were a sloth, I unbuckled the seat belt and said, "I'm OK." Except for my still clenched stomach.

Dan said, "Let's get out of the truck."

I opened the passenger door and slid down to the slickness of the road, my feet in their smooth-soled high tops slipping on the ice. I held on to the door to keep myself upright as Dan grabbed something from behind the seat and crunched around the front of the truck in his boots.

"Are you sure you're OK?" Dan's face was worried as he glanced at me and then over at the overturned truck. He draped an old jacket over my shoulders, on top of my pretty, but far too lightweight, Easter jacket. "That guy probably needs help."

I nodded and waved him away, shrugging into the jacket,

grateful for the extra warmth. Shivering from a combination of dread and cold, I hoped the person in the truck wasn't dead.

"Stay out of the road. Climb up on one of the snowbanks, out of the way," Dan called back over his shoulder as he walked over to the truck, putting his feet down carefully.

The Dodge was lying on the driver's side. Dan bent down and peered into the front window and then walked around to the passenger side, his body a black silhouette as he passed in front of the headlights. In their snow-reflected glow, I saw him climb up on the frame and try to pull the door open. When nothing happened, he called to me, "Clare, can you reach under the front seat and get the flares? There should be two of them."

I nodded, even though I didn't think he could really see me in the eerie darkness. I climbed/slid down off the hill of packed snow I'd been standing on and found the flares. There was a blanket and some work gloves behind the seat, so I brought those too as I slide-walked my way across the highway to Dan. The air smelled of gasoline and winter. My teeth began to chatter and the tip of my nose felt frozen.

Dan was still tugging on the passenger door. It finally popped open and fingers waved out. Dan bent down, grasping the reaching fingers and asked the person inside if they could move, were they injured.

"I bumped my head pretty hard on the headliner, but I think I'm OK," a raspy voice said. "Can you help me out of here?"

Dan reached in with both hands and in a few minutes, a skinny guy who looked to be only a few years older than me, was leaning up against the truck. He didn't appear to be bleeding anywhere, but his legs weren't doing a good job of holding him upright. I glided the final few steps to his side while Dan climbed off the frame, rocking the truck slightly.

A thousand anxious questions later, we ascertained that the boy was unhurt, except for feeling bruised and having a knot on the top of his head. The boy, Tim, said he lived in Placerville but had a girlfriend in South Lake Tahoe. He'd been anxious to show her his new truck. "Now look at it," he said mournfully.

"I don't think we can get it off the road," said Dan, "but we can see if it will slide a little." He wouldn't let Tim help. "You might have a concussion, so just lean up against the snow pile while Clare and I try to rock it."

Tim looked at me doubtfully but let me help him over to the piled up snow on the side of the road. I wrapped the blanket around him and slipped my way to where Dan was waiting. He made me put on the work gloves. I hadn't even realized that I couldn't feel my fingers anymore. The work gloves recalled my attention to the fingers, but weren't much help in providing warmth.

Pushing a big, heavy truck over to the side of the road sounded like a crazy idea, but maybe if we could get the truck moving just a little, it would slide on the slippery ice. Still, even with my caffeinated super strength, neither Dan nor I could get any real traction on the ice to push. After my slick-soled feet slid out from under me for the second time, Dan patted my back and motioned me back to Tim. He lit the flares and placed them on the road on either side of the truck. The hissing of the flares and the crunch of Dan's boots as he made his way over to us were the only sounds in the snowy silence. Maybe all the bears and mountain lions were hibernating; it sure seemed as if all the cars in the world were doing so.

"Come on, we'll take you to Tahoe where you can get

checked out at the hospital and you can call your girlfriend," said Dan. Tim protested, saying he didn't want to leave his truck, but Dan took his arm gently and said, "No one is going to steal your truck, believe me. We'll talk about your options on the way."

Dan put Tim in the middle of the pickup's bench seat and before we climbed in on either side of him, he leaned close to me and said, "I put the boy in the middle so he can't lean his head on the window and fall asleep. If he has a concussion, we have to keep him awake." He squeezed my shoulder, "Good job helping, by the way."

I felt my stomach finally unclench.

Dan's trusty turquoise pickup slid a few times when it started to move, but, finally, we were in the right lane and headed toward Tahoe. I looked back to see the flares casting a satanic red glow over the piles of plowed snow while the headlights of the disabled truck reflected the sheen of the black pavement. If I'd thought it was an eerie scene before, it was definitely freaky now. Dan said leaving the headlights on would wear down the battery, but the additional light might make the truck more visible and prevent another accident.

We were only a minute or so away from the summit and soon the lights of lake communities sparkled against the darkness as we started down into Meyers, a few miles outside South Lake Tahoe. "There's a convenience store in Meyers and I'm sure they'll have a phone we can use to report the accident," said Dan. "They can get a tow truck up there to move your vehicle," he told Tim.

At this, Tim moaned. Dan and I swiveled our heads toward him in concern, but he said, "I've only had my truck three days. I haven't even paid my first insurance premium yet and I sure can't afford a tow truck."

Dan and I looked at each other. There wasn't any other

way Tim was going to get his truck back. I felt bad for him and from the expression in Dan's eyes I could tell that he did too, but I also knew Dan's thoughts about reckless driving. Tim's speeding had been partly to blame for the accident and he was going to have to deal with it.

The convenience store was open and the man behind the counter called the CHP himself. Dan talked to an officer on the phone, telling him where the vehicle was and that we would take Tim to Barton Hospital in South Lake Tahoe. An officer could talk to him there.

Officer McGruder was waiting for us at the hospital entrance, a fact that made Tim moan yet again. He'd said almost nothing in Dan's pickup or in the convenience store. I'd kept my eye, and my elbow, on him, making sure he was awake, but I think the destruction of his new truck had him tongue-tied. Sitting on a plastic chair in the emergency room waiting area, still wrapped in the blanket, he looked miserable.

While the ER doctor was examining Tim, Officer McGruder took statements from Dan and me, as witnesses. He assured us that another officer was en route to the site. Tim reappeared, with a fistful of forms and still wearing the blanket. The ER doctor accompanied him. The doctor must have thought we were Dan's family because he told us Tim had a mild concussion and he gave us instructions about his care. He would need rest and he might have a headache, the doctor said. Tim nodded at this and winced as he did so. The doctor said he could take acetaminophen for the headache. "He'll be fine," he said before leaving us in the waiting room.

Tim shook his head slowly and winced once more. "Never going to be fine again."

I didn't think he was talking about the concussion. Officer McGruder suppressed a smile and left the waiting room.

Dan used the hospital pay phone to call Miggie and tell her why we would be late. Then he got the girlfriend's phone number from Tim and called. Tim probably could have done this himself, but he was still looking a little dazed.

"Well, they're on their way," Dan told Tim a couple of minutes later.

Tim's eyes opened so wide that all I could see was white. "They?" he said in a quavering voice.

I could tell that Dan was trying not to grin. "Yeah, your girlfriend and her dad."

Tim gave a dramatic groan. I edged over to Dan. "Could we stay until they get here?"

Dan nodded. "Exactly what I was thinking, darlin'."

We sat down in plastic chairs on either side of poor Tim, trying to bolster him with our presence, and in ten minutes, a scared looking girl about my age, and a burly middle-aged man wearing an old plaid flannel jacket, a Bass Pro fishing hat and a frown, barreled through the ER doors.

The girl flew over to Tim who was slumped in his chair, eyes closed. He opened them at her touch, managing to look both gratified and pathetic. His expression and posture changed dramatically at the sight of her dad looming up behind her. Jerking himself upright in the chair, Tim looked like a soldier who expects to be shot at dawn.

"You the guy who called?" The burly man's voice was too loud in a place for the sick and injured; it was too loud for the parking lot outside; it was just plain too loud.

Dan stood up from his chair and nodded. The man shook his hand. "He doing OK?" he boomed. Under his plaid jacket, I could see a gray thermal shirt, frayed at the collar, and he wore a pair of stained jeans that looked as if he'd cleaned fish in them. Maybe he had, since the aroma of fish seemed to emanate from him like a cloud.

Tim closed his eyes once more and allowed the girl to fuss over him while Dan filled in the dad about the concussion, the doctor's instructions, and the accident. As they were talking, Officer McGruder returned and said that another officer was already at the accident location and a tow truck was on the way. Our work being done, Dan and I said goodbye to Tim and friends and left.

We had almost reached the outside hospital doors when "Hey!" echoed off the tiled floor and the walls behind us. We turned as one to find the dad chasing after us, the smell of fish rolling toward us. Dan stepped in front of me as though protecting me from His Burliness, but the man grabbed Dan's hand and shook it again. "Thanks, man. We'll take good care of him, make sure his parents know he's OK."

Dan must have looked doubtful because the man grinned and nodded at me before saying in what he must have thought was a lower tone of voice, "You got a kid; you know how it is. You have to act tough or they'll walk right over you." He looked back through the ER window at his daughter, sitting next to Tim, comforting him. "Merrilee would have my hide if anything happened to that boy."

He fished into his jacket pocket and produced a business card which he handed to Dan. "You ever need any help with taxes, you let me know. I'll make sure you're OK."

When he went back inside the ER, Dan showed me the business card, which read "Charles Hudson Whitney III, Certified Public Accountant." The thought of our fishy friend hunched over piles of forms during tax season made us both laugh all the way out to the truck.

The drive home through Luther Pass was a piece of cake after that, despite snow and ice. I was proud of Dan for stopping to help Tim, for taking charge of the situation and for staying with him at the hospital, and I told him so.

He smiled at me and said, "Thanks, darlin'. You were pretty great at taking care of the boy, yourself. He's still wearing the blanket you wrapped around him."

I'd thought about retrieving it, but Tim looked so pathetic, I couldn't bear to take one more thing away from him. "You think Tim's girlfriend's dad is going to be hard on him?" I was a little worried about what might happen after we left.

"It's my impression that Mr. Whitney is more loud bark than bite," joked Dan. "I don't know what Tim's own parents will say about this, but I think he's in good hands with Charles Hudson Whitney III, CPA."

"Would you ever be like that? Try to intimidate a boy if he dated me?" I had a few prospects in mind, and while Grammie could be scary enough when she wanted to be, I wasn't sure how Dan would react to a prospective suitor.

"I don't think I have the volume for it," said my slender, soft-spoken stepfather. We chuckled and then he said in a more serious tone, "But, if you're ever with someone who's not treating you right, then you let me know. There's just some things I won't tolerate."

Our eyes met. In his, I could see resolve. In mine, I hoped he could see gratitude.

Chapter Twenty-Two

"I don't want to go." Barty clenched the door handle of Miggie's Camry as if preparing to leap out of the car. I'd told him where we were going as soon as we'd gotten on the highway. I'd felt sneaky about telling him (and Dan and Miggie) that we were going to Carson City to pick up some Easter candy and visit the U. S. Mint. Instead, we were driving to Virginia City to meet up with Ravi. I was determined that my brother should meet his biological father.

"Look, you're thirteen—practically a man—and you need to meet your father." I couldn't identify, even to myself, why Barty needed to meet our father—I just knew that he did.

"I *have* a father, remember?" Barty's voice was still changing so the beginning of his sentence started out baritone and ended up soprano with a sort of warble in the middle. Three years younger than me, he was already taller than my five feet by four inches. "Dad is the best dad, ever. I don't need another one, especially one that doesn't even seem to know I'm alive." His skinny frame was leaning away from me, rigid and angry.

I kept my eyes on the road, concentrating. Miggie seemed relieved to have me use her Camry to drive Barty and Jacob around, but the furthest I'd driven in six months had been the twenty-six straight-as-an-arrow miles from Placerville to the Folsom outlets on Highway 50 with Grammie. Virginia City, where Ravi had moved, was only thirty miles from Minden where Barty lived with Miggie, Daddy Dan and Jacob, but I had to change highways four times and the road looked like it would get curvy once I got onto Nevada State Highway 341. I'd tried to enlist Barty's chivalry when we got into the car by telling him he could be my navigator, but when he found out where we were going, he'd refused.

"C'mon, Barty. I've never driven this way before."

"So, turn around." He sounded furious and I couldn't blame him. I hadn't realized how he felt about Ravi ignoring him, and worst of all, I hadn't invited him to go—I had simply made the decision for him. Who knew if Ravi would even be home?

It had sounded like such a heartwarming, Hallmark kind of idea when I'd dreamed it up a month ago. After his single visit, Ravi had begun calling me once every two months, "checking in" as he called it. I never asked him to check in and each time he'd called, our conversations had been brief and forced. In every call, however, I had made it a point to include news of Barty and how well he was doing. In the last call, Ravi had asked me whether Barty was good in school. Surprised, I'd said that school and Barty were not friends, but he was good at lots of other things, especially with animals.

Ravi's low chuckle came to my ears. "School and me weren't friends, either. I just hated having to sit and be bored."

It was when I got off the phone that I got the idea Barty needed to meet Ravi. He'd relocated to Virginia City just after Dan and Miggie had moved to Minden, a fact I had neglected to share with my mother. I had no idea why he picked Virginia City, but I didn't think he knew that Miggie lived only thirty miles away from him. He'd given me his address and in our bi-monthly conversations, he'd indicated a slight interest in Barty. Even though Barty had never said he wanted to meet our father, I thought that psychologically speaking—psychology was my newest interest—it would be a good thing for him. So, I had hatched this plan for Easter vacation and not wanting to deal with any possible nay-saying, I hadn't said anything to anyone about it. Till now. And Barty wasn't having it.

I wriggled my toes in my new purple Converse. Red was my signature color, but purple was my concession to Easter. Barty sulked against the passenger door, staring out the window. We didn't see each other all that often, and I didn't want him to be mad at me during the short time we had together.

"Barty, I'm sorry. I really thought this would be a good thing. Last time I talked to Ravi, he asked about you and I thought we could have an adventure together to see him."

Silence.

Waves of guilt and remorse began to flood me as the Great Reconciliation Idea began to feel more like The Really Stupid Idea. I took a breath. "Can you forgive me?" I pleaded. The exit to the next freeway was coming up soon—somewhere. Either I turned off and followed my plan or I turned off and turned around.

Barty looked over at me, just a brief glance, but it was packed with resentment. "Why do you think I need to meet him?" His voice was low.

"Well, don't you think you should—sometime? Do you want to wait until you're thirty or something?" I couldn't prevent the tone in my voice from suggesting that waiting so long, until he was, like, middle-aged, was unreasonable.

"He calls you. He doesn't call me."

That had been, still was, a stumbling block for me, too. Why wouldn't Ravi have contacted both of us? Because he didn't know where Miggie was or because he was scared of talking to her? I caught my breath—here I was making excuses for a man I barely knew. And putting my much loved brother into a situation he hadn't chosen and didn't want.

I saw the exit for Highway 50 to Dayton and Fallon coming up and took it, being careful to use the turn signal and slow down. Then I said, "Help me figure out how to get back on the freeway to Minden."

Barty got us turned around. Back on U.S. 395, with only light traffic, we cruised along, listening to the radio.

He turned down the volume on "Kryptonite" and said in gruff voice, "Thanks, Frezzie."

"Don't call me Frezzie," I growled, but I smiled at him. He grinned back and turned the radio up. "Kryptonite" morphed into Shania Twain's "Man! I Feel Like a Woman" which bounced around inside the Camry. We started singing at the top of our voices, Barty pitching his voice to falsetto on the chorus as he put his hands on his hip and batted his eyelashes. We were laughing so hard that it took a few minutes before I realized that I was having trouble keeping the car straight. I slowed and turned the radio down. The car was veering to the left and I could hear the thumping of a tire.

Barty's eyes were wide as he said, "I think we've got a flat."

Heart pounding, I slowed again, put the turn signal on and limped to the shoulder of the freeway. As the few cars whizzed past, we slid out of the car and viewed the damage. Flat tire, right rear. I looked at Barty; he looked at me.

"Have you ever changed a tire?" I asked. He shook his head. "Me either. Daddy Dan walked me through it when I first got my license, but I think I must have. . . blanked out."

Barty shrugged. "There are two of us. How hard can it be? First, we need a jack."

I opened the trunk. No jack in or under Miggie's tote bags of jewelry. No spare tire visible either. Crapadoodle.

Barty and I tore the car apart searching for the jack and tire. They had to be there because Daddy Dan would never let Miggie drive a car without them. At last, we found a little hole with a ring in the bottom of the trunk. I pulled up on the ring and, voila! A spare tire. We pulled it out and there was the jack, nestled under the tire well along with some other tools.

We spread out all the tools and stared at them. I tried to remember what Daddy Dan had shown me. "So, I think," I began, trying to talk my way through the process, "you have to jack up the car and take off the old tire and then put on the new one. Simple."

"Lug nuts," Barty muttered. I looked at him, thinking I had heard those words before, but not remembering when or where. "After you jack up the car, you have to loosen the lug nuts on the tire." He looked at me, certainty in his eyes. "Dad told me that you had to do that."

I remembered that lug nuts figured somewhere in Dan's directions, but unfortunately, I didn't remember what they looked like. We peered at the tire, searching for lug nuts.

There was a crunch of gravel behind us and the hot, rumbling breath of a vehicle. Barty and I turned in tandem. A lime-green pickup with a beige camper shell farted blue smoke. Of all the highways, in all the towns, in all the world—

there couldn't be two lime-green pickups with ugly beige camper shells, could there? Crapadoodie. Barty was going to meet Ravi after all.

"Hey there!" Ravi's cheery voice called out. "Need some help?" Gravel crunched under his feet as he walked up to us.

Barty looked over at him and said, "Maybe, a little." His voice was cautious, but hopeful.

I turned slowly to face my father. He was standing next to Barty and looking down at the tire. Then he looked up and our eyes made contact. Ravi's eyes widened comically and he broke into a huge grin.

"Well, I'll be! It's you!" He reached forward with his hand as if he were going to take my hand and shake it or maybe pull me toward him. I backed up and flicked a look at Barty. He was crouched by the tire, still looking for lug nuts. Ravi's eyes followed mine and I saw him do a double take— just like one of the Three Stooges. If nothing else, our father had one expressive face.

Barty looked up in surprise at Ravi's words. He glanced at me, caught the expression on my face and looked back at Ravi. Barty frowned in puzzlement and looked back at me. Ravi looked at me. Crapadoodie.

"Uh, Barty, this is Ravi." I didn't add, "Our father." I hoped I wouldn't have to.

Ravi now looked as if he had eaten a bad hotdog. Barty's rigid face wore the same look. It could have been funny, but it wasn't. Not yet anyway.

"Uh, where did you come from?" I managed.

"I was on my way back home from Carson and I saw the car pull off the freeway." Ravi was looking at me, but darting lightning looks at Barty from the corners of his eyes as though Barty were a dangerous dog. "The road was pretty quiet, so I flipped a U-ie and came to see if anyone needed help."

Barty was standing up straight and glaring at the back of the car. "We don't need any help. It's just a flat tire." His voice was formal, as rigid sounding as his face looked. He picked up a jack as if he knew exactly what to do with it.

We had no clue how to change the tire. But I didn't know if Barty could handle having the father who hadn't ever talked to him fix our flat. And then what? We all go out for a burger like a happy little family?

I saw Ravi take a breath. The feather on his cowboy hat fluttered in the breeze. In a quiet voice he said, "I'm sure you're capable of changing this tire, but sometimes those lug nuts can be a bear. I've got a lug wrench in my truck." He walked back to his pickup.

When he was out of earshot, I said, "Barty, I'm sorry. I had no idea . . ."

His eyes looked like stones.

"But . . . we could use his help."

He glared at me.

"Just this first time. Then we'll know what to do." I heard the pleading tone of my voice. Even though there was no way I could have planned this, I still felt guilty.

Silence.

Crunch, crunch, crunch. Ravi was back, wielding a tool that looked just like one of the tools that had been tucked in with the jack. Barty stalked away to the passenger side of the car and slid inside. Ravi glanced at his back and then at me. In a hearty voice, he said, "Well, I see you did all the hard work—found the jack and the spare!"

It took him about twenty-five minutes to change the tire with my hovering. He detailed every step in the tire-changing procedure in a voice that sounded like he was trying to reach the back rows of a huge theater. Barty had to have heard that voice, but he never moved out of the passenger seat.

I paid attention, noted that the wheel cover had to be removed before you could loosen the lug nuts (before you could even find the lug nuts) and you had to put rocks under the other tires so the car didn't roll. Lug nuts had to be loosened, not removed, and *then* you jacked up the car. Then the lug nuts could be removed. By the time we were done, I realized that lug nuts were a big part of the whole procedure.

While Ravi was retightening the lug nuts I had tightened, he whispered, "Is he going to be OK?" He nodded toward Barty's still turned back.

As we put the wheel cover back on, I whispered back, "What do you think? He thinks you don't even care if he's alive. I don't know what he feels, but maybe you should take an interest, you know?"

His lips, under the bushy mustache, tightened. He tucked the bag of tools and the jack into the wheel well in the trunk and dropped the flat tire on top. Then he wiped his hands on a rag that I later realized was one of Miggie's workout shirts and said, "I'll talk to him."

While I put the cover back on the wheel well and checked to make sure everything was back in the trunk, Ravi walked up to Barty. He said something to Barty's back, waited for a minute, and then walked back to me. His face was grim, even his mustache drooped.

"Thanks for helping us," I said.

He nodded once. "No problem. Take it easy getting back on the road and make sure you get that flat fixed soon. Why were you out here, anyway?"

"I was bringing Barty to meet you."

His eyebrows quirked up. Now I felt guilty because I hadn't asked Ravi either.

"Well, we met."

He walked back to his pickup and climbed in. He pulled

into the nearest lane and then crossed the median to make an illegal U-turn onto the freeway going in the opposite direction.

I turned back to the car. Barty was already seat-belted inside. It was going to be a long ride home.

Chapter Twenty-Three

Miggie sighed with relief as Barty enticed Jacob away from the screaming siren of the fire engine that had become his new favorite toy. The two of them went outside, Barty calling over his shoulder that they were going to look for wild horses as Einstein barked in joyful agreement. Miggie bent her head back over the red jasper pendant and added another bead of solder to the ring of solder beads outlining the oval stone. What were they doing home so early? And thank god they were—that firetruck was going to be the death of her.

Both Clare and Barty were acting strangely: Barty hadn't even said hello before he hustled Jacob outside and Clare was standing by the kitchen doorway looking as if she expected something to fall on her. Miggie paused in her work, letting the heat of the soldering iron build. "You're home early. What's up?"

"We had a flat tire."

Miggie slid her eyes sideways toward her daughter. "So, what did you do?"

"We couldn't remember all the steps that Daddy Dan had told us about how to change a tire, but . . . a man drove up and changed it for us. Then we just came home."

It was said casually, but Miggie felt her heart freeze. "A stranger changed the tire for you?" She thought of what Dan would think of this but kept her voice neutral. At least they were home and safe. She tried to breathe.

Clare flushed, stared at her shoes. Then she mumbled, "It wasn't a stranger. It was. . . Ravi."

Miggie paused, soldering iron in hand. "Who?" She looked confused.

Clare rolled her eyes. "You know, Ravi, our father, the one who used to be Byron Macy Ingersoll?"

Miggie raised her eyebrows at the sarcastic tone. "Yes, I know the man; I just find it hard to believe that, of all the billions of people in the world, your father happened to be driving down a road where you had a flat tire and he stopped to change it for you."

Clare looked away. "Well, he lives in Virginia City and he was going home. There weren't very many cars on the highway."

"He lives here?" As Miggie's voice scaled up, she heard in her own voice an echo of her mother's. That bothered her more than learning that Ravi was living thirty miles away in the same state. "Since when?"

"He moved there a year after you guys came to Minden."

"And you didn't tell me?" She couldn't help it, her voice seemed to stay in that upper register. If she'd known that Ravi was living in Virginia City, she would have tried to make sure they relocated to Oregon or somewhere far, far away, like Kansas. Had her mother known about this?

"You never wanted to talk about him." Clare paused,

then said, "You know I talk to him, right? On the phone? Grammie told you?"

Miggie knew that Ravi called Clare and that he had stopped by to visit once. Ellen had let Miggie know about that proposed visit before she had agreed to it. At the time, Miggie thought Clare was old enough to make her own decision about whether or not she wanted to see her father, but now, with the man living so close, she was surprised at the anger she felt at the thought of him with her children. "What does he say when he calls?"

"Nothing much. He's building a pottery studio and he tells me about it; he asks me about school." Then, as if the words had been forced out of her, Clare blurted, "He never asks about Barty and it makes me mad."

Still—after thirteen years, thought Miggie. What an asshole. Carefully, she added another bead of solder.

"Why isn't he interested in Barty? Barty is his son." Clare's voice sounded as if she were going to cry.

"When I knew him, all he was interested in was making things out of clay. Doesn't sound like *that* has changed." Miggie didn't care if Clare and Barty thought their father was a self-centered prick, which he was, but she did not want them to know the reason Ravi shunned Barty.

"Well it doesn't make any sense. They should know each other."

"Barty doesn't need him—he's got Dan."

"That's what Barty said." Clare turned her back slightly.

Miggie couldn't see her daughter's eyes, but there was something in the tone of her voice. She decided to change the subject and circle back to it later. Clare could be stubborn if pushed. Instead, she asked, "Did you get the Easter stuff?"

The question took Clare off balance. "No." She waited a beat before adding, "Barty didn't want to go shopping."

Chapter Twenty-Three

"Why not? He was all excited about picking out the candy and plastic eggs."

"He was mad at me." Too late, Clare realized an honest answer might not be a good idea

"Because . . ." Maddeningly, Miggie held the tip of the soldering iron up, waiting. Smoke wafted toward Clare along with the acrid odor of melted solder.

"Because I was taking Barty to meet Ravi and I hadn't asked him first. He didn't want to go." Now that she'd said it, Clare heard how awful it sounded. Not only had she not taken Barty and Ravi's feelings into consideration, she hadn't thought about how her mother might feel. Actually, she'd avoided thinking about it since she'd heard it was sometimes better to ask forgiveness than permission. This didn't sound like one of those times. The Great Reconciliation Idea was not only a flop, it was an epic flop.

Miggie set the soldering iron down on its holder. Slowly, deliberately. Clare felt her stomach tense. Her mother's next words made it turn over.

"Why didn't you ask us?" "Us" was Miggie and Dan, Clare knew, not Miggie and Barty.

"You didn't mind when Ravi came to see me." Clare winced at the defensiveness in her voice

"I mind." The two words came out like cut crystal.

Clare knew she was pushing, but she wanted more of an answer: "Why is it alright for me to talk to Ravi, but it's not OK for Barty?"

"Leave it alone. Leave Barty alone. Stop interfering with his life." If Miggie's voice had gotten any sharper, it would have shredded Clare into pieces. Her mother looked like an angry, rigid stranger.

Clare boiled with frustration and curiosity. Everything in her wanted to shout "Why? Why?" But she didn't know what the stranger would do so she closed her mouth and left the room.

Miggie laid the soldering iron in its cradle. She picked up the pendant, smoothing the cool jasper with her fingers. The deep red color reminded her of Clare's constant Converse. Clare didn't remember where her first pair had come from, and yet she clung to them as a footwear choice.

She sighed—Clare was angry with Ravi, and now with her, but how would she feel if Miggie told her the truth? Maybe she'd been wrong to assume that it was something the kids didn't need to know, especially Barty. Dan was a good man and a great father, but maybe Clare and Barty needed a connection with their roots. God knows why. For the first time in a long, long time, Miggie wanted her mother.

Chapter Twenty-Four

October 2002

"That girl is so stuck up." Alanna jerked her chin in the direction of Kelly Martindale, a tall girl with jealousy-producing hair who was hurrying down the crowded hallway of El Dorado High School. I popped open the locker Alanna and I shared and took another look at Kelly's retreating back. There was something about her today . . . something different.

Before I could say anything, Alanna shoved her chemistry book onto the top shelf of the locker, pulled out the novel her English class was reading and said, "She thinks she's so hot just because she's a cheerleader. She never talks to anyone except her boyfriend and his friends. Girls are just. . . beneath her." Alanna rolled her eyes and mimicked a haughty, disdainful face.

Alanna was a good friend and I loved her, but she could be overly sensitive. If someone didn't say hello to her or she got a broken cookie, she took it personally and woe betide the person who forgot the hello or handed her the cookie. I pulled out my Algebra 2 textbook and broke my granola bar in half. Handing her the big half, I said, "See you in P.E." Not buying into Alanna's drama today.

We did a gentle high five and walked off in our separate directions. Reaching my algebra class, I saw that Kelly Martindale was already in her seat at the back of the room where the jocks sat. I slid into my seat in the front on the opposite side of the room. I was struggling with Algebra 2—heck, I had struggled with Algebra 1—and was always so focused on the board that I never talked to anyone in class. But, today, Mrs. Delander was a little late and I let my eyes slide toward Kelly. She was half turned toward her boyfriend, Kirk Tracy, who had a possessive hand on her arm. As I watched her, looking for evidence of Alanna's claim, I felt something I hadn't felt for years—my baby radar.

Was Kelly pregnant? I peered at her more closely and saw that, despite her thick caramel-colored curls and beautiful face, Kelly looked utterly miserable. She wasn't talking with the jocks or her boyfriend; her face was crumpled as if her dog had died. Kirk on the other hand, was laughing and joking with his friends.

Mrs. Delander rushed into the room and class started. "Alright, today we're doing a review of adding and subtracting complex numbers . . ." As I continued to watch Kelly, Mrs. Delander's voice faded away, replaced by the sounds of Kelly's baby singing his song. It was very faint, as if the baby was far away or maybe, Kelly wasn't very far along, but my baby radar honed in on it. The math lecture and the sounds of my classmates disappeared.

For a few minutes, all I heard was the baby song, but then I began to sense a cloud of misery enveloping Kelly. Confusion, fear and panic swirled through the misery cloud, overwhelming me and making me squirm in sympathy. From the intensity of her panic, it seemed that she hadn't yet told Kirk about the baby. Alanna was right, Kelly never seemed to talk to any other girls—it felt like she was carrying this secret all alone.

My last class of the day was P.E. and while Alanna and I were changing out of our sweaty shorts and T-shirts, Alanna began ragging on Kelly again. "Just last week, I tried being nice to her, saying hello and smiling," she said. "I even invited her to come over to swim, but she just shook her head. Didn't even say a word."

I wrapped a towel around myself and headed to the showers, Alanna right behind me. As we soaped up, Alanna's complaints vied with my remembrance of Kelly's fear and panic, causing me to rush through the shower.

By the time we got back to our lockers and were changing into our street clothes, Alanna was really on a roll. I kept seeing Kelly's miserable face. My stomach felt full of churning rocks. Alanna had to stop talking about this.

I looked over at Rhoda Tibbets whose locker was next to mine. Biggest and meanest gossip in school. Kelly's pregnancy wasn't my secret to share, but I had to stop Alanna's complaints before I threw up. I leaned toward Alanna and whispered, "Alanna, Kelly has a lot to deal with at the moment, cut her some slack."

"What? What are you saying? Have you ever even talked to her?" Alanna's voice ratcheted up.

"Shhh," I cautioned. Rhoda's back was toward me, but you never knew. "She's in my algebra class and. . . she's pregnant. She's really scared."

"How do you know?" Alanna whispered back.

"I, uh, just . . . know—I can't tell you."

Somehow, I finished dressing and got out of the gym,

Alanna following and peppering me with questions I was determined not to answer.

The next day at school, everyone was talking about Kelly Martindale being pregnant. I caught Alanna at our locker and asked her in a furious whisper who she'd told. Indignantly, she told me that she hadn't told anyone—she hadn't even believed me since I wouldn't share how I knew. I knew that she was telling me the truth; Alanna always turned red when she lied.

Slamming the locker shut, Alanna stormed off. I spent the next hour in Civics wondering how people had found out about Kelly. Maybe Kelly herself had told someone. I hoped so, otherwise, it was probably Rhoda. If she had overheard Alanna and me, it would have been her sworn duty to make sure the world knew. It was all my fault.

I felt horrible. I could barely drag myself to algebra that afternoon. Kelly wasn't there; the girl in the desk in front of me told another girl across the aisle that she had gone home before lunch. Kirk sat staring straight ahead and his jock friends were silent for a change.

For two days, a tornado of rumor and innuendo swirled through the school. Alanna and I weren't speaking, although I tried to apologize for accusing her. Kelly didn't come back to school. Each day, I felt worse. I even tried listening for the baby song, but I heard nothing.

Walking home from school on the second day, I was sure Kelly had gone home because she'd heard all the gossip. And maybe she hadn't even told Kirk yet; maybe she wasn't actually sure. I worried about what she might be feeling and wished I'd kept my mouth shut, that I'd ignored that stupid baby radar which might not even have been accurate.

Our local newspaper, *Mountain Democrat*, was in the mailbox when I got home. On the front page, under the fold, was an article titled, **"High School Student Dies."** Horrified, I read that Kelly Martindale, age 18, had died as the result of an accident at her home in Placerville. She was found in an upstairs bathroom where she had bled to death.

The breath whooshed out of my body; I felt like I might pass out. The article in the *Democrat* hadn't said what caused Kelly's death, just that it was an accident, but I still worried that somehow, I had been responsible.

Grammie came home to find me curled up in my favorite chair. "Honey, are you feeling OK?" Her face was worried as she laid her cool hand against my forehead.

"I'm OK, Grammie," I lied. "It's just . . . my period."

"Well, you don't feel hot. I'll get you some Midol if you're having cramps." She turned to go down the hall toward her bedroom but stopped. "Did you hear about that girl who died? She went to your school."

I pointed to the newspaper, crumpled on the coffee table.

"Did you know her?" Her face was full of concern for me, concern I didn't feel I deserved.

"Not really."

At school the next day, Alanna, having decided to talk to me once again, told me that Kelly had attempted to give herself an abortion with a coat hanger. No one else had been home and she had tried to staunch the bleeding with towels. Alanna said she had heard this from her mother who worked with a friend of Kelly's mom. Her eyes huge and filled with tears, Alanna said, "I feel bad that I was talking so mean about her." Then she peered at me and said, "But you knew she was pregnant—how did you know?"

I couldn't speak, I couldn't stand without holding onto the locker door. It *was* all my fault. Finally, I let go of the locker and began walking. Alanna followed, asking me if I was OK. The bell rang, Alanna tugged on my blouse. Words came out of her mouth, but I couldn't hear them. "I gotta go to class," I managed to say.

Reluctantly, she turned around and headed down the hall. My feet took me out to the front of the school. I felt the solidity of the sidewalk under my Converse and I just kept walking as visions of blood and Kelly's miserable face filled my head. I walked and walked, tears coursing down my face, until, somehow, I found myself in front of Grammie's house with no idea of how I had gotten there.

I went inside and curled up in the swivel rocker. I wanted Grammie. I wanted to spill my words and my tears to her and feel her warm protectiveness. But I remembered how Aunt Nita had avoided me after I told her about her baby, how Grammie had told me that indulging in psychic fantasy would bring nothing but trouble. Grammie had shut me down before—I couldn't tell her that I had disobeyed her and now someone was dead. I didn't want to see the concern on her face turn to anger, or worse, disgust. And she was right— the baby stuff brought me trouble, fear, pain—even when it helped, like with Jacob. There was nothing I could do except to never, ever let my baby radar surface again.

Part Two

Chapter Twenty-Five

2004

I looked over as Donna, my perennially late roommate, slid breathlessly into a seat near the door. Dr. Whiteman, who had already launched into a joyful debate with the geeky looking guy from the Washoe dorm, glanced back at her and frowned, but didn't pause in his argument.

It was my second semester at the University of Nevada, Reno, and the usual scenario for Philosophy 101.Whiteman debated one student the entire class period as the rest of the class doodled in their notebooks and waited for Whiteman's last minute assignment of chapters from John Mill or Socrates.

There was something special about Donna today. I looked at her again, trying to puzzle out what it was. Her straw-blond hair shone, her round face was lightly freckled and her blue eyes looked bored, as they usually did, in Whiteman's class. When she looked over and caught my glance, she gave a tiny smile before rolling her eyes.

I grinned back and looked down. Donna's legs, clad in jeans, were stretched out in front of her, crossed at the ankles. As a bona-fide Southern California girl, Donna wore flip-flops despite Reno's March weather. Her toenails were polished a rose pink and her ankles looked puffy and swollen.

A thunderclap went off inside my head. I shot a look back up at Donna's face, now focused on her notebook as she doodled. Donna was pregnant.

To the background of Whiteman's droning voice, thoughts whirled around in my head. I focused them on the past few weeks. Donna had none of the signs that I associated with pregnancy. She hadn't fainted, thrown up or turned pale. She didn't look as if she'd gained weight. All she had were two swollen ankles. And a tiny presence in the center of her being that was making my baby radar ping like crazy. Baby radar that I had refused to acknowledge since that awful day in high school.

Determinedly, I focused on Dr. Whiteman's spirited rebuttal of the frat guy's argument, using all my mental strength to push the presence of the baby out of my mind. Not again, I was not going to do this again.

Minutes went by and all I could think was why hadn't Donna told me? We shared everything: clothing, notes, purloined food from the student dining room and our hopes and fears. She even knew my real name. Together, we analyzed each of our dates over Cheetos and M&M's, pulled each other through Philosophy and English Composition, and snuck alcohol into our dorm. Had my determination to ignore baby radar blocked Donna's baby? Then why was I sensing her now?

Class ended a hundred years later. Slowly, I gathered my books and my thoughts. Donna waited for me at the door.

"Want to pick up some lunch? My botany lab was

cancelled today—both the TA and the prof have the flu. What a break!" Donna's eyes sparkled.

"Sure," I nodded without looking at her. My next class wasn't until two. Maybe Donna wanted to tell me during lunch.

"What's up, Clare Bear? Something bothering you?" Donna asked as we cut across the red brick quad toward the student union.

I looked at her from the sides of my eyes, but I couldn't think of what to say. Was it possible that she didn't know? Finally, I croaked out, "Got a headache."

She nodded. "I should have, after the bottle of wine Steve and I killed last night, but I feel great."

A whole bottle? The fetal alcohol syndrome slides from my high school health class flashed before my eyes. Donna must not know she was pregnant. She wouldn't do that to a baby . . . would she?

Trying to escape the sudden blast of March wind, we walked quickly, taking shortcuts toward the protection of buildings. There was a sudden commotion behind us as we reached the student union and we turned to see two men barreling down upon us, wearing nothing but ski masks and hiking boots. We jumped to one side of the walkway as they charged past groups of laughing students, shrieking a Tarzan yell. Catcalls and hoots followed them.

Donna said, "I think I know that guy on the left."

Our eyes met and, despite my agitation, I burst into laughter.

Still laughing, we hurried into the student dining hall. It felt good to be out of the wind, and I snickered at the thought of how thirty degree weather might affect streakers. Streaking was a throwback to the 1970s, but it was new to those of us who weren't born until the eighties. Probably a fraternity stunt—a dare to flash in the frost.

It was a little after eleven, early for lunch, but the student dining room was already beginning to fill up. Lunch selection was quick since we were both scholarship babies on budgets. Hot tea was free and a bowl of white rice with gravy was cheap. Carrying our trays, we slid into seats at our favorite table near the windows overlooking the campus lake.

I dug into my rice and waited. Donna chattered about her botany class and her scatter-brained lab partner, the vacation her family was planning to take during spring break, and Steve, her new boyfriend of three days. I sipped my tea and waited, steaming as hot as my beverage.

I couldn't talk to Donna about the baby—not until she brought the subject up, if she ever did. I'd learned from Aunt Nita and from that horrible experience with Kelly in high school, that my baby sensing could cause trouble. I would wait, like a normal person, until Donna decided to talk. And then, I would act as if I was like everyone else, only getting my information about the baby from the baby's mother.

My resolution lasted three days. Donna and I were studying for tests and I was writing a paper for my English comp class, but it was rough going—at least for me. Donna's baby sang and sent out distress calls when Donna sat for too long or snacked on her favorite habanero pistachios. It was like trying to think during a kid's birthday party.

But, when Donna closed her laptop, saying she needed a break and was going to a frat party with Steve, a frat party in which there would be plenty of alcohol, I had to say something.

"Do you think that's a good idea?" I asked, resting my fingertips on the keyboard of my laptop. Donna's eyes widened; she looked astonished. "I mean . . . there will be a lot of alcohol."

"Man, I hope so!" she laughed. She slung her purse over one shoulder and said, "What's the deal? Since when are you against alcohol?"

Donna and I had been to plenty of frat parties together. I had discovered a fondness for wine coolers and vodka with cranberry juice. Donna was more partial to wine and tequila, beverages that babies definitely didn't require.

"But . . . you're pregnant!" I blurted.

There was a shocked silence—my shock at letting it slip, Donna's shock at what I had said. She cocked her head at me and said, "I am not." Her mouth was open and her brows knit in indignation. It didn't look like an act. "Where would you get such a crazy idea?"

Not again. Grammie's stern determination to avoid any mention of anything even remotely having to do with psychic abilities had caused me to go underground with baby channeling. Indulging in psychic fantasy just got you into trouble. And yet, I had done it again.

Then, Donna straightened and her face changed as if something had suddenly come into focus.

"Oh," she said as the air whooshed out of her. I could see her thinking, ticking over things in her mind like turning over rocks and finding something unexpected under one of them.

As I waited for Donna to say something, a feeling of peaceful contentment came over me. I felt as if I were floating lazily in a warm pool. Despite my agitation, Donna's baby was coming through loud and clear, the way she had been for the past three days.

Meanwhile, my roommate had her fingers spread out in front of her and was flicking them up and down in turn as if she were counting. She stared at something only she could see and then she said, "Oh, my god. I think you're right."

"You do it. Please," Donna pleaded. She clutched the shopping cart for balance and cast wild looks around her, as if being pursued by cannibals. "I'll be in the hair care aisle. We need shampoo, don't we?"

The anguish on her face got to Clare. "Ok. I'll get it. But we don't need shampoo."

"We have to put *something* else in the cart. Something . . . big."

"Fine. You find something to put in the cart that's not shampoo, and I'll find you."

Donna nodded like a Bobblehead and wheeled the cart around, sprinting for another aisle, any aisle except the pregnancy test aisle.

The pregnancy tests were mid-aisle and there were a few thousand choices. Stacks of cardboard boxes were neatly lined up between boxes of tampons for those not worried about becoming an unwed mother, vaginal washes for those who wanted to have a "spring flower" booty call, and vaginal lubricants to make that booty call carefree.

There were pregnancy test strips in boxes of twenty-five and forty; double packs of midstream test sticks; tests that promised rapid results in one minute with 99 percent accuracy; a generic brand that was four dollars cheaper; early detection tests; tests that turned color or had a plus or minus sign as an indicator; tests that promised a clear readout of "pregnant" or "not pregnant."

There was a test that provided both test and confirmation (what did that mean?), one that came with a urine catcher, one that provided a "triple check" which just looked to be three tests, and the most expensive—a combo pack with digital readout, rapid detection, and a smart countdown.

Sheesh, who knew? Clare didn't want to stand there any longer than she had to. Her usual stop in this particular aisle lasted about thirty seconds—just long enough to grab a box of tampons and put it at the bottom of the pile of other goods, so no one but the cashier would notice that it read "super" in gigantic letters. It was cheaper to buy the massive box of sixty, but Clare could never make herself be that frugal.

Donna wasn't exactly a slob, but she didn't pay attention to details. Something was always spilling out of a drawer, falling out of her blouse, or being lost. Still, she was so freaked out, Clare knew that she wouldn't want any maybes or probablies about pregnancy, so Clare opted for the combo pack with its promise of early, rapid detection with words instead of plus or minus, and double confirmation, whatever that meant. Yes, yes or no, no?

She turned around, box in hand, and saw Carmen from their dorm walking past the aisle. Carmen would be more than happy to share the information that Clare was buying a pregnancy test. Stuffing the box under a fold of her parka, Clare reversed direction, backing down the aisle. She peeked around the next aisle and saw that the coast was clear. Walking rapidly past antacids and probiotics, Clare came out into the main throughway of the store, still concealing the pregnancy test beneath her jacket, and saw Carmen's back disappearing down the hair care aisle. Clare sprinted out toward the middle of the store, looking for Donna and hoping she wasn't buying shampoo after all.

After peering fruitlessly down five aisles, Clare was standing in the middle of the store's main thoroughfare, hoping Donna would emerge, when someone tapped her on the shoulder. She turned like a top, almost flying out of her

Converse, and found her nose even with a belt buckle. Peering up, up and up, she saw the blue uniform and the embroidered patch that read, "security guard."

Twenty minutes later, after a humiliating interview in a store office that looked like every interrogation room she'd ever seen on television, Clare was escorted out of the building sans the pregnancy test. As soon as the security guard left her in the parking lot to go back into the store, Clare managed to look up from her shoes to see Donna hovering by the car.

"Where have you been?" Donna whisper-shrieked. Her eyes darted around the parking lot and flew back to Clare whose stony expression froze her in position. "I waited and waited, but I couldn't find you and then I saw Carmen. I just left everything in the cart and ran outside."

Clare didn't speak until she was safely buckled into the passenger seat. Gritting her teeth, she said, "I have just spent the most embarrassing, humiliating, awful moments of my life with a cop wannabe who threatened me with years of incarceration for hiding a pregnancy test under my coat."

"You weren't going to shoplift it, were you?" Donna looked shocked. In the nick of time, before she decked her roommate and best friend, Clare remembered that Donna was a pregnant person. As calmly as she could manage, she said, "We'll have to go to Rite-Aid." She scowled, "I've been banned from Walmart."

Minutes later, still smarting with humiliation, Clare marched into Rite-Aid, determined to get in and get out in record time while Donna cowered in the car. At least she'd winnowed the selection down in Walmart. In the tampon/feminine hygiene/personal lubricant/pregnancy aisle, she picked the pregnancy test off the shelf and paid for it, looking at the clerk directly, challenging him to say one word, one single word. But he didn't.

Chapter Twenty-Six

Donna and I stared as the word, "Pregnant" appeared. The double-duty confirmation appeared. Really pregnant. Donna moaned and slid to the floor of the dorm bathroom. Crapadoodie.

Between Donna's moans and wailed predictions of what her parents would do to her, I felt something odd. Not something—someone. I took Donna's hand and pressed it comfortingly, both to calm her and to quiet her so I could concentrate on what I was sensing. As I sharpened my focus, Donna's wails faded away. The lazy floating I had felt earlier was gone; the baby felt frozen in place, tight and drawn in. Donna's anguish was being mirrored by her baby.

"Stop. Donna, you've got to calm down." I took her hand and used the firmest, most calm voice I could summon. "You don't want to let everyone know, do you?" She shook her head so hard the gold hoops in her ears jingled. "Then let's keep cool and get some sleep. Tomorrow we can see the doctor at the university clinic and find out for sure."

Someone knocked on the door. The sound acted like a

cattle prod for Donna who bolted up, wild-eyed. I splashed some water on her shirt, gave her a reassuring look and opened the door.

"Sorry, just a little chemical mishap." I said, motioning to Donna's sodden shirt as we walked past an impatient dormie. "All better now."

The doctor confirmed Donna's pregnancy and gave a due date of September 21. Somehow, Donna pulled through the last week of classes before spring break, but we were both quivering messes as the week drew to a close. I tried to send calming thoughts to the baby and keep Donna from bursting into tears every few minutes. The baby was much easier than my roommate.

As we packed for the break, I asked Donna if she was going to tell her parents. While I waited for her answer, I could feel her tiny child rolling inside the infinity of her womb, singing and radiating joy. It made it hard to focus on folding underwear.

Donna sat down on her bed amid the chaos of shoes, shirts, dresses and shorts, looking like an orphan adrift in a church clothing closet. "I don't know," she confessed. "I don't know whether I am going to . . . keep it. I don't want to tell my mom and dad if I don't have to. They'll be so disappointed in me."

I knew, from meeting her family, that Donna was close to both her parents and her younger brother. She seemed to be more worried about what they would think than about bringing a baby into the world.

"What do you think I should do?" Donna's question wailed out of her, piercing my ears and my heart.

I couldn't answer that question objectively. For one thing,

I didn't know how Donna really felt about becoming a mother and how she would support a child if her parents washed their hands of her. But, more importantly, I couldn't stop hearing her daughter. Theoretically, I believed in a woman's right to choose and, if she didn't want to be a parent or couldn't care for a child, she should be able to terminate a pregnancy. But I heard that joyful singing, felt the baby's contentment when Donna was relaxed, knew when the baby felt anxious. Later, I knew I would sense her hiccups and sneezes, just as I had with both my brothers and my little cousin, Taylor. And so, I couldn't bear to think of that tiny voice being snuffed out.

Donna was my friend. She listened to me. For her sake, I couldn't have an opinion, couldn't make a list of pros and cons. "It's a big decision. I can't help you with it," I finally said, "But whatever you decide, I support you and I will help in any way I can."

She hugged me and we finished our spring break packing. Two hours later, I drove Donna to the Reno airport in her car. She had lent me her car so I could drive to Minden, saving Dan a trip. We loaded a cart with her luggage and I walked her to the check-in. The new rules since 9/11 meant that we said goodbye there instead of being able to go to the gate.

We hugged again and I whispered "Good luck," into her ear. She looked at me with an uncharacteristically serious face and nodded before getting into the check-in line.

It was a long week with worrying over Donna and her decision niggling at me. On the plus side, Barty had just turned sixteen and was chomping at the bit to get his driver's license. Despite his eagerness, he had waited until I was home for break, which touched me more than I could say. He was scheduled for his driving test that Monday, so we spent the weekend practicing in Dan's turquoise pickup. Jacob clamored to go with us, but Dan thought he might be too distracting. We finally got permission to take him, firmly seat belted into the old truck when we were on the back roads. Barty was a careful driver, especially when Jacob was with us.

When I drove, Jacob, tucked between us, squealed with joy and excitement. Through the open windows, the chill spring air rushed around our heads and pulled our hair. The tires made a high-pitched sound and Jacob screamed, "Squeak the tires! Squeak 'em, Clare!"

Barty and I started laughing like crazy people while our five year-old brother bounced up and down and hollered for more squeaking. I don't know what he would have done if I'd been able to get the truck up to fifty.

Despite the fun I was having with my brothers, my thoughts about Donna and her baby, as well as Dan's constant weariness and Miggie's preoccupied manner, filled me with concern. Dan was working two jobs—one at an auto body shop and the other out of the garage at home doing small engine repairs. Miggie always seemed to be thinking about something else. Whenever I talked to her, she acted startled. I watched Dan and Miggie together with narrowed eyes, trying to see if they were having marital problems. At last, from discreetly questioning Barty and my own observations, my fears about that were laid to rest. Dan still adored Miggie and showed it. Miggie didn't show her feelings often, but I saw her leaning into him when he touched her. She made sure that at least one of his favorite foods was always a part of the dinner menu and even made his lunch for work occasionally. Once, I came into the kitchen and found them in an embrace, which both embarrassed and pleased me.

With Jacob, Miggie was more demonstrative than I remembered her being with Barty and me, but then we all were. He was Barty's shadow and mine as well. We played with him, carried him around and chased him. He was like a pet tornado that talked. All the time. He carried on a running commentary on everything that happened around him, explaining things to an eagerly attentive Einstein the dog or to an imaginary audience. He questioned everything, encouraged the plants to grow and the animals to stand still so he could pet them, protested carrots and naps and demanded ice cream and tire squeaking. When Dan got home from work, however, Barty and I became old news as he threw himself into his father's arms and commanded hugs and stories.

Jacob was slightly less boisterous with Miggie, but when he started getting sleepy at night while we watched TV, he would climb into her lap for a cuddle. Usually, he fell asleep right there in her arms and then Dan would scoop him up and carry him to bed. Just when he was all tucked in and you were safely tiptoeing out, he would wake up and demand a story. He liked stories with animal or vehicle sounds which we tried to reproduce and when I gave the characters different voices, he was awe-struck.

We celebrated Barty's victory at the DMV with ice cream, of course, and Dan presented him with the turquoise pickup as his own vehicle. As Barty posed his lanky 5'10" frame against the side of the truck for a photo, I realized how very handsome and tall my little brother had become. His wild dark brown curls, so like Ravi's and mine, had been cropped, showing off his clean-cut features and gleaming hazel eyes. He had a great smile, too.

I wanted to talk to Miggie about what was going on with her, but there was always either someone else around, or Miggie was busy with her jewelry and Jacob. And it had always been challenging for us to talk about real things—like Ravi or my baby channeling. Even after Jacob was born, all she'd said about my psychic knowledge was to thank me for alerting Dan and to make an observation that I could still "do it"—still hear babies like I had heard Barty and Taylor. I had felt at the time that she had accepted my baby channeling, just as I accepted her ability to know color through touch, but even when we weren't around Grammie, we hadn't talked about it. And now, there didn't seem to be any segue I could use to expand the conversation.

The only conversation we'd ever had that might have led to talk of using my superpower was when Miggie asked about Donna. On the few occasions I had brought Donna home to visit, she had been a big hit with my family, especially with Barty who thought she was hot.

In response to Miggie's question, I couldn't talk about Donna's secret, even though I was dying to do so, until she had made her decision, so I shut down that conversation. "Oh, you know—excited about getting a tan and checking out surfers during the family week at the beach."

Miggie smiled and nodded and that was that.

At the end of the week, I drove Donna's car back to UNR, wondering what she was going to do about the baby. After checking in and unpacking my things, I hung around and greeted returning friends until it was time to pick her up at the airport.

When she emerged from the terminal doorway, Donna looked tanned, keyed up and not pregnant. We piled the luggage in the back and I hadn't even driven out of the airport before she blurted out, "I'm going to keep it!"

Chapter Twenty-Seven

Not only had Donna decided to keep her baby, but she had told her parents about it. Her mom had hysterics, according to Donna, bewailing the fact that Donna had thrown away her education and opportunities. Her dad had gone completely silent. By mid-week, they pulled it together and told her that while they were disappointed, she could have the baby and live with them if that's what she wanted to do. It was Donna's decision to make, since the father was a guy she'd hooked up with one night at a party when she was home for Thanksgiving vacation. He had been visiting a friend and she didn't know where he lived. Or his last name.

When Donna unpacked her suitcase in our room, we found out how much her mother had accepted the situation. On the top of Donna's neatly folded clothes was a brand-new copy of *What to Expect When You're Expecting,* and a bottle of pre-natal vitamins.

Two weeks after we returned from break, I came back to our dorm room after my geology lab, my head still sorting rocks by category. It was a Tuesday, one of the days that Donna and I usually met in the dorm before going to early dinner in the dining hall. I dropped my backpack onto my bed just as Donna burst into the room.

"I felt it!" She looked like she was on fire—hair awry, face flushed, arms and legs in constant movement.

"What?"

"The baby moved! In my legal ed class!" Before I could joke that legal ed sounded like something that could make me move—right out the door—Donna squealed, "It was so cool—like a flutter. Then it moved again when I was sitting on the bench in the quad. It's alive!" She grabbed my hands and started jumping up and down like a kid who's been told they're going to Disneyland.

When she let go of me, I grabbed the copy of *What to Expect When You're Expecting*. It had become our go-to study guide, much to the detriment of our regular homework.

It was the end of April. Donna was at the tail end of her fourth month, just the time, according to the book, that movement might be felt. Looking over my shoulder at the words on the page, Donna shrieked, "I'm normal—it's normal!" Her grin covered her whole face.

I beamed back, glad for her, but also relieved that I was no longer the only one feeling the baby with my Spidey-senses. Donna still didn't know that I had those Spidey-senses. After the day in our dorm when I'd blurted out that she was pregnant, I'd been careful to let Donna tell me what was going on. At the time, I had been relieved that she was too upset to ask me how I knew, but now, I wondered why she hadn't.

"I gotta call my mom." Donna called over her shoulder as she dug around for her cell phone.

Donna's mom was calling three times a week to check on

Donna's health and to offer advice. Flurries of newspaper and magazine articles about best practices in child rearing, gestational nutrition and advances in obstetrics, were daily mail offerings. She was going to be over the moon about the flutter.

After what we named Movement Day, the baby became real to Donna. More real, anyway than it had been before. We poured over *What to Expect* every night, measuring out how big the baby would be and what new developments would have happened. I nicknamed my roomie, "Donna Madonna," even as she began to play with names herself.

Several times a day, she would announce, "This is it," and then she would tell me the absolute, definitive name for the baby: "Lucius Andrew Middleton if it's a boy and Amanda Anne Middleton if it's a girl." Hours later, something in one of her classes or a conversation with a friend would have triggered a new set of names. "Mackay Paul Middleton" came from our Nevada history class after John Mackay and Paul Laxalt—a Nevada silver baron and a U.S. senator. "Julia Sarah Middleton" came from Julia Bulette, a famous prostitute, and Sarah Winnemucca, a Native American activist. Every hour brought something new and different. Donna barely had time to study.

Since I already knew that the baby was a girl, the name thing was funny at first and then, one day after Donna had tried out at least thirty names on me, I was over it. "Just pick out a girl's name and decide whether you're going to color her world pink or introduce her to the rest of the color palette," I told her.

"What makes you think it's a girl? Is it because of the way I'm carrying it? Did you read something? Is there some sort of old wives tale that you know about? Should we do that thing with the ring on a string?" Donna started rummaging through her desk drawer, presumably looking for a string. Or a ring.

"No . . . I just know things about babies." I couldn't believe the words were coming out of my mouth after all the bad memories I carried regarding baby channeling and all my good intentions to keep the baby radar to myself.

"What? All babies? What do you know?" She stopped rummaging and sat down on her bed.

Grammie's stern face came back to me, but Donna was my friend. I couldn't let her do this alone if I could help in any way. Despite my misgivings, I told Donna about my experiences as a baby channeler. When I was finished, Donna stared at me, mouth slightly open.

"So, *that's* why you knew I was pregnant." Then she shocked me. "How cool! Can you, like, talk to them?"

What? Donna had completely accepted my claim that her baby was female and that I could know what the baby was feeling. She hadn't been mad at me for sensing her pregnancy and, now, she accepted this so easily, without any of Grammie's disapproval.

While I was wrapping my head around Donna's easy acceptance, she repeated her question. "Can you talk to babies?"

I'd never tried. Not even with Jacob. I just sent reassuring thoughts out into the universe, hoping they would help. "I don't know."

"Let's try it. First, what is she thinking right now?" I focused my attention on the baby. Nothing happened. Maybe she was sleeping. I started to tell Donna that, but suddenly I felt her wake up. And stretch. It was a weird sensation, feeling my right leg reach out into space when in reality, it was crossed over my left leg as I sat on the edge of my bed.

"She's stretching and . . . she's hungry. Really hungry."

Donna squealed and dragged me out of the dorm to the dining hall for dinner.

When we got back, I decided to take a shower, despite Donna's pleas to find out if we could talk to the baby. "I need to concentrate," I told her. "And I can't do that if I'm thinking about whether I smell."

Really, I just needed time to think about it. I didn't want to disappoint Donna or have her think that I had made up a story about my baby abilities. Also, I still felt the weight of Grammie's dictum not to talk about anything psychic. The shower helped ease a bit of tension, but I was unsure about what I was going to do. Robed and toweled, I opened the door to our room to find Donna doing jumping jacks in our shared floor space.

"What are you doing?" I tried to edge past her to my side of the room without getting an elbow in my eye, but she quickly sat down on her bed, one hand on her negligible baby bump. A look of intense concentration came over her face as she held up a finger. I unwrapped the towel from my head. After a couple of minutes, Donna's look of concentration changed to one of disappointment.

"I'm trying to get the baby to move. I read an article that said if you did jumping jacks and then sat down really fast, it would make the baby move. Do you have a flashlight?"

This was getting weird, but I reached under my bed and felt for the little box in which I kept my tools and emergency equipment. Pulling out my small flashlight, I tossed it to Donna who immediately flipped up her shirt and switched on the flashlight, shining it on her bared belly.

Sitting on my bed, I sensed the baby moving away from the light, like a jellyfish propelling herself into the familiar darkness. "Did you feel that?"

Donna stared at me. "Maybe. Wait, what do you mean,

'feel that?'" She sat up, leaning toward me, hands on her knees. The flashlight lay forgotten on her bed and her blouse fell back over her belly.

"The baby pushed away from the light."

Donna looked at me appraisingly, as if she was wondering if I was playing a joke on her. "I didn't feel anything." Her voice was hard, disappointed, disbelieving. "You did?"

"No, I just . . . sensed her movement." How to explain something I didn't understand myself? Was Donna just now realizing how strange this all was? "Let me get changed and then we'll try to talk to her."

While I changed into sweats and a T-shirt, Donna played with the flashlight and her belly. Finally, I sat down beside her on her bed and said, "I don't know if this will work—I've never tried to talk to them before."

I hoped she wouldn't be mad at me if nothing happened. I rested my hand gently on Donna's neon pink and green-covered stomach in the spot where I sensed the baby lay, took a deep breath, and let it out slowly. An electrical charge moved up my hand and into my arm, surprising me. I focused all my attention on the baby and sent a thought directly to her. "Hello."

There was a stillness as if the baby were startled and listening, confused. I sent my thought again and again, concentrating so hard that the room faded away, Donna faded away, even the barrier of her stomach faded away. I was floating. Dark fuzzy images of something I didn't recognize but that felt somehow familiar, came to me. Then a clear, crisp voice inside my head said, *"Help you."* It wasn't the baby—I could still feel her confusion as she turned back toward my hand.

The voice again, *"Sister."*

What was this? Did Donna have twins in there? I reached my thoughts toward the baby, and felt her and only her, directly under my hand. Surprise. Curiosity. Nothing else came from her.

"Help you." The genderless voice was from outside myself, yet within me. It was . . . unsettling. I focused my thoughts now on the voice.

"Who are you?" Mentally, I sent the question to the Voice.

"Sister" came again.

I sensed the baby moving toward the warmth of my hand. The voice said, *"Move up."* I slid my hand up a little higher on Donna's stomach and immediately felt the baby propel herself in that direction.

I sent a thought, making it as clear and direct as I could. "I want to talk to the baby."

Equally clear and direct came the Voice's response. *"Ask."*

Donna, watching my face during this silent process, said "Are you hearing anything? What's she saying? Ask her if she needs anything." If I hadn't been concentrating so hard, I would have laughed.

Still, the Voice had said to ask, so I sent my question. "What does the baby want?" I didn't know whether I was talking to the Voice or to the baby, or whether it even mattered.

Immediately, against the black curtain of my mind's eye, I saw a dim image of a strawberry and had a strong feeling of repugnance. I pulled back in confusion. What a bizarre thought—like the ones that would flit through my mind every time I tried to meditate in the yoga classes Grammie and I had taken together. Monkey mind, they called it.

"What's wrong?" Donna's voice sounded panicky as she studied the look on my face.

"It's OK, I just need to focus." I soothed her. I put my hand back on her stomach and concentrated on my breath. In, out, in, out. There was the image of the strawberry again, the feeling of repugnance and then another image. This was of a peach and it was accompanied by a feeling of pleasure.

Donna switched her gaze back and forth from my face to her stomach, as if she were watching a tennis match. "Can you hear her?"

"I feel . . . something, but I don't know. I saw a strawberry and felt disgusted and then I saw a peach and felt pleasure. I'm sorry, I guess I must still be hungry."

Eyes wide, Donna said, "I had some strawberries during the break before Legal Ed class and I almost threw up in class —just before the baby moved. But, when we went to dinner, I was craving peaches like crazy and they didn't have any. Do you suppose she hates strawberries and loves peaches? I wonder if anyone on the floor has peaches? Maybe we should drive to the store." She sat up, preparing to hunt down a can of peaches.

It seemed like a stretch to me, but I hadn't known that Donna had eaten strawberries and she hadn't mentioned any craving for peaches at dinner. Maybe I wasn't talking to the baby at all; maybe I was just tuning into Donna. But, later, there had been that voice—what was that?

I went to bed wondering about the Voice. Nothing like this had happened with Jacob or Taylor. Of course I hadn't tried to actually talk to them, either. But, to hear a voice, one that seemed to be both within me and beyond me, was disturbing. Could this be the onset of mental health issues brought on by the stress of college? Was the Voice real? How could it be? Was Grammie right that playing with psychic stuff could get me into trouble?

For a few days after the first encounter with the Voice, I thought about it all the time, trying to puzzle out what it was, where it came from. Donna was convinced that I could talk to babies. I wasn't so sure, but, though the Voice disturbed me, I did want to know more. Donna had accepted my baby channeling, but I didn't tell her about the Voice. I didn't want to scare her, and the possibility that I was having some sort of auditory hallucination scared me. But, because she wanted to know about the baby, who we had nicknamed "Whozit," and I wanted to know more about the Voice, we began having nightly sessions in which I would try to contact our third roommate.

Each session began the same way: Donna would lie on her back on her bed and I would put my hand on the place where I sensed the baby. We'd tried it with Donna standing or sitting up and it was just easier to find the baby, and less embarrassing for me, to have Donna lie down. As Whozit grew, it became easier to find her and to sense what was going on with her.

When I placed my hand on Donna's growing belly, the Voice would guide me to the baby's position. I asked the questions Donna wanted me to ask and the Voice seemed to interpret the answers into images and words. It greeted me each time with "*Sister.*" I found that I couldn't ask the Voice questions about itself. It would grow silent, unresponsive until I asked something about Whozit. I only heard the Voice when I was trying to contact Whozit, which was slightly reassuring, as far as my mental health was concerned.

The Voice gave me a feeling of calm and comfort when I

heard it, but when I *thought* about the Voice, I felt anxious and fearful. And guilty, as if I were doing something forbidden. What if hearing voices meant the onset of schizophrenia? I didn't understand it; I didn't want to hear a voice any more than I wanted to hear babies and yet I wanted to help my friend and the Voice seemed to be helping me do that.

We consulted Whozit about our dinner choices and included her in our conversations as if she were sitting in the room with us, which technically, she was. We consulted her about our movie options. Scary movies like *Aliens*, which Donna loved, were banned after we discovered that little Whozit had a strong reaction to Donna's delighted terror, kicking and bumping around like crazy inside her mother and distracting her from the movie experience. At night, while studying or watching TV, I would feel Whozit's lazy contentment or sense her need for activity. I felt it when she reached out a limb to explore, to stretch and when she turned away in distress.

One night, I asked Donna if she thought my baby channeling was weird. I still wondered about her easy acceptance of something that was so forbidden in my family.

"Of course it's weird," she laughed. "But in a nice way." She shrugged. "I'm kind of used to weird because of my Aunt Ria. She's a psychic—she knows when there's going to be an earthquake, when someone's husband is cheating, what the stock market is going to do, stuff like that. And she's really accurate, so she has a group of clients who consult her about all their life decisions."

My face must have shown my shock, because Donna continued, "Everybody in my whole family is used to it, so it's no big deal."

I wished I could say the same about my family.

Donna kept her pregnancy quiet. A few of the girls in our

dorm knew, but it wasn't something she felt comfortable discussing. A hundred years ago, even thirty years ago, being single and pregnant would have meant having to leave college, but not in 2004. Instead, Donna wore baggier clothing and fielded daily calls from her mother asking whether she was taking vitamins and resting. She stopped dating Frat Party Steve. Caught up in Donna's drama and trying to finish my first year of college with decent grades, I took a break from the dating scene too.

"Mom was pretty upset about this," Donna told me as she waved a hand toward the gentle curve of her stomach which was just beginning to pooch out over her jeans. "But I swear, now that it's a done deal, she's all over it. Yesterday she told me that she'd signed me up for Lamaze classes during the summer." She paused and looked at me. "Do I want Lamaze classes?"

I lifted my shoulders in a puzzled shrug. "I guess it's a good thing to think about—giving birth, I mean."

Donna shuddered. "I don't want to think about any of that, yet. Besides, don't you have to have a coach or something? Who's going to be my coach?" There was a note of self-pity in her voice until it hit us at the same time.

"Your mom, "I said just as Donna exclaimed in horror, "My mom!" Then we collapsed into giggles.

Chapter Twenty-Eight

"Whoa!" Donna lay on her bed, hand resting on her stomach. Her eyes were round and wide. "Oh my god, you gotta feel this."

I was sitting on the edge of her bed, chatting with her about my weekend trip to Minden. My hands lay loosely in my lap. Donna grabbed one of them and placed it atop her stomach. Little Whozit and I had connected many times, but I had never actually felt Donna's baby move. Now, as my hand rested lightly on Donna's cotton-covered tummy, I felt a light thump, a fleeting touch that was gone as quickly as it had surfaced. The skin rippled all over my body.

Donna watched me, her eyes dancing with excitement. I left my hand in place, waiting for Whozit to resurface. Ah, there it was again, a tap I could barely feel. A sensation of warmth and joy flooded me and I heard singing—no words, but it was a song of contentment and peace nonetheless.

Then in my mind's eyes, I saw Whozit—not as a fetus, but as she might be in a couple of years—with Donna's round face and her own almond-shaped blue-green eyes, startling against the background of her creamy brown skin. A cluster of medium brown curls rioted around Whozit's head and she was waving both her chubby hands in the air. Adorable.

I couldn't stop grinning—this was utterly amazing. It was like meeting a friend you'd only known through emails.

"Isn't that cool?" Donna was thrilled at my reaction.

I flew off the bed and grabbed a sheet of paper. Donna's colored pencils were in a jar on her desk and I used them to draw, as best I could, the face I had seen. Donna peered over my shoulder as I told her what I was doing.

"You actually saw her?" Her voice scaled up in delight.

"Yeah, look. . . . She looked like you except her eyes were almond-shaped and more green than blue and she had these beautiful ringlets and . . ."

Donna was suddenly silent, staring at the paper where I had started coloring in Whozit's face with the brown pencil.

"Did she have a tan?" Donna's voice was tiny.

"I don't think so," I said. "She didn't have freckles and her hands and neck were all the same color. And . . ." Whatever I was about to say, faded away at the look on Donna's face.

She muttered something that sounded like, "Not the party guy."

"What?"

"Whozit's father—I don't think he's the guy from the Thanksgiving party." She looked puzzled. "I think it might be Derrick."

Donna had dated Derrick, a black student from Los Angeles, for three months in our first semester. He was smart, funny and a huge flirt. As much as I'd liked him, Derrick had seemed too interested in other girls when all of us had gone out together. Partway through the semester, Derrick decided that UNR was not his thing and he had given up his tennis scholarship to return to Los Angeles. Donna had pined over him, but he hadn't even given her his home address, so she had tried to forget him in a whirlwind of parties and dates.

I did a quick calculation in my head. "Derrick left just before Thanksgiving break and the doctor said you're due on September 21. Isn't that kind of a long pregnancy?"

Donna flushed. "He came back up here in December the weekend before finals—when you were at your grandma's. He said he missed me. We were using protection, but maybe . . . it didn't work." Her mouth turned down and her flush deepened. "I didn't tell you because I found out from his friend Carl, that Derrick only came back to pick up some things he'd left at Carl's house and to get the last paycheck from his part-time job—I was just icing on the cake. Carl said that Derrick has been engaged to his high school girl-friend for months and they're getting married in June. When Carl told me that, I felt humiliated." She looked down at the floor. "I didn't want anyone to know that I had been so stupid."

I felt bad for her and scorchingly angry at Derrick. But, as I patted her shoulder and wondered how to sabotage Derrick's wedding, something else occurred to me. "Well, even though Derrick was a jerk, you did care about him, didn't you?"

She gave a reluctant nod, distress filling her face.

I checked at the misery I saw, but then continued. "So isn't it better that Whozit's daddy is someone you know and that you cared about instead of a one-night party hookup?"

"Ye-es." But the look of misery on Donna's face remained.

"What's the real problem?" It had to be more than Derrick's fickleness.

She sighed. "It was hard enough telling my parents that I was pregnant and that there wouldn't be a wedding, but I don't know how I'm going to tell them that their grandchild is bi-racial. They aren't racist, but they are pretty conservative and so are all their friends."

Sounded racist to me. "Are you going to tell Derrick?"

"I don't have his address and I don't know if Carl would give it to me," Donna said slowly. "And after what Carl told me, I never wanted to see Derrick again."

"But now that you know, doesn't that make a difference?"

"Maybe . . . Oh, I don't know," she wailed. "Maybe you're wrong about the way Whozit looks. Maybe Derrick isn't her dad."

I could be wrong . . . but I saw Whozit's little face again in my mind, eyes the same shape as Derrick's and sparkling with mischief. I recognized Derrick's devastating dimples in a little girl's face. But Donna looked ready to implode so I said, "You're probably right, Donna Madonna—you know I can't draw."

Donna was almost six months along when finals came up. Between studying and heartburn, she was a mess. She looked pregnant to me—not from the back which looked the same as always, but from the front . . . definitely pregnant. With the baggier clothes she wore, though, most people would probably think she had put on the Freshman Twenty. Her mom sent maternity jeans with an expandable pouch in the front which horrified both of us, until Donna tried them on and heaved a huge sigh of relief. The maternity T-shirt with an arrow pointing down to Donna's belly with the words, "Baby here" was not a hit.

We made our plans for the summer: Donna going home to wait for Whozit's arrival and I off to Minden to work at Groovy's Ice Cream Parlor and hang out with my family. Already, I dreaded the coming separation from Donna and

Whozit. We promised each other that we would stay in constant contact, neither wanting to lose this precious friendship.

About the Voice I was still unsure. I would miss it—but should I?

Chapter Twenty-Nine

It was the summer of many things—of torpedo-shaped dragonflies in gunmetal gray, busy over a sprinkler-soaked baseball field, hot sun shining through double sets of wings; of secrets revealed; of fear and love; of exploring what might be and moving past what once was; of endless possibilities. It was the summer that spun Clare's life into new directions.

From the dorm window, she watched the turquoise pickup circle the parking lot and settle in the closest space. Expecting Dan or Barty, Clare was astounded to see her mother emerge from the vehicle. Miggie strode across the lot, sun glinting off her golden-blond hair, long legs peeking in and out of the slit in her ankle-length skirt, Birkenstock sandals on her feet. Clare thought she looked like a student throwback from the seventies. Several frat guys checked her out, heads turning to follow her path. Clare thought they might have been checking out the truck as well, but in any case, Miggie didn't look like anyone's mom.

Miggie had never picked her up before. Although Minden was only about fifty miles away from UNR, Miggie didn't drive distance and she didn't like freeways, despite having driven to Utah and back. And the truck, needed to haul all Clare's dorm paraphernalia, clothing and laptop, could be a challenge with its sticky clutch. After the move from California to Utah years earlier, Miggie had sworn off both pickups and freeways.

Clare raced downstairs to meet up with her mother in the lobby. After brief hugs, Miggie stepped back and said, "Are you packed yet?" and "Aren't you hot in those things?"

Clare didn't need to look down at her red Converse to know what her mother was talking about. Miggie had never liked Clare's constant choice of footwear. "Yes, I'm packed and no, not hot." She punched the button for the elevator thinking that if it had been Dan or Barty, they probably would have taken the stairs up to her third floor room. Miggie wasn't a race-you-up-the-stairs kind of person.

Again, her mother surprised her. "Let's take the stairs instead of waiting for the elevator." She started up the stairs, her sandals slapping the steps as she went. Clare followed behind, short legs trying to keep up.

In the dorm room, Miggie surveyed Clare's neatly packed boxes and Donna's empty side. Donna's dad had already picked up her big stuff a couple of days earlier. This morning, Donna and Clare had finished packing the rest of Donna's things into her car and then Donna had squeezed herself behind the steering wheel, and headed back to Huntington Beach, tears streaming down her face at the thought of leaving her friend.

"Are you and Donna going to room together next year?" Miggie asked. "It seemed that you two hit it off pretty well."

Clare couldn't keep the dismay she felt off her face. Donna wasn't coming back; Donna's reality and her own were going to be very different.

Miggie saw her face and said, "What's wrong? Did you two have a fight?" Her voice sounded concerned as they stacked boxes on the dolly Clare had borrowed from the equipment room.

Putting her suitcase on top of the stack, Clare muttered, "I'll tell you later, when we're on our way." She wasn't going to talk about Donna's condition here, in the dorm where anyone might hear. She maneuvered the laden dolly out into the hallway and down toward the elevator. Miggie closed the dorm room door and followed.

Out in the parking lot, after hitting a few sidewalk cracks that almost derailed the dolly and its burdens, they loaded the boxes into the bed of the pickup. Clare brought the dolly back up in the elevator to her room. She stacked another box of clothing and one of books and notes on the dolly and placed her precious laptop on top before taking a final look around, saying goodbye to the place where she had spent her first year of college and made a friend for life, no matter what direction that life took each of them. Unexpected tears welled up in her eyes, but she shook them away and went out the door.

Inside the pickup, Clare watched Miggie wrestle the clutch. "So, how come you picked me up?"

"What, can't a mother pick up her own daughter from college?" Miggie's tone was light but it sounded wrong to Clare's suspicious ear. She gave her mother a look of incredulity.

Miggie saw it and snorted. "We're not ready for Barty to drive that far on the freeway yet and Dan had to finish rebuilding an engine that someone needs by tomorrow." She paused, "And I needed a break." Another pause, "I thought we could talk."

Another first. This was getting scary. Was Miggie going to tell her that she and Dan were getting a divorce? That Grammie had cancer? That Barty had been in an accident? Had something awful happened to Jacob? Clare's heart began to pound. "Has something happened?" she managed to choke out. Then she noticed that Miggie hadn't gotten on the freeway. Instead, she was driving up University Avenue, appearing to look for something.

"What?" Miggie cast a preoccupied glance over at Clare as she pulled into the parking lot of a little café known for its healthy options. They'd gone there when the whole family brought Clare to UNR the previous August. Jacob hadn't liked it because they didn't serve ice cream and Barty had complained about no hamburgers except ones made out of plant material, but Miggie and Clare had liked the veggie burritos. Miggie parked in front of a window and said, "I thought we'd have lunch before going home. We can keep an eye on the truck while we eat or maybe we can eat outside." She nodded toward the small outdoor dining area dotted with colorful umbrellas.

Anxiety shot sparks up Clare's back and into her neck. This must really be serious. She got out of the pickup on legs that felt as if they could collapse at any moment.

"Why don't you get us a table outside and I'll go in and order," said Miggie. "Do you want the veggie burrito?"

Clare nodded. "And the raspberry ice tea." She slid into a chair parked under a red and white striped umbrella. Staring at her shoes, she conjured up disaster after disaster, until Miggie appeared bearing two plastic glasses of ice tea, straws, a handful of plastic utensils and paper napkins.

They busied themselves defrocking the straws and splitting up the utensils. Clare added sugar to her tea which made Miggie grimace. A girl in a sunflower bedecked T-shirt and black shorts delivered the burritos and a bottle of hot sauce. Neither of them spoke until after their first bite of food when Miggie said, "I'm taking a class."

Clare looked at her sharply. "In what?"

"Well, it's sort of a class in living your best life. I was going to a counselor, but it was too expensive, so she suggested a class that she teaches instead." Miggie dug into her burrito, basmati rice and black beans spilling out onto her plate, the fragrance of cumin in the air.

"Are you and Dan having problems?" Clare couldn't keep her voice from cracking. Her burrito tasted like dirt as her stomach shriveled up.

"Not really." The concern in Clare's eyes spurred Miggie into being more specific. "It's not Dan—he's great. It's me . . . I've been going through some things." Her voice trailed off.

Clare sipped her tea. Waited. Sent an encouraging look. Finally, Miggie set her burrito aside and said, "Something happened seven years ago and it . . . changed me. Our class instructor says that part of healing is to tell someone about it. I wanted you to be the one I told."

Despite feeling touched that Miggie had chosen to tell her, and relief that Dan and Miggie weren't on the rocks, Clare asked, "Why? Why tell me?"

Seven years ago, Clare had been eleven, going on twelve. That was the summer Clare had bailed on her mother after the Calaveras County fair, the summer that Miggie returned early from her craft fair circuit. When she became so preoccupied and started spending more time with Dan. When they got married and moved away, leaving Clare behind.

Chapter Twenty-Nine

Miggie quirked up an eyebrow, her usual response when Clare was asking a question Miggie thought impertinent, but she said only, "Because I want us to understand each other. Because you need to know."

Chapter Thirty

Miggie took a sip of her sugarless tea and then pushed it away. I could see her steeling herself for something—the deep breath, the jut of her chin, the tense rise and fall of her shoulders. I didn't know what was coming, but it didn't bode well.

She began abruptly. "Remember when I borrowed Dan's van and took my jewelry to all the fairs?"

I nodded, keeping my eyes on her face. She looked up at me and seemed to take heart in what she saw there, enough to continue, anyway. "The first summer was fun, easy. I made some money so I made big plans for the second summer. I had all the county fairs and festivals mapped out. You even helped me with the first one in Calaveras, remember?"

As if I could forget Fred Pyne being frenched by his frog, Lipstick Lily.

"I was doing pretty well until I drove to the fair in Andersonville. The van was low on gas and I got kind of lost out in the sticks. But I never worried in those days." Miggie pulled at a strand of long hair and repeated, "No, I never worried.

"I pulled into the campground and there was a sign on the check-in station that the host was called away, but campers should pick an empty site and the host would collect the fee in the morning. I found a campsite at the back of the campground above the river and close, but not too close, to the bathroom. There wasn't anyone else in that part of the camp. I felt lucky to have it all to myself. I got out my camp chair and was fixing some dinner when a guy walked into my camp.

"He said he was parked in the front section and he'd been excited to see a Corvair Greenbrier drive in—his uncle collected them. I asked him if he knew a place I could get gas since my van was on fumes. He said he had a gas can and could give me a few gallons to get me to the closest station which was about ten miles away. He got the gas and put it in my tank and then we sat and talked. Smoked a joint. He asked if he could look at how the inside of the van was arranged, because he was thinking of talking his uncle into converting one of his Greenbriers into a camper.

"The van doors were open and I stood back when he went inside. He asked me a question about the storage cabinets and when I leaned into the van to look at what he was talking about, he pulled me in and slammed the doors shut."

Miggie stopped speaking. With dread in my heart, I knew what was coming and I tried to spare her from telling me in words. "You don't have to . . . ." I began, but Miggie interrupted.

"Yes, I do. It's been inside me all these years, poisoning the good things, making me a stranger to myself. Please, let me do this."

I could see her need and so it became my turn to steel myself. She told me, in halting words, of the stranger's assault, how he left her with two gallons of gas in her tank and bruises all over her body. But the bruises weren't the worst part. "It was the shame, the feeling that I had caused this by flirting with him so I could get gas for the van."

After he left her, Miggie said she crawled into the driver's seat and maneuvered the Greenbrier through the campground, struggling between tears to find the main road. She drove to the little town with the gas station and filled the van. Then she drove home.

"All the way home, I replayed every word I'd said to get him to help me with the gas; smoking the joint, even the drive from the last fair; what I had done at the fair, the fair before that and the fair before that." She shook her head. Tears poured down her face, but she didn't seem to notice.

Tears spilled out of my own eyes. I remembered how different she had seemed when she got home that summer, a month early: Quiet, preoccupied and more distant than usual. She spent almost all her time at Dan's place—clinging to his hand when they walked or when she was next to him. At the time I had wondered. Now I was beginning to understand.

"I felt it was my fault—I'd been reckless and careless, the way Mom always warned me would get me into trouble. My whole life felt like one big screw-up. I began to think they had been right, all those people who told me that I was making poor choices. They were right and I had been wrong all along." The words came out of Miggie as if they were runaway horses and she'd been holding them back with reins that had suddenly been torn from her hands—jerky and fast with breathless gasps.

"I decided to do everything people told me that I should have been doing all along—I married a nice man, I followed him into the desert and tried to make a nice home. I gave him a son. I took care of Jack until he died, and I did my best to be a better mother to you and Barty since I'd always sucked at that. I even tried to become a Mormon."

Her voice sounded so sad, and yet I couldn't help analyzing her words—remembering the Bible Bitches and Miggie's lack of underwear and thinking that "I followed him into the desert" was a weird, sort of Biblical-sounding way to describe Uncle Jack's sheep ranch. Miggie had also twice used "nice"—a word she used to say had no value to interesting people. But more than anything else, Miggie's recognition that she hadn't been much of a parent took my breath away.

A window had opened into Miggie's mind and I saw that the scenery there was different than what I had always thought. Pieces began to fall into place.

Pushing my wayward thoughts aside, I looked at my mother and really saw her. Maybe for the first time, ever. I saw that her hair was still long, but there was silver mixed in with the gold. She was wearing a sarong type skirt, a long-sleeved white tunic with embroidery around the neck, and sandals—it had been years since I'd seen her in short-shorts and tank tops. She was still slender, but it was a solid-looking slender. There were lines at the corners of her eyes. She did look like somebody's mom, after all. My mom.

Even with tears coursing down her cheeks, Miggie looked bewildered as she said, "All the things I did, all the ways I tried to change, just didn't work. The more it didn't work, the more I thought of all the times people thought I was wrong, different. Even way back with Ravi." She took a breath, her tears turning into a gasp of shame. "You always wanted to know why Ravi didn't want to talk to Barty or seemed to care about him. Well, that's because of me." Miggie looked directly into my eyes before continuing. "You came along a little more than a year after Ravi and I took off together. He loved you—you were his little pumpkin—but he wasn't really interested in being a father and he didn't want any more children to slow us down. After a couple of years of moving around, we went to South Lake Tahoe and shared a cabin with Sam and Ariel. Do you remember them?"

I shook my head, no. The earliest thing I could remember was snow—being surprised that the flakes, which looked soft, were instead cold and wet.

"Sam was into leather crafting and jewelry and Ariel made candles. We all got along and helped each other out setting up for festivals and craft fairs. Sam showed me how to make big pieces of jewelry like pendants instead of just earrings and bracelets. He loved kids and he gave you little pieces of leather to chew on when you were teething. He was a good guy." For a moment, Miggie's face was wistful.

"Ravi was gone a lot—looking for gigs to play, working at a lumber yard to help pay the rent, or cleaning up at a pottery studio so he could use the kiln for free. Sam and Ariel and I spent a lot of time together." She took another breath. "And then I got pregnant again. Ravi was furious. He said that it wasn't his baby, that I was a slut. He accused me of sleeping with Sam. And then he left.

"Sam and Ariel heard everything. I was so ashamed—not because Sam and I had ever slept together—but because, sometimes, I'd wished that Ravi would be more like Sam and because I'd spent so much time with him, learning about jewelry making." The look on Miggie's face was the same one Barty had worn when he peed his pants in second grade.

"When the guy in the campground attacked me, it all came flooding back—the shame, the feeling of being wrong, of it somehow being my fault."

I looked down at the table where the ice had melted in my tea, at the forgotten burrito on my plate looking like a marooned submarine. A used napkin was wadded in my clenched fist. There was no air in my lungs. It was too much, too much all at once. I was drowning, trying to keep my head above the waves of shock, guilt at my own thoughtless actions, sorrow for my mother and a welter of other emotions I didn't even want to try to identify.

So much to process—it couldn't be done in an hour, or even a day. Slowly, I pulled my thoughts back into some kind of order and glanced over at my mother. She looked as if she were waiting for the sky to fall. I would have questions, many of them—I had plenty of them already—but not today. Today, she needed me; today my mother, who'd trusted me with the most painful secrets in her life, needed me.

I put my hand over hers, clenched around her glass, and put all the love I felt for her into my eyes. Her shoulders relaxed, the tightness around her mouth fell away. She bent her head down, touching our joined hands with her forehead. Sometimes there are no words.

Chapter Thirty-One

After Miggie's revelations, we threw our mostly uneaten burritos away and got back into the pickup. We were silent, except for my brief directions to Miggie about how and where to get on the freeway to Minden. I offered to drive, but she shook her head, "I need something to focus my attention."

Miggie's decision to drive was probably for the best, despite her dislike of freeways. Both my head and my heart were so battered—one with thoughts and questions and the other with a morass of emotion—that my ability to do more than sit upright was in jeopardy. The heaviest emotion was guilt—guilt that the rape was my fault—if I hadn't left Miggie after Calaveras, maybe that guy wouldn't have attacked her.

I didn't know which event was more disturbing to me—Miggie's rape or Ravi's accusation and abandonment. Both seemed like violations, one more physical than the other, but both boring into Miggie's soul, ripping away her sense of self, her feeling of safety in the world. And Ravi's abandonment had left Barty and me vulnerable as well.

Now I could see that the changes I'd attributed to Miggie becoming more like a mom—cooking, doing laundry, taking care of Uncle Jack and Jacob—were like a cloak of penitence, one that she'd put on over her real self, to cover her pain. Who was my mother, anyway? How had she been able to cope with all this and still keep Barty and me, and now Dan and Jacob, together? Grammie had been there for her when Ravi left, and Dan was there for her now, but it didn't sound like either of them knew the whole story.

Despite her revelations, there was still so much I didn't know. Her trust in me was a gift, but one that felt like a responsibility. How could I help her?

I wanted to tell her about Donna and about the Voice, but they seemed like such miniscule worries in comparison that I said nothing, just kept replaying Miggie's words, trying to process the hugeness of what she'd revealed.

About ten miles from Minden, Miggie broke the silence. "Do you think I should tell Dan about . . . about that guy?"

Dan loved my mother. I couldn't imagine him being angry with her for the attack or not trying to understand and be sensitive about her feelings, but I'd never been in a long-term relationship. I'd dated in high school and college, had crushes on guys who never seemed to notice me, and I'd had a steady boyfriend in my senior year for two whole months before his possessiveness drove me crazy, but nothing more.

"Mom, I don't know very much about being married, but I think he might want to know." I spoke slowly, trying to feel my way through. "Knowing might help him understand some things that he could be worried about." I didn't know what things I was talking about, but Miggie had said "not really" when I'd asked if she and Dan were having problems.

Miggie drove in silence, but she looked over at me and nodded.

I took another plunge. "And if you haven't told him about Ravi's accusation, maybe that too." When she looked at me this time, I could see shame and fear in her eyes before they welled up with tears.

"I don't know if I can do that."

I reached over and squeezed her shoulder. "It's OK, if you don't. Dan loves you and he's going to keep on doing that."

She took her hand off the steering wheel and touched mine.

For the next fifteen minutes, until we reached Minden, Miggie and I were silent. I was chewing on the big bites of revelation about Miggie's rape and Ravi's betrayal. Maybe Miggie was too.

When she pulled the pickup into the driveway of the house in Minden, Dan, Barty, Jacob and Einstein emerged from the garage. Dan and Barty were smiling from ear to ear as Jacob hurled himself into me, wrapping his arms around my legs while Einstein whirled in joyous circles. After peeling my little monkey of a brother off and exchanging hugs all around, each of us grabbed something from the back of the truck and hauled it into the house, unloading the vehicle in far less time than it had taken Miggie and me to load it.

My bedroom, cool and inviting, with the leaf-green walls I'd painted last summer, was soon stuffed with boxes. I decided to unpack later—much later when my swirling thoughts would allow me to do so. I followed my family back into the living room where Miggie sat by herself on the end of the couch, looking lost in thought while Dan, Barty and Jacob stood beaming at me as if they had been witnesses at a clown revival. Jacob was full of the wiggles, a-buzz with something that yearned to burst forth, but that he was trying to keep in check. Something was up—I knew they were glad to see me and I was certainly happy to see them—but all this wiggling and grinning seemed a bit much. Dan cleared his throat and said, "C'mon out to the garage. Barty, Jacob and I have been working on a project."

I didn't want to see a project—I wanted to wrap my head around the conversation I'd had with Miggie, I wanted to process my own part in the things that had happened to her, I wanted to check on Donna, I missed Whozit and the Voice, and I wanted to take a damn nap since Donna had gotten me up at four to help her finish loading the car—but Jacob grabbed my hand and with every ounce of his five- and- a- half- year-old's energy, he pulled me out of the house.

We walked out to the detached garage/workshop, Barty leading the way in a loping semi-gallop. Dan reached out a hand to Miggie and pulled her up off the couch. She leaned into him and they followed Jacob, Einstein and me out to the garage. Barty disappeared through the open door and as I stepped into the dim interior of the workshop, I heard four sets of "TA DA!"

Dan flicked the overhead light on as Barty pulled the cover off a shiny red VW Beetle. Jacob shrieked, "Look at the dots! Just like a real ladybug!"

A car of my own! My heart soared. While I didn't remember ever saying that I liked ladybugs, it was impossible to keep the huge grin off my face as Jacob pointed out the big black dots scattered over the red surface. And it was a convertible! With a black top.

As I walked around my beautiful little car, Barty proudly pointed out the newly reupholstered seats that he had worked on while Jacob showed me the ladybug gearshift knob he had found in a car catalog. Dan talked to me about the newly rebuilt engine and transmission, the brakes, and the refurbished, but original, parts he'd found for it, but all I really heard from any of them was . . . love.

I hadn't had a car at UNR; in a choice between a laptop computer and a car, the computer won. In Minden, I borrowed Miggie's Camry and in Placerville, when visiting Grammie, I just borrowed her Corolla. But now, I had a car of my own, lovingly crafted by my family. And, as Jacob later pointed out, it matched my shoes.

Chapter Thirty-Two

I called Donna later that evening. Her mother answered and told me Donna was sleeping. It was only seven o'clock.

"She got here around three and she was so tired that she just went straight to bed. Sleep is good for babies. Gives them growth time," Mrs. Middleton informed me.

I had never heard this, but I refrained from mentioning it and just asked her to have Donna call me the next day. Donna called in the morning while I was making breakfast for Jacob.

"Are you OK? Did you have any problems?" I asked as soon as we'd said hello.

"You mean outside of having to pee every half hour and wanting to take a nap?" Donna laughed. "I'm great, but my mom has decided that I need to eat more to nourish the baby, so she made me eat a breakfast as big as the buffet at MGM Grand."

"Yeah, I heard about the growth properties of sleep when I called last night."

"This might be one loooonng four months." She paused, "I wish you were here. I miss you already and I know I'm going to miss talking with my little Whozit. Will you be able to come to the shower?" Her mother was giving Donna a baby shower sometime in July or August.

The thought of not talking with the Voice and little Whozit caused a painful twitch to run through me, but I said, "I'll be there and I'll arrive in style."

I told her about my "new" 1978 Super Beetle, complete with dots. Donna demanded that we come up with a cool name for the Bug. Since I had already been through a bajillion changes with the baby's name, I didn't hold out a lot of hope, but while I was telling her about taking a few days to play before going to work at Groovy's, the place I'd worked during the previous summer, Donna suddenly shrieked. "I've got it! Coccinella! Only because the Bug is a car, you could spell it Coachinella! Isn't that great?"

My silence, engendered because her shriek had temporarily deafened me, must have seemed like disapproval, because Donna immediately started telling me that Coccinella was the Italian word for ladybug, and, of course, with the dots, the name had to have something to do with ladybugs. And besides, it was so cool. I stopped her before she went into a full-on sales pitch, by agreeing that Coachinella was a great name and telling her that Jacob was currently driving me crazy as he jumped up and down on the kitchen floor, waiting for his promised ride in Coachinella. We hung up, agreeing to talk next week and then Jacob and I raced each other out to the garage, my mind set at ease about Donna, but my heart still missing the connection with the Voice.

Chapter Thirty-Three

The summer began in earnest with Clare's managerial job at Groovy's Ice Cream Parlor. The owner, a Wavy Gravy lookalike who wore nothing but tie-dye T-shirts, pull- on shorts, and flip flops, greeted her with a hug when she walked into the shop. "Welcome back, kid! I see you're wearing your lucky shoes."

Clare glanced down at her red Converse which harmonized with the bright red shorts and red and white striped T-shirt she wore. She didn't usually wear red, except for her shoes, but working in the ice cream parlor and driving her shiny new car seemed to beg for something bright and cheery to match it.

Wavy, whose actual name was Myron, produced a bib apron and matching ball cap tie-dyed in shades of orange, pink, yellow and turquoise, and handed them to her. "I made these myself!" he chirped, almost quivering in excitement. "Whaddaya think?"

The tie dye was definitely bright and clashed horribly with her red and white outfit. Still, it was a nice spot of color in a shop that was almost entirely white—shiny white tile floors, white subway tile on the wall behind the counter, white painted walls, white-topped round tables and white wrought iron chairs. The open tubs of ice cream in the cold case and Myron himself were the only bits of color.

"Very cheerful," Clare said, smiling at Myron. It was her second summer working at Groovy's and Myron's tie dye enthusiasm had grown on her.

"Exactly!" He beamed at her before adding, "Let me show you the changes I've made since last year."

After Myron had talked her through the operations of the new cooler and the hot fudge machine and shown her the new ordering system he was using, it was almost time to open. He told her that he'd hired a part-time person for weekends and evenings when it got busy, reminded her that they were closed on Mondays, and made sure she had his numbers in case she had to call with questions. Then, after she put on her apron and tucked her hair into the ball cap, he left. Clare knew she wouldn't see him again until she left to spend a couple of weeks with her grandmother in Placerville before heading back to school. The shop was only open April through October, but after working April and most of May, Myron said he needed a summer break. Clare had no idea where he went or what he did, but he always called back if she had an emergency like last summer's refrigerator failure.

Promptly at ten, she unlocked the front door to find two customers already waiting outside in the warm sun. She welcomed them in and within thirty seconds, she was scooping Zingalicious Jazz into a waffle cone.

The part-time helper turned out to be a frizzy-haired high school junior named Norm, who said he couldn't work at

McDonald's because the french fry grease in the air made him break out. He was built like a fishing pole and talked non-stop, but he came in every evening from six to eight p.m. which gave Clare time to do the ordering and take an uninterrupted break.

Working ten hour days, six days a week ate up her summer, but Clare needed the money for the school year. Her scholarship paid for tuition, books and some living expenses, but she didn't want to ask Miggie and Dan for more than they were already giving her. Last summer it had worked out well—she had put away enough money in her bank account that, with careful management, it got her through the school year. She was determined to get her four year degree in four years, although she knew a lot of people were taking longer. She just wished she could decide on a major more specific than liberal arts. She had a few more required courses left to take, but it didn't feel as if she had a purpose, a goal that reflected who she was and what she wanted. Her scholarship was partially based on the awards she'd received for her creative writing in high school, but although she loved to write, a career in writing sounded more like a starving artist's career than one that could pay the rent.

And just who was she, anyway? What *did* she want from life? As the summer progressed, Clare drew up a list of things she wanted to do, hoping they would reveal a direction, a path she could follow. *Help people, Travel, Make the world a better place,* went on the left side of the paper. On the right side she wrote her interests: *Writing, Reading, Exploring, History, Driving Coachinella, Playing video games with Barty,* (although this last entry seemed overly specific to her). Added to the list were classes she'd really enjoyed, like English composition and psychology.

On the porch after work, Clare made a list of her skills:

Organization, Problem solving, Cleaning. It seemed like an awfully short list. She didn't include *Baby Channeling or Ice Cream Scooping.* On a weekly call, Grammie suggested that she add *Care giver* and strengths like *Empathy* and *Kindness* as well.

"Maybe you could be a social worker," she said. "That would allow you to use some of your strengths to help people. Or you could use your writing skills to be a journalist."

Grammie's suggestions were good, but although Clare wanted to help people, she wasn't sure that social work was the way she wanted to do it. And, after working on the high school newspaper, she'd discovered that reporting facts wasn't as much fun as writing fiction, so journalism wasn't a career that drew her, either.

Each night, Clare trundled home in Coachinella at eight-thirty, tired and hungry for something other than ice cream. Miggie usually had something for her to eat and they sat together on the front porch, watching the light from the long summer days fade. Sometimes, Barty and Dan joined them for an hour, but Dan went to bed early since he had to be at work by seven. Barty, who worked at the auto body shop with Dan, also had to be to work at seven, but he often met up with friends after dinner and was rarely home before his midnight curfew. Clare was glad he had so many friends, but disappointed that the only time she got to talk to him was when he stopped by Groovy's for some daily taste testing. What could Barty and his friends be doing? Minden was hardly a hot night spot and her sixteen-year-old brother wasn't of age to indulge even if it had been. She hoped he wasn't getting into trouble.

Clare wanted to talk to her mother about the revelations

Miggie had shared; she needed help in processing the information. But Miggie hadn't brought the subject up again and Clare hadn't wanted to rush her. She wanted to tell Donna about what Miggie had told her, but it seemed like something you should do in person, not over the phone—especially since she didn't know what to do with the guilt Miggie's disclosures had engendered. And even though Grammie was both a mentor and a confidante, Clare knew she couldn't share what Miggie had told her, particularly after Grammie's reaction when Clare had shared the news of Donna's pregnancy. Avoiding her own involvement with Whozit and the Voice, she'd told Grammie about what they had learned from *What to Expect* and all of Donna's baby names, expecting her grandmother to chuckle. But Grammie had gone silent. Clare had called her name and gotten no response for a minute. When Grammie finally replied that she was still there and no need to shout, her voice had been shaky and faint. It had frightened Clare who promptly added unwed pregnancies to the short list of things in Grammie's Forbidden Zone.

After two weeks of waiting for her mother to bring it up, Clare decided to broach the subject of the revelations herself. On a warm night as the bitter, herby scent of sagebrush filled the air, Clare and Miggie were sitting on the front porch watching the night sky pepper with stars. Clare asked, "Have you told Dan about . . . the guy, yet?"

Scrunched against the back of the huge wicker armchair she'd rescued from a garage sale, Miggie looked away, off into the mountains. A cricket sounded; its chirp making a lonely dent in the silence. An eternity later, Miggie said, "No . . . it hasn't been the right time."

It felt like the same old Miggie, shutting her down, but since Clare wasn't sure what *would* be the right time, she nodded in support or agreement or just because, and continued to rock in the old wicker chair.

"You never did finish telling me about Donna," Miggie said. "When we were loading you up, you said you'd tell me later. So, isn't she coming back to UNR?'

Clare knew Miggie was deflecting the conversation away from herself, but it did seem as if she were trying to keep communication happening between them. Clare rocked slowly, thinking, her back comfortable against the faded chair cushion. It felt like years had passed since she had waved goodbye to Donna and her fully loaded car bound for Southern California. So much to tell: things Clare had grown used to, like Donna's pregnancy, the millions of names she'd explored, the excitement of Whozit's progress and movements, their nightly talks with the baby. And the Voice.

"Wow," she said, "it might take a while to catch you up. "

Miggie smiled, "I've got all night."

So Clare unraveled it all. The unplanned pregnancy had Miggie's nod of remembrance, the near arrest in Walmart for a pregnancy test got a smile, while the plethora of Donna's name choices and her cravings brought a laugh from her.

"Big job ahead of her," Miggie commented. "She's lucky that her parents are supportive."

The tone of her voice made Clare think that perhaps Miggie hadn't been so lucky. She stopped rocking, thinking about this, before saying, "We spent a lot of time this semester learning about pregnancy and reading this book called *What to Expect When You're Expecting*. And . . . I learned to talk with the baby."

"Talk . . . not just sense, actually talk?" Miggie picked up on the difference right away. Her glance at Clare from the depths of her chair, just barely visible in the twilight, was curious, but not doubting.

Clare let out a breath she hadn't realized she was holding and began rocking again. "I think so—at least I was able to communicate with her—I got images of what she wanted or didn't want, answers to questions. But, I might have been talking to something else. Or someone else." Clare stopped rocking, unsure how to explain the Voice without sounding as if she heard voices. Because she did. Just one.

Miggie frowned. "What are you talking about?"

"Well, every time I tried to communicate with the baby, a voice would greet me. It offered to help with the baby and maybe it did, because I never talked with Barty or Taylor or Jacob before they were born—I just sensed things about them. The Voice always called me 'Sister.' " At this, Miggie blinked as if she were startled.

Clare took a breath, feeling again both the warmth of connection with the Voice and the fear that she had been carrying most of the semester—that she might be schizophrenic or have some other mental health issue. Her voice came faster and higher as she said, "I don't know what this voice is. It seems to be helpful, but I don't know, I just don't know. But it's weird, I miss it, miss this connection I felt like I had with it." Fear overcame Clare—fear of being ridiculed, fear of being thought crazy. She stopped talking and felt herself beginning to shake as she clenched the arms of the rocker.

Her mother reached over. When she found Clare's hand, she held on to it as if both their lives depended on it. The warmth of Miggie's hand began to calm her and when Miggie said, "It's OK, it will be OK," Clare felt, for the first time, that it really might be.

Moments went by. Miggie began speaking in a quiet voice. "You know, even though your grandmother won't talk about any possible psychic abilities," here, Miggie grimaced before continuing, "she did tell me a day or so after Barty was born, that you knew when Barty got stuck in the birth canal. The doctor had to pull him out with forceps and you told Grammie that it made you shiver when his head got 'squeezed with the silver things.' When I was pregnant with him, you were always telling me that the baby didn't like garlic and that I needed to rest."

In the darkening night, Clare nodded. Miggie kept her voice calm and quiet, as if she was gentling a skittish horse "Remember, the other day, I told you about Sam and Ariel when we lived with them in South Lake Tahoe?" Clare nodded again, although she didn't think her mother could see it. She kept her hand in Miggie's, gave it a gentle squeeze. "Well, Ariel was a psychic and used to give readings at the fairs. She told me that you were getting messages from your twin."

"Twin?"

At the confusion in Clare's voice, Miggie clarified: "I was pregnant with twins when you were born, but I didn't know it. The other baby miscarried early—I thought I'd lost my baby—but then we found out that I was still pregnant with you." She squeezed Clare's hand again.

Clare was entranced. This talking with her mother about baby channeling, the warmth of Miggie's hand holding her own, felt so amazing. Just to be able to freely admit her connection with Whozit, instead of being shut down was like being liberated from a great weight. And a twin—no one had ever mentioned a twin.

Miggie's voice rolled on into the night, "Before Barty was born, you had an imaginary friend. You called her Sissy and you would play with your toys for hours, talking to Sissy as if she were sitting with you on the floor. I thought it was kind of creepy, but Ravi thought it was cute because he'd had an imaginary friend too. Ariel was convinced that Sissy was actually your twin and that she stayed around you to protect you. Maybe that's who you're connecting with now."

Did her mother have any other revelations to rock her world? Rape, betrayal, abandonment and now a protective, hovering twin? Clare cast her mind back as far as she could, but no memory of an imaginary friend surfaced. Still, the twin thing was oddly . . . comforting. As if something long missing had suddenly clicked into place. Maybe she wasn't crazy—maybe she just had a twin. Although, communicating with a twin who was never born sounded kind of crazy.

"So, you don't think I might be having some mental health issues?" Clare held her breath as if doing so would influence the answer.

"Because you have an ability that most people don't have?" Her mother's voice sounded amused. "Because you might have a connection with a twin? We both love Grammie, but don't let her attitude toward things she doesn't understand make you doubt yourself." Miggie's voice now sounded sad. "I know—that's what happened when I was growing up. Her concern about my being able to sense color made me feel like a freak, like I wasn't acceptable." She sighed, "So I made sure I wasn't acceptable. I did just the opposite of whatever my mother thought I should do. And I deliberately teased both my mother and Nita with my color thing—just to make them mad . . . like they made me."

More pieces of her mother fell into place. Grammie was Clare's favorite person, but it had been hard feeling so shut down about her baby channeling. And now, it seemed that Miggie had felt the same way.

Clare wrapped her other hand around their clasped hands, feeling a release of the tension she felt she'd been carrying her whole life. Talking with Miggie about this, hearing the lack of judgement in her voice, the understanding of how Clare felt, was a gift. It was too bizarre to think that the Voice might be her long-dead twin, but at least Miggie didn't think she was crazy. And, at last, she could talk to someone about her baby channeling. What other amazing things might happen this summer?

Chapter Thirty-Four

Summer flew along in the air-conditioned coolness of the ice cream parlor; in windblown Mondays driving Coachinella to Lake Tahoe to hike and swim with Jacob; in wonderful talks about real things with Miggie; in weekly chats with Donna and Grammie, and in sage-scented evenings shared with all the family barbecuing and listening to the coyotes call. But, as precious as my developing relationship with my mother was, the summer also included worry about Barty and Donna and missing my connection with Whozit and the Voice.

Donna told me about the Labor and Delivery class and the Lamaze instruction that she and her mother, who was going to be her birthing partner, attended at the local hospital. Her mother made nutritious meals for Donna and nagged her into daily walks and exercise.

"All I want is a latte and a greasy cheeseburger," Donna moaned during one call. "And a huge margarita with plenty of salt on the rim . . . that I can sip during my parenting for dummies class, the only class I'm taking by myself."

We laughed about it, but I began to hear an undercurrent of worry through the humor as the pregnancy progressed. At first, it was little things that Donna let slip, like her joking concern that she might have to live with her parents forever since she wasn't going to be able to fit all the baby paraphernalia into an apartment. Or a remark about how they didn't make bikinis big enough for pregnant people and maybe she would have to resign herself to wearing a one-piece for the rest of her life to hide the stretch marks. The remarks sounded like jokes, but they weren't. I could tell that she was worried that she wouldn't be able to take care of Whozit on her own and that, for the first time in her life, she felt fat and unattractive—maybe permanently. It also sounded as if Donna's mother was attempting a coup on Donna's pregnancy with her constant attempts at controlling Donna's diet, how long she slept, what exercise she did and what things she learned about babies. By late June, Donna's remarks were less humorous and more pointed.

"Clare, I wasn't even a good babysitter," Donna said one night. "What if I suck as a mother?" Before I could say anything, she continued, "I miss our talks with Whozit. I felt like, when you were listening to her and telling me what she felt, that we were a team—that we were all so connected. But now, even though I can feel her move, it's not the same. My mom has been great, but it's like she's taking over. I feel . . . alone." Her voice was wavery, and she sounded scared.

It felt, to me, that Donna was losing faith in herself, that her mother's good intentions had almost usurped Donna's ability to make decisions about her life—as if she thought Donna was a little kid having a kid. But, even with all the help that her mother would give her, Donna was the one carrying the baby, the one who would give birth, and she would be ultimately the one responsible for her child. For at least eighteen years. It was a sobering thought.

Maybe a stronger connection with her baby would help Donna feel that she had some control. Even though I couldn't be there with her, I might be able to help with that.

"I really miss Team Whozit too," I said. And the Voice, especially the Voice. "But, this is *your* baby and it's important that you feel connected to her. Maybe . . ." I was talking my way through this, making it up as I went along. "Maybe, you could spend some time every night, like we did in the dorm, and try to talk to Whozit. You know, lie down, put your hand on your stomach where you can feel her and just close your eyes and think of her."

"Yeah, I could do that," said Donna. "But I don't have your gift."

"You have something better—you have a baby inside you."

We laughed. Donna said she would try it.

When I got home from work the next evening, Miggie told me Donna had called and wanted me to call back. It was after nine o'clock, but I called anyway.

"It didn't work," Donna wailed as soon as I said hello. "I did just what we always did and nothing happened."

I thought for a minute before saying, "OK, how about you try it again. This time I'll be on the phone with you and talk you through it. "

Donna agreed willingly and, since she was talking on the phone in her bedroom, it was only a minute before she reported that she was lying on her bed with her hand resting on top of the baby.

From yoga classes, I remembered one instructor doing a guided meditation, so I attempted to do something similar—talking in a low, soft voice about relaxing her body, quieting her mind and imagining that she was floating, surrounded by a warm bath of fluid, completely safe and content. After a few minutes, there was a soft sliding sound in my ear and I realized I could hear a heartbeat. "Donna, Donna?" I called. There was no answer except the heartbeat. Then, as I strained to hear whatever Donna was doing, I heard the Voice.

"*Sister.*"

A great surge of joy flooded me at the greeting from the Voice. I felt a wave of something I can only call recognition; I felt utterly known and accepted. And loved. The depth of wholeness and belonging that filled me brought a flood of tears down my face. I struggled to calm myself and respond.

But, I needed no words—actually, I wasn't capable of words at that moment. I simply sent back the love and acceptance I felt I had received. "*Sister*" the Voice always called me—she'd been telling me who she was the whole time. My sister, my twin, my missing piece. What had sounded crazy now felt real.

As the intensity of emotion began to subside, I felt a familiar presence—Whozit. And she was hungry. I called out to Donna, but heard nothing but a heartbeat and then . . . a gentle snore. Guided meditation had put my friend to sleep. From the Voice I heard nothing more, but Whozit's hunger call was deafening. After whistles and calls failed to elicit any response from Donna, other than a snore, I hung up the phone. Maybe the dial tone would wake her up. As for me, I was still glowing from the connection with Whozit and the Voice, my twin.

I went to the Minden library to look up information about twins. There wasn't much available, so the librarian referred me to the Carson City library. In a funny twist, she also told me that the UNR library probably had the most information available because of the medical school. I knew where I would be spending most of my free time when school started.

The next night, after work, I fell asleep out on the porch sitting in one of the wicker chairs. Miggie had already gone inside, but I wanted to sit in the quiet darkness and let myself feel the night.

I dreamed that I was in a sea cave, dark and cool. The entrance to the cave was in front of me and through it I saw waves marching endlessly to their destination on the beach. I felt smooth pebbles and cool, damp sand under my feet. Stepping out of the cave, I turned right, into a sort of cove tucked inside a half-circle of boulders. The beach stretched away in a beige crescent on the other side of the cove, disappearing around a headland. There was a person sitting atop one of the boulders ringing the cove. Barefoot, she was wearing a white garment fitted to her slender shape. And she looked like me. Almost exactly like me. Her dark, curly hair was longer than mine and her face was rounder, but we could have been twins. Then, with a surge of excitement, I realized that we were.

When she saw the realization on my face, she jumped up from the boulder and waved as she laughed down at me. I bolted up the face of the nearest boulder, toward her. But, as fast as I climbed, I couldn't seem to make any progress. My twin kept laughing, the musical sound floating over the sound of the waves and the huff of my panting breath. At last, I fell back to the sand. She smiled and waved again—this time a goodbye instead of a hello. Then she was gone.

. . .

The rumble of Barty's pickup woke me. As I struggled to maneuver myself out of the chair and pull myself out of the dream, I heard the slam of the truck's door and the crunch of gravel under Barty's feet.

"Hey, Barty," I said as he stepped onto the porch. He jumped back as if I had shot him. The moon was full enough that I could see the spooked expression on his face, so exaggerated that I started to giggle.

When he saw it was me, Barty stepped back onto the porch and flung himself into Miggie's chair all in one movement. "You scared the crap out of me," he panted as he shook his head. "What are you doing out here?"

"I could ask you the same thing, little brother. In fact, I am asking you that." I looked at the luminous dial on my watch. 12:04. He was home by his midnight curfew, not that I cared, or would have said anything to Dan or Miggie if he had gotten home later, but it bugged me that his nightly forays were something he wouldn't talk to me about. "Have a girlfriend?" I said it teasingly, but he shook his head in firm denial.

"No, I do not." He got up from the chair. "And I don't have to tell you what I do with my friends."

I had never heard such a hostile tone from my brother—except for the time I tried to take him to meet Ravi. "Whoa brother, what's eating you? I care about you—I miss hearing about what you're doing these days."

His answer was gruff, but his tone softened as he said, "Don't worry about me. I'm OK."

Like *that* was a comforting response.

Before I could say anything else, he'd disappeared into the house, letting the screen door close quietly behind him.

I missed my brother, missed talking with him and sharing our ideas. During the years when we lived in different places, even in different states, we had still remained close. Our phone calls were brief, but frequent, and even though he was always succinct, he told me about his friends and the things they did. All of our school vacations were spent together and that's when we really talked. And always it was as if we had only been apart minutes instead of months. But now that we were living in the same household, at least temporarily, it was as if we were still in two different states, and one of those states was making me worry. A frisson of unease crept over my spine, causing me to shiver despite the warmth of the summer night.

Chapter Thirty-Five

Barty didn't stop by the ice cream shop for his usual flavor tasting the next day. When I got home from work at nine that evening, Miggie greeted me with her specialty, a warmed-up, formerly frozen, burrito—one of the staples of my childhood. Miggie sat on the porch with me while I ate and then Dan came out onto the porch, carrying an unconscious Jacob.

"He snuck out of his room to watch TV from the hallway and fell asleep." Dan grinned. "I used to do the same thing, myself." He hefted Jacob a little higher on his shoulder. "Just wanted to say hi before I turned in." He gave me a one-armed hug and kissed the top of my head. Miggie was about to follow them, but I stopped her.

"Is Barty home?"

Dan answered over his shoulder, "Nope. Said he was having dinner at a friend's house."

"I hardly ever see him," I complained.

Miggie said, "I know. He's either at work or hanging out

with his friends. He's always home by curfew though—I can't fall asleep until I hear his tires on the gravel."

She'd always seemed so lackadaisical about our comings and goings. Another change in Miggie.

After two days, I began to suspect that Barty was avoiding me. He still hadn't resumed his morning taste testing at Groovy's and he always seemed to be out with friends or asleep when I got home. Asleep at nine o'clock? Dan maybe, but not my night-owl brother.

While I was scheming up ways to find out what Barty was up to, the invitation to Donna's shower arrived. It was scheduled for July 31, a Saturday almost two months before her due date of September 21. Donna's call followed the invitation's arrival.

"I'm so sorry I fell asleep. I'm blaming it on Whozit making me so tired all the time," Donna apologized. "Will you be able to come? You can stay with us and maybe we can go shopping afterward and get you some back-to-school clothes—if I can fit into Coachinella."

"Well, you might have been asleep, but Whozit was wide awake and hungry!" I took a breath, "And . . . I heard this Voice. I haven't told you, but I always hear a voice when I connect with Whozit, but it's not Whozit. It's someone else." I hadn't told Donna about the Voice before because I was worried that I might be having some sort of mental health episode. But Miggie's twin explanation and my own reconnection with the Voice had somewhat allayed my fears about mental illness.

I filled Donna in on the "*Sister*" greeting "And, believe it or not, I'm a twin. Miggie miscarried my twin at around twelve weeks and she thinks the Voice might be my twin sister." I described the feeling of wholeness and acceptance that connecting with my twin had given me .

There was a silence and then Donna said, "Whoa, that is bizarre."

Another silence, this one long enough that I started to feel that maybe this was more peculiar information than my friend could handle. But she surprised me.

"This is so crazy—remember I told you that my Aunt Ria does psychic readings? Just for friends and people they refer." Donna said this in a matter of fact manner as if her aunt worked at Macy's. "Anyway, one of her friends had this problem with always feeling that something in her life was missing. She kept trying to fill it with buying things. It was getting her into trouble with her husband. My aunt did a reading for her and told her that she had a twin brother who had died at birth—that was why she was always looking for something to fill the space. The lady talked to her mother and Aunt Ria was right! The mother had never mentioned the twin because it made her too sad. So, my aunt helped the lady do a ceremony to acknowledge her twin and to release her own grief at the loss. Now the lady says she's happier and she's trying to do things she feels her twin would have done, instead of shopping all the time. I think she even went skydiving last week."

I'd have to think about that. It sounded too weird to miss someone that you never even knew existed, but I remembered all the times I'd found myself missing . . . something. Maybe it was someone. I'd tried to fill the space with interesting words and writing stories, but it was still there, in the background of my life. A ceremony to release your grief at the loss of someone you'd never met seemed a little extreme, but it was interesting.

We set a time to try another guided meditation—Donna promising to sneak in a cup of coffee to stay awake. Then, I changed the subject to something that had been at the back of my mind, niggling at me. "So, have you mentioned to your parents the possibility that Whozit might be bi-racial?" It had been a while since Donna and I had talked about this. I didn't want to be a nag, but wouldn't a good friend try to help her friend deal with issues instead of pretending they didn't exist?

There was a silence on the other end of the phone making me wonder if I had overstepped the boundaries of friendship.

"I've been trying to, you know, feel out how they might react, without being obvious about it," she said. "But mostly, I've been trying to figure out how I could deal with some of the problems she might face, starting with the probability that her mother and grandparents will be a different color."

I was glad that she wasn't ducking the issue altogether but I wondered what she was thinking about race issues.

Before I could ask, Donna said, "Once, when Derrick and I were dating, he was driving us to a concert in my car and he was going a little fast. We got pulled over and the cop asked for license and registration. Derrick handed over his driver's license and I got the registration out of the glove compart-ment. The cop took one look at it and said to Derrick, 'This isn't your car. I'm calling this in as a stolen vehicle.' Both of us told him that it was *my* car, but the cop acted as if Derrick had stolen it and possibly abducted me. It was awful, but you know what the worst part was?" Her voice sounded both indignant and sad. "The worst part was that when we were finally allowed to drive away, with a speeding ticket for going eight miles over the limit, Derrick shrugged it off. He said it happened all the time; he was used to it. He didn't want to talk about it, though, and I could see how tense he was." She paused before saying, "How will I deal with that if it happens to Whozit? What if kids tease her because her mom's white and she isn't? What if people treat her as if she is not as capable or intelligent as white kids? What if she wants to know about her black heritage and all I know is how to be white?"

Donna said she'd been thinking about it a lot. She continued, her voice falling, "When I was ten, my parents gave a dinner party. During dinner, the adults started talking about how their taxes were going to support people who didn't want to work, people 'of color' like blacks and Latinos. It was the first time I'd ever seen someone use air quotes," she snorted. "My parents didn't join in, but they didn't say anything against it either. So it makes me wonder if they secretly think that way too."

Donna's questioning concern made me realize what a great mom she would be if she was already wondering how to help her child through racism, even the kind that pretends it isn't racism. Maybe that is how to change the world—one mom, one kid at a time.

"Donna Madonna—you're already trying to protect Whozit," I was so proud of her. "You're going to be an awesome mom. Those things you're worrying about might happen, but I know you're going to figure it out. Maybe your parents didn't say anything because they didn't want to start an argument at their dinner party, but don't you think it would be a good idea to prepare them, instead of blindsiding them? Maybe having a bi-racial grandchild will give them a reason to speak out."

"Maybe." Donna said slowly. "I've been thinking more about the problems; maybe I should be thinking that Whozit could be a positive force for change."

Chapter Thirty-Six

One Monday, unable to wait until school started, I drove to Reno and checked out a few books on twins from the UNR library. One book introduced me to the "vanishing twin syndrome" in which twins were conceived but one of them died before birth, leaving a "womb twin" survivor. It sounded exactly like what Miggie had told me happened to her.

In some cases, the twin who died was partially or completely reabsorbed by the mother's body—literally vanishing. In other cases, the fetus was compressed and flattened into a parchment-like state. This was horrifying to me, but the information that sometimes the dead twin was absorbed by the surviving twin seemed even worse. Was that what had happened to my twin? Had I eaten her? Or had I sucked up all the nourishment, leaving nothing for her? Were you still a twin if your twin didn't survive?

I felt a sense of overwhelming guilt. Was the Voice the one who lost the fight for the shared resources of Miggie's womb? On the way home from work each night, I analyzed myself: I knew I was a fighter, but only when I had to be; a worrier but also a problem solver; a person who longed for the closeness of family and friends, but who often felt alone or as if something was missing even when surrounded by them. Was I such a fighter that I could take the room and the food from another in order to survive? I didn't want to be that person.

In addition to stewing over my possible evil womb deeds, I worked out a plan to follow Barty when he got off work. I'd have to borrow a different car since a bright-red, ladybug spotted Volkswagen is hardly inconspicuous. Norm, the kid who worked at Groovy's with me, drove a white Ford Horizon. He would probably swap cars for a few hours since he thought Coachinella was the coolest thing he'd ever seen. I felt a pang at the thought of someone else pushing back her seats, adjusting the mirrors, perhaps grinding the gears. Did Norm even know how to drive a stick? Still, if Barty was doing something that could get him in trouble and I could stop it, a few ground gears and a mirror adjustment was a small price to pay.

On Saturday morning, the little bell over the ice cream shop door jingled and a man in a cowboy hat stepped inside. Ravi. The last time I'd talked to my father had been at school, the week before summer vacation started. I'd told him about my summer plans and about the job at Groovy's. He told me that his band was doing well and his pottery studio was building a reputation with the tourists. As usual, he had not asked about Barty directly, just said he hoped that Barty wasn't doing drugs. Ravi said that he had started experimenting with drugs at Barty's age and told me that I should keep an eye on him. I had to bite back a quick retort that he had no business giving me orders, especially since he wasn't willing to talk to Barty himself. But now, seeing my pony-tailed father saunter into the shop for the first time since I had been working there and with Miggie's revelation about his treatment of her fresh in my mind, I was furious. I shot Ravi a glare full of resentment.

He stopped in front of the counter, staring at my angry face in comical surprise. "Hey, I didn't need a reservation for this place, did I? You look a little annoyed."

I took a breath, cast a glance over at Norm who was wiping down a table, and managed to tone down some of the death rays being emitted from my eyes. "No reservations required. What can I get you?" The words were polite, but my tone was frost-covered.

Ravi cast an interested look over the silver bins neatly filled with colorful ice cream. After he had walked up and down the entire counter, he walked back to me and said, "I'll have a scoop of vanilla. In a cup."

I'd been thinking maybe the magenta-colored Zingali-cious sherbet or perhaps the lurid orange Papaya Punch with its swirls of neon-green lime ice cream. Probably two scoops in a waffle cone. Not *vanilla*. In a cup with a tiny spoon. Please.

I quirked up an eyebrow. Ravi saw it and grinned. "I like vanilla."

I scooped a generous amount of ice cream into a white cardboard cup, added a wooden spoon—Myron didn't believe in putting plastic in your mouth—and handed it to Ravi. "That will be $2.50."

He handed me a five and, as I busied myself making change, he leaned over the counter and said, "Tell your brother to stay out of the clubs."

"What?" The word was shocked out of my mouth. Norm,

having finished cleaning the table, had moved behind the counter, preparing to take over when I went on break. His interested gaze flickering between Ravi and me propelled me out into the lobby where I removed my ball cap and apron before walking outside. Ravi followed.

Still processing Ravi's unbelievable words, I took my time finding just the right outside table. Ravi joined me, leisurely eating his ice cream with dainty bites.

"What are you talking about?" I demanded as soon as he sat down.

"Your brother has been hanging around the clubs and lounges in Carson City, Reno and Sparks. I've seen him with his friends a few times at places where I've had a gig."

"How would they even get into a casino?" I couldn't imagine Barty and any of the friends I'd met being able to fool a security guard into believing they were of legal age.

"They take turns, come in one at a time like they're on their way to a restaurant or the bathrooms, then they meet up in front of where a lounge act," Ravi pointed his spoon at himself, "is performing, and watch until one of the security guards starts moving in their direction. At the bars, they hang around outside the doors, not close enough to see inside, but too close to be just passing by. Some shady characters hang out in those places—he and his friends shouldn't be there."

Ravi finished his ice cream and put the spoon in the cup, wiped his moustache with a paper napkin and got up to throw the cup and spoon away. I stared at him, trying to puzzle through his words to the truth. Why would Barty do such a thing, and why would Ravi care?

Ravi nodded at me and said, "Make him listen, pumpkin." Then he walked away, getting into a white van with a magnetic sign on the driver's side door that read "Greenware —the band and the legend" followed by a phone number and a cartoon of musical notes and long-haired musicians. I wasn't sure it was an improvement from the lime green pickup with the beige camper shell, especially after the van clanked to life and ejected a puff of smoke from the tail pipe before pulling out of the parking space and onto the roadway.

Chapter Thirty-Seven

I drove home that night, rehearsing what I was going to say to Barty. He'd just started talking to me again and I didn't want to make him so angry that he stopped talking altogether, or come across as a bossy sister interfering with his life. But he needed to know how serious his playing chicken with security guards and hanging out in front of bars and in casinos could be. What if he were arrested? Would he go to juvie? Have a record? What could he be thinking?

I was still wrestling with how to approach him when I walked up onto the porch of our house. Apparently, I didn't hear Miggie the first time she called to me, so she whisper-shouted, "Clare!" Startled, I looked up to see her perched on the edge of her seat on one of the rockers. Even though it was after nine o'clock, there was enough light to see that she had been crying.

The last time Miggie cried was the day she picked me up from UNR. I stopped, frozen with my foot on the first step, staring at her, waiting for the bomb to drop.

"I told Dan."

She didn't have to identify what she had told Dan, but her tense posture and those red-rimmed eyes didn't give me any confidence that their conversation had gone well. My heart dropped—I had so believed that Dan would be understanding and supportive.

Before I could say anything, Miggie said, "He was so sweet, so loving and understanding." To my mind, this didn't explain her obvious agitation, but then she said, "I don't deserve him. I don't deserve any of you. I've been so selfish."

That brought me all the way up onto the porch and into the rocker next to her. I took her trembling hand. This sad and agitated person was so not the mother I knew. I had never thought in terms of deserving the people in my life before. It was clear to me now that Miggie truly loved Dan and somehow she thought she needed to be a better person to deserve his love.

"Can't you have something good just happen—to kind of —I don't know, show you that it's OK? That you're OK, just the way you are?" I asked.

Miggie stared at me as if I had just said something unthinkable. It didn't seem so strange to me, but maybe I was wrong. Maybe you only got good things if you were a good person. No, that didn't explain Mr. Kerwick who won $27 million in the Lotto. He was the mean guy who lived down the block from Grammie in Placerville. He drank and often staggered around in his front yard, yelling at kids who dared to walk on the sidewalk in front of his house which almost burned down when he fell asleep in his recliner while smoking. He was also the local drug dealer, attracting a host of scary types into the neighborhood. Barty and I always crossed the street on tiptoe rather than walk in front of his house. When it burned, we expected that he would leave since he didn't have insurance, but instead, he won the lottery, which didn't seem fair at all. Mr. Kerwick rebuilt his burned up house with the lottery money and sold it for twice what he had paid for it, according to neighborhood gossip. When he moved, much to my relief, gossip placed him in Colorado, living with a super model and giving fabulous parties in his new mansion.

Maybe Miggie was thinking of Mr. Kerwick too. In a soft voice, as if she were exploring something completely unknown to her, she said, "Maybe it *isn't* all about being perfect and always doing the right thing—maybe you can just be lucky." She leaned forward and gave me a hug, awkward because we were both in rockers. She kissed me before saying, "I'm lucky to have you." She added as she got up, "There's a burrito in the kitchen. I'm going to make some jewelry." Miggie's go-to calming device.

She went into the house. I stared at the burgeoning stars a few minutes thinking about luck and wondering whether it just happened or if it was something you could make happen. Reaching no conclusion, I fetched my burrito and went back out to the porch, preparing to wait for my brother and hoping I would get lucky in getting answers to my questions about his activities.

Chapter Thirty-Eight

Hours went by at a crawl. The moon moved, the stars twinkled, but Barty's pickup did not appear. At midnight, his curfew, he wasn't home. No big deal, I thought, he usually rolled in exactly at midnight or a couple of minutes past. But, at 12:40, there was still no Barty. My thoughts about talking to him turned to thoughts of possible disasters that might have happened. The burrito in my stomach began to feel like lead.

By 1:15, I was seriously worried. Was Miggie still awake, waiting to hear the crunch of gravel under the tires of Barty's pickup? What was the time at which I could stop worrying about getting my brother in trouble with our parents and feel legitimately justified in waking them? One-thirty? Two? What if he had been in an accident? What if he'd been arrested at one of the casinos?

At 1:30, a pair of headlights appeared at the end of our drive. As the vehicle approached, my heart sank, realizing from the wheeze of the engine and the distance between the headlights that it couldn't be Barty's pickup. And it wasn't.

The vehicle moved slowly, as if the driver wasn't sure where he was going or he wasn't sure the engine would make it, or both. I stood up on the porch, trying to see who it was. One of Barty's friends, bringing him home?

As the vehicle finally pulled up in front of our house, parallel to the porch, moonlight revealed a white van with a sign on the side. "Greenware—the Band and the Legend."

Crapadoodie.

Involuntarily, I glanced behind me at the house, expecting Miggie to come flying out, maybe with her soldering iron in hand, but the house remained quiet. The side door of the van opened and Barty climbed awkwardly out, just as Ravi rounded the front of the van from the driver's side. It looked as if Ravi put a hand on Barty's arm which Barty shook off. As I went toward them, I could hear Ravi speaking in a low and urgent tone as Barty stood, rigid, staring straight ahead. When I reached a patch of moonlight, both of them turned toward me. Ravi said something else to Barty who gave a curt nod. Then. Barty strode past me into the house, giving me a brief nod as well.

Ravi was already opening the driver's door when I reached him. I could see another man in the passenger seat, middle-aged and balding but with giant muttonchops.

"What's going on?" I whispered.

Ravi turned to me after first casting an uneasy glance back at the house. "I just brought your brother home," he whispered back.

I rolled my eyes. "Yeah, I got that. Why?"

"He can tell you." He looked at the house again and put a foot inside the van and said in a rushed whisper, "I gotta go. I'm taking Beanie home. We gotta put the equipment away."

Muttonchops, aka, Beanie, gave me a small wave as Ravi pulled himself all the way inside the van. I realized the engine was still running and was mildly amazed that it was able to do so. I put my hand on the frame of the open window to stop them from leaving, but Ravi leaned his head out and said softly, "He's OK. Not drunk, not arrested, not hurt." I left my hand on the door frame. He patted it and said, "You're off work today?"

I nodded.

"Then, meet me at the Nevada State Museum in Carson City. Around noon?"

I nodded again and stepped away from the van as it wheezed its way back into the road.

Chapter Thirty-Nine

I went into the dark, silent house and knocked softly on Barty's closed door. There was no answer. If Miggie had been waiting up to hear Barty's pickup, I couldn't tell as the door to Miggie and Dan's bedroom was also closed. I checked on Jacob who was sprawled in a welter of sheets as if he were sleeping in the eye of a hurricane. Exhausted by a full day of work and a full evening of worry, I went to bed myself.

The next morning, Barty and Dan were already gone when I pulled myself out of bed. Jacob greeted me in the living room with his usual flying leap onto my back and we wrestled and tickled each other into the kitchen where Miggie was clearing away the breakfast dishes.

I chased Jacob out of the kitchen with a banana, one of the few edibles he wouldn't eat, and did a side-eye glance at Miggie to check on her mood. She smiled at me and said, "Good morning." As she slid dishes into the sink and squirted a little soap on them, I could hear her singing under her breath. It sounded like "You Make My Dreams Come True" by Hall and Oates. Her feet weren't moving, but the rest of her—head, shoulders and hips—kept up a gentle movement to her song as she washed the dishes and stacked them in the drainer. Miggie did not look like a parent who had just grounded one of her children.

I busied myself making tea and toast, sneaking occasional glances over at my singing, swaying mother. How had Barty explained his missing truck?

I couldn't stand it. "Did you see Barty this morning?"

Miggie turned my way and nodded. "He caught a ride to work with Dan. One of his friends brought him home because his truck wouldn't start." She gave me another dreamy smile before saying, "After you and I talked, I went to our room. Dan was still awake, so we started talking." She laughed softly and shook her head. "We talked so long that we just fell asleep—I didn't even hear Barty come home!"

Well that explained a lot.

Obviously Miggie wasn't aware of the Barty/Ravi connection, and I wasn't about to inform her, especially since I didn't know anything about why Ravi had brought Barty home. I couldn't wait to talk to Ravi and find out what was going on, so I grabbed a quick breakfast and then flew around, getting dressed. Just before eleven, with my hand on the front door, I told Miggie I was going to Carson on an errand and disappeared out onto the porch before she could suggest that I take Jacob with me.

My mind swirled between Barty and Ravi, Miggie and Dan. I used the half hour drive to force myself to focus on the first task at hand—wondering what had happened to Barty. He was working, so I couldn't talk to him yet—I would just have to trust that Ravi would tell me what I wanted to know and then I could take whatever action needed to be done.

. . .

I got to downtown Carson City a little before noon and found a close parking spot which seemed like a good sign to me. Ravi had found one too—I passed his white van on my way to the museum and speeded my steps. He was waiting right next to the Nevada State Museum sign. The sandstone brick edifice that housed the museum was imposing, but we walked around to the rear of the building to the other part of the museum, a modern glass pyramid, and then we kept walking.

I told him I hadn't seen Barty yet. "He shut himself in his room last night and wouldn't answer the door. Then he left with Dan this morning before I was up." As we rounded a corner behind the museum, I demanded. "You've got to tell me what happened."

Ravi gave a sigh and then said, "We were playing a gig at the Barbarossa last night—one of our usual spots. It's a little rough around the edges, but the owner is cool and the customers like us." He nodded at me as if to confirm that I knew the Barbarossa.

Everyone knew of the Barbarossa. It was a bar, right off the highway. Its beat up dark wood exterior suggested that it was left over from the days of the Comstock silver strikes, but Dan said it had been built in the 1970s and named after a pirate. The interior décor boasted skulls with eyepatches and tri-cornered hats, stuffed parrots and a nautical theme that was out of keeping with a desert mining town two hundred and forty miles from the nearest ocean. Dan said it was mostly a biker hangout due to the proximity to the highway. You could see a line of motorcycles parked out front almost any time of the day or night.

"Well, we were taking our last break and I went outside in the front to get a breath of air." He grinned, "It's pretty smoky in that place. I gotta breathe to sing."

He sang? I didn't even know what instrument he played —or whether he did.

"I heard this altercation going on." Again, he grinned, "There's always an altercation going on at the Barbarossa." I gave an impatient huff and Ravi stopped grinning and started talking again.

"I wasn't paying any mind to all the fuss, but then one of the boys that hangs out with Barty flew past me, running down the frontage road like an Olympic sprinter. A bunch of dudes were running after him, but not putting much into it. Another kid peeled off in the opposite direction and Barty ran toward the back parking lot. He was moving pretty fast, but there's nowhere to go once you get to the back unless you can hop a chain link fence with barbed wire at the top of it." He looked at me to see if I was understanding how serious this was, so I nodded, wanting him to finish.

"The guys chasing him realized it too. They sounded like a pack of hounds after a rabbit, yelling how they were going to beat the shit out of him for smarting off. The dudes chasing the other two boys had given up and doubled back, so the whole pack was after Barty. I ducked back into the bar and out the back door. My van was parked way back on the left of the parking area, sort of between the back fence and the side fence. I saw something moving out behind it and figured it was Barty, so I grabbed one of my guitars from the back room where we kept our extra equipment and walked out to the van.

"The crowd was yelling that they were gonna kill him. Some guys were trying to climb the fence; the rest were peering through it to see where he had gone. One dude even had a flashlight and was shining it around the lot and into the desert beyond the fence. I opened the side of the van. Barty was crouched down between the side fence and the back tire on the side away from the crowd. A few guys had turned at the sound of the door opening, but I stepped around to the front of the van and waved, holding up my guitar and they went back to baying like hounds. I stepped back, told Barty to get in and he did. I told him to stay down and I locked the door. Then I walked up to the crowd and asked one dude what was going on. He said three punks had been hanging around outside the bar and had knocked over one of the bikes. When the biker who owned it found out, he and his friends started hassling the punks and one of the punks sassed them and then it was on."

I frowned. "What happened to Barty's friends?"

"Barty told me later that they had parked down the road a piece. They were able to get to their car and take off." Here, Ravi gave a one-sided sneer as if disgusted with boys who deserted their friends.

"The crowd broke up and most of them came back inside for the rest of the show, but a few of them hung out in the parking lot, waiting to see if Barty would sneak back—like maybe his car was parked back there. I figured he was as safe in the van as he could be, providing he kept down low, so I went back inside to finish my set." He shrugged.

"You didn't call the police?"

My indignant words drew an eye roll from Ravi who followed it up with, "The cops take their time responding to calls from the Barbarossa. And I would have lost any future gigs at the Barbarossa for being a snitch and Barty would have been busted for being where he shouldn't have been." He gave me a look as if even a kindergartener would have been able to figure this out.

I suppressed my anger that he seemed to be more concerned about his future at a bar than about his son and settled for, "Where was Barty's pickup?"

"At his friend's house. They'd taken the friend's dad's car. I told Beanie what was going on and after we finished our set, Beanie and I loaded up the van while the other guys stayed inside for beers. We told them that Beanie had to get home which was true because his old lady freaks out if he stays out drinking. When we left, those dudes were still in the parking lot, waiting for Barty. Not a real bright bunch." Ravi shrugged before saying, "We drove over to where he said his friend's car was parked, but it was gone. Barty was too worried about missing curfew to go over to the friend's house to get his pickup. He just said he would pick it up later. You know the rest."

All my questions were answered except why Barty was doing this. "Did you guys talk about why he is going to bars and casinos?"

"The kid wouldn't talk to me except for yes and no. But, when I asked him if he and his friends followed any other bands, he just shook his head."

We had continued our endless rounds of the buildings, so absorbed in our conversation that I had noticed nothing about our surroundings. As Ravi finished his sentence, we stopped walking and I looked around. We were behind the museums in a quiet shaded area. There was a bench and as we sat down, Ravi cleared his throat and said, "I think I know why he comes around. Not bragging, but I think he wants to know me. Know who I am. And . . . I think I want to know him too."

That Barty had chosen this way to learn about Ravi made more sense than developing a sudden taste for classic rock performed by middle-aged men. That Ravi had finally decided he wanted to know his son was more surprising to me.

"So, what are you going to do?"

"I . . . don't know," Ravi admitted, his eyes on his pointy-toed boots.

"What do you mean? Just say hello to him, for God's sake, or write him a letter or call."

"Clare, I've spent his whole life pretending he wasn't my son."

"Why?" From Miggie I already knew, but I wanted to hear what Ravi would say.

Ravi sighed. "I didn't want kids. Didn't want them to slow me down. When you came along, I tried to deal with parenthood as if we had gotten a puppy. Miggie carried all the load; I was too busy doing my art." He looked at me and shrugged. "It wasn't fair, but I told myself that I was the real artist; Miggie was just a crafter.

"But, when she told me she was pregnant again, I was so damn mad. I could see my whole life turning out just like my father's—he'd told me over and over again that I needed to get a 'real job' and settle down; I had to be a man and support my family, buy a house, move up the corporate ladder, buy a bigger house with a pool and a Mercedes. I had to be like him and that was the one thing I never, ever wanted to be."

He got up as if the bench had suddenly become red-hot and stalked a few steps away before pacing back to the bench. I saw red spots on his cheeks above the mustache. He paced back and forth; I waited, silent. Finally, he seemed to have worked off some of the emotion driving him and he slumped down on the bench speaking in a voice so low I had to lean forward to hear him.

"So, I left. I grabbed a few things and hit the road. And I didn't look back—not for a long, long time."

I stared at my father as if he had suddenly turned green. Ravi didn't look up from the concrete beneath his feet. The silence between us grew like a mushroom cloud. So, he still wasn't going to come clean about what he had done to Miggie?

Finally, I said, "You just left—without saying a word to Miggie?" I waited.

My father kept staring at the concrete. He peeked up once and looked at me, then his gaze shot back to the concrete. I cleared my throat. Waited.

In an almost inaudible voice, Ravi said, "Uh, we had an argument. I . . . uh, told her I didn't think the kid was mine."

I saw again the shamed misery on Miggie's face. Pity and rage at how Miggie had been left, on her own, with two babies, and sorrow at how Barty had been discarded by his own blood overwhelmed me once again. It had been building, without an outlet, all summer, since Miggie's confession, and now with the addition of Barty's near escape from a beating and possible mutilation, it morphed into fury. I jumped off the bench.

When Ravi looked up at me, I was almost choking with the effort of trying to hold my rage in check. Probably thinking I really was choking, Ravi flew off the bench, grabbed me and began pounding me on the back.

I fought away from him, smacking him hard on the chin. As Ravi stepped back and saw the blaze of anger in my eyes, he took another involuntary step back, half falling against the bench behind him.

I had never been so angry in my life. I couldn't speak, couldn't make any coherent sound with the dam of rage blocking my throat. I stood over my father who was sprawled awkwardly against the stone bench, my fists and teeth clenched, my eyes feeling like they were on fire, my entire body rigid as a granite boulder. I struggled, until at last, a huge scream broke the dam choking me.

"ARRAAHHHG!" The sound echoed off the buildings

in front of us, roiled around the trees in the park and returned in full force. Ravi froze. Stunned at the sound that had just been torn out of me, I too, remained rigid, my mouth open. An elderly couple rushed around the corner and stopped at the sight of Ravi and me. A nano second went by and then the gray-haired woman, her red water bottle upraised, charged, her husband a half-step behind.

"You leave her alone!" she shrieked as she brought the water bottle crashing down on Ravi's head. Being made of plastic, the bottle didn't break, but the top flew off and water cascaded down Ravi's face. The woman whacked him again as Ravi tried to stand and fend her off.

Her husband appeared to be trying to restrain both his wife and Ravi as well as comfort me. A tangle of arms, legs, heads and water bottle began to move slowly away from the bench to the accompaniment of the woman's shrieks, Ravi's protests and the white-haired man's grunts. My rage had dissipated in surprise, but I had to stop this.

I produced another gut-wrenching scream and everything came to an abrupt halt. With the tiny bit of breath I had left, I forced out, "I'm all right. It's OK." I repeated my words over and over as the man tried to ask what happened and the woman, minus her weapon, glared at Ravi as if to skewer him on a non-existent rapier. Ravi, wisely, said nothing at all and tried not to look at his attacker.

Finally, my rigid muscles relaxed and I was able to move. I unclenched my fists and smiled apologetically at the couple. "I'm so sorry I frightened you," I told them. "I really am fine." I took a breath and glanced at a motionless and streaming wet Ravi, before turning back to the couple. "I was just so angry at something *he*," I nodded at Ravi, "said, that I had to scream."

The woman's glare at Ravi became incandescent, as if her

non-existent rapier had become red-hot and could burn through his entrails. I stepped between them. "Really, it isn't anything to worry about. He didn't threaten me or anything. I just got mad, that's all. I'm sorry, sorry . . ."

Gradually, the older couple seemed to calm themselves. "You're sure you're not hurt?" the woman asked, obviously believing that I was being suborned by wicked Ravi into pretending that nothing had happened.

"Thank you so much for coming to my rescue." I smiled and touched the woman's arm. "You were so brave. It was my fault for screaming. See," I turned around in a circle in front of the couple, "I'm not hurt at all. *This*," I said, through gritted teeth as some of my anger returned, "is my father and if there's anyone who can make you scream in anger, it's your father. Well, my father, anyway."

Another apologetic smile from me and the couple slowly moved away, the husband with his arm around his wife who was still trembling with adrenaline and glaring back over her shoulder at Ravi, daring him to make a move, any move.

As they disappeared around the corner of a building, Ravi said, "Sure glad that wasn't a glass bottle."

Between his bedraggled appearance and my own hysteria, I was tempted to laugh, but my anger had returned and I wasn't about to let him off the hook.

"I wish I had a glass bottle now." I said, glaring at him as he stood, wiping the water that dripped off the ends of his moustache. "Or a sledgehammer."

Ravi looked at me warily, running a hand across the top of his head as if checking for bumps. "Look . . ." he began.

I wasn't having any of it. After a whole summer of fermenting, my rage had found words and he was going to hear them. Every single one of them.

Chapter Forty

After my torrent of words, accusations and frustration had spent itself, I was exhausted. I slumped on the bench still trembling with adrenaline as Ravi began to speak. His voice was slow and gentle as if he were trying to soothe a wild beast, which I pretty much had been for the past fifteen minutes. He didn't deny or rush past any of my furious tirade. Instead, Ravi talked about how he knew he had caused great turmoil and grief in our lives and how stupid he had been, at which point I nodded in agreement.

Then he said, "I think—I think maybe Barty wants to get to know me."

I opened my mouth to object, but Ravi held up a hand. "Why else would he come to my gigs? There's any number of hole-in-the-wall joints he and his buddies could get into. Why only where I'm performing?"

It made sense in a weird way. Maybe my years-ago attempt to connect my brother and father had made Barty curious. I looked at my father, cocking my head to one side, wanting to know more.

Ravi rubbed his head and then pulled on his mustache. He took a breath. "I've been a dick and I want to tell him that and apologize for ignoring him, but I think we need to get to know each other first. If he wants to."

For the first time, Ravi sounded like a grownup to me—the world's oldest teenager deciding to be an adult. Softening my voice, I said, "That's a good idea, but I think you might want to apologize to Miggie first. And find out if she is OK with Barty getting to know you. She's got some big-time baggage around that."

Ravi managed to look mulish and sheepish at the same time. Finally, the sheepish part won out and he said, "You're probably right. Gonna need to get my head around it first—give me a couple of days and I'll call her."

No way was he going to weasel out now if I could help it. I drew myself up to my full five feet, my lucky red Converse digging in. "Nope, this is going to have to be face to face. Man up, Ravi, you insulted her face to face, so any apology needs to be the same way."

He stared at me for a long moment. Then he said, "OK, you set it up—when I call you. But maybe you could talk to her first. Sort of get her ready."

Crapadoodie. Who would have parents if they didn't have to?

Ravi continued, as if he hadn't just handed me a commission that might take years off my life, "There's stuff I should tell him, about our family, about how the world works and about finding out what's important—stuff that my father never told me. Stuff that might have made a difference." He looked away, off into the distance. I couldn't see his face, but I could see the tenseness in his shoulders hunched around his ears.

It made me happy that Ravi apparently wanted to acknowledge Barty and talk to him as a father should, but a little part of me wondered why Ravi didn't seem to want to tell me those things too. Until this day, all of our conversations had been about what he was doing or questions about what I was doing. It sounded like Ravi wanted to talk to Barty about real things. Wasn't I important enough for that too? He'd abandoned all of us, not just Miggie. A shaft of pain speared me. Wasn't he my father too?

I pushed away the feeling—I was an adult, or mostly, anyway. I didn't need another parent, and maybe Barty didn't either, but he did need some sort of connection with his father. I already had a relationship with Ravi, even though it was more like one with a weird uncle, the one who shows up unexpectedly and whose lifestyle makes no sense to you, than with a father. Dan felt more like my real father. In his own way, Barty was reaching out to Ravi, and if Miggie allowed it, then I wanted him to have the chance to build his own relationship with our father, even if Ravi was a weird uncle.

Chapter Forty-One

Miggie stared at her daughter. Had Clare just said that Ravi wanted to talk to her about Barty? Since when had Ravi cared about Barty? She picked up a kitchen towel and began wiping down the already clean counter.

"Mom, Barty's been hanging around the casinos and the bars where Ravi and his band are performing."

Clare was facing away from her and looking down at her shoes, the back of her neck under her upswept curls a dull crimson—always a telltale sign of distress—that, and calling her "Mom." Those shoes, Ravi's last gift before he left them. Clare didn't remember where those first red Converse had come from, but Miggie did, and they had always pissed her off.

Why was she thinking about Clare's shoes? "How do you know?"

"Ravi brought him home the other night." Clare looked at the wall "You know, the night Barty said that a friend brought him home because his truck wouldn't start."

Miggie wondered why she ever thought it might be fun to have a baby. Of course, she didn't think that until she found out that Clare, no *Fresno*, was on the way. She could feel her daughter's anxiety—probably Clare was worried about Miggie's feelings and how upset Barty was going to be when he found out that Clare had told on him. Clare had always been a worrywart. But protective—something Miggie had always relied upon.

"Are you saying that Barty has been following Ravi?" Miggie felt the muscles in her throat constrict. She tried to relax, tried to follow her counselor Emma's advice about breathing through emotion, letting herself feel that emotion without losing control. Miggie hated being at the mercy of her feelings. She always pretended to be calmly above it all, like a Buddha. It drove other people, like her mother, crazy, so that was another plus. But Emma was teaching her how important it was to allow herself to feel her emotions instead of stuffing them away to fester. She wondered if Emma had children.

"Ravi said that Barty and his friends have almost gotten busted by security a couple of times and Ravi had to sneak him past a pack of bikers at Barbarossa's a couple of nights ago." Clare's pleading eyes were now fixed on Miggie's face. "Barty doesn't want to talk to me about it, but maybe he just wants to know Ravi, find out what kind of person he is."

Breathe, breathe. Miggie looked away from Clare. Maybe Emma was right about not suppressing your feelings, but letting loose the hurt and anger threatening to choke her now wasn't going to work. Breathe. The kitchen towel was clenched in her hands.

When she felt like she could speak without screaming, Miggie said, "So why are you bringing this up?"

She saw Clare take a breath. A big one.

"Ravi wants to get to know Barty, too. He asked me to set up a meeting with you so he could talk to you about it."

Miggie's breath came out in a huge burst of sound. "Are you kidding me? After sixteen years of pretending Barty doesn't exist, he wants to swoop in like nothing ever happened? Where was he when Barty broke his arm? Where was he when we had to eat ramen for a week? When we moved to Utah? Where was he when you graduated from high school? Where was he all this time?"

No breathing exercises were going to help now, and dammit, she was feeling every single one of those feelings of abandonment, humiliation, fear, rage, pain and resentment now careening through her body like pinballs.

Miggie saw Clare's eyes widen as she leaned away from her mother. She could tell that Clare was wishing she were anywhere on the planet except this kitchen. Miggie felt the same way. She felt as if she might implode.

"Why, why, why should I let him talk to Barty?" Miggie's hands flew out in front of her, the kitchen towel slipping to the floor. "He left us!"

Clare remained silent, fitting herself in the corner of the kitchen wall. After a few moments, Miggie heard the silence —the silence of someone trying very hard to be unnoticed. She recognized the technique—her sister had been a master at becoming invisible whenever their mother found fault with them. Miggie never mastered invisibility—she always had to say something.

The realization that Clare was trying for invisibility calmed Miggie, somewhat. She bent over and picked up the towel. Not looking at her daughter, she said, "I can't talk about this right now." Tossing the towel on the counter, she walked out the side door.

Chapter Forty-Two

The Saturday after her conversation with Miggie, Clare was up early and getting ready for work. She didn't have to be at the shop until after nine, but weekends were the busiest days at the ice cream shop. Besides, the atmosphere around the house had been tense since Miggie's explosion, and even though her mother had calmed down, Clare didn't mind being out of the house.

She yawned her way into the kitchen and found Dan pouring coffee into his thermos just as he did every weekday. His motions were quick and jerky, almost spilling the carafe of coffee. Dan's eyes flicked toward her, but his usual smile and greeting were missing.

"Isn't this Saturday?" Clare asked. She'd never seen Dan angry, but the grim expression on his face, which he turned away from her, seemed angry. "Is everything OK?"

"It's Saturday. Fine." The terse words jerked out of Dan as if he were trying to hold them back. He capped the thermos, opened the outside kitchen door and disappeared, the screen door banging behind him.

Clare stared after him. On weekends, Dan often did car repairs out in his workshop to bring in a little extra money, but usually he slept in and had breakfast with the family before he headed outside.

Jacob came into the kitchen in his jammie bottoms, sleepy-eyed and clutching his furry yellow blanket. The color and texture of the blanket had reminded Clare of a baby chick, causing her to christen it "Chicky." Jacob walked directly into her midsection and wrapped his arms around her, Chicky tickling her bare leg below her sleep shorts. A slow, quiet and clingy Jacob was weird, very weird.

She pulled him back to look into his face. "You seem very quiet this morning. Are you still sleepy?"

He snuggled back into her. "Mommy's crying and I think Daddy is mad. He was yelling."

Miggie must have finally told him about Ravi's request. Clare thought Dan might have objections, but she hadn't thought he would be angry. It was all her fault for trying to manage everyone and bring about a happy ending. She should have just told Ravi to go away and stay away. She had to make this right, somehow.

Clare gave Jacob a gentle squeeze and said, "I'm going to go out and talk to Daddy. Before I do, how about some breakfast?"

He slid into a kitchen chair, Chicky now wrapped around one arm. "Not hungry." Jacob's head hung down.

Alarmed, Clare said, "Look, I'll talk to both Mommy and Daddy and they will be fine. OK? I promise." Her little brother looked up at her solemnly. Clare smiled back, hoping he would believe her. She waited, still smiling until, finally, he nodded.

"OK then, how about some cereal?"

"French toast. With butter and syrup. And power sugar,"

he ordered. Inwardly Clare groaned. French toast would take forever and who had ever let him have syrup *and* powdered sugar in this almost all-natural household? Probably Barty.

"OK, you get out the bread and I'll get out the egg and milk." If she were really fast, she could slap out a couple of pieces in five minutes.

Eight minutes later, Jacob was trying to spear four pieces of toast on one fork and fit it into his mouth. Clare backed him down to two pieces and reminded him to chew. She put the syrup and sugar away before he could decide he needed extra, and flew to her bedroom to change.

Outside, Dan's Explorer was still parked in the driveway along with Barty's pickup, Coachinella and Miggie's Camry. Clare walked to the barnlike structure that housed Dan's workshop.

Dan usually blocked the doors wide open to let in light and air, but today the doors were almost closed. Clare slipped inside and stood, letting her eyes adjust from the bright sunshine of the day to the dimness inside the workshop.

She heard him before she saw him. The ratcheting sound of a socket wrench tightening a bolt echoed around the shop. Clare walked toward a Chevy Impala and peered around until she saw Dan's jean-covered legs poking out from underneath it. The 1970 Impala was his friend's baby, its bright orange color blazing even inside the darkened barn.

Clare crouched down. "Hey there." She heard him grunt. "I just thought I'd come out and visit since we haven't had much time to talk lately."

Silence. After a couple of minutes, she heard, "Don't have time to talk."

"Maybe I can just hand you tools, then."

Silence, then more ratcheting. Banging. "Crescent wrench."

Clare looked at Dan's array of tools on the floor. She could see the crescent wrench. She handed him a pipe wrench.

"No, the crescent wrench, please." His voice had an edge to it. His hand waved the pipe wrench at her.

Clare took the pipe wrench and handed down another socket wrench.

"Clare, you know what a crescent wrench looks like. Take this thing." The socket wrench was waved impatiently at her.

She took the wrench and handed him a hammer.

"What the hell . . ." Dan rolled out from under the Impala like a rocket, his eyes blazing. Clare held out the crescent wrench.

"This one?" She gave him an impish smile, inwardly hoping that he wouldn't use the hammer on her.

There was a second when both of them were holding tools and staring at each other. Dan broke first, blowing out his breath and shaking his head. An unwilling grin crept across his face. "You brat."

"That I am, but only sometimes." Clare grinned back at him, as she handed over the crescent wrench. In a softer voice she asked, "So, what's going on?"

Dan rolled the creeper all the way out from under the car and sat up on it, wiping his hands on one of the blue work towels he kept in his pockets.

"Ravi wants to see Barty."

Clare nodded.

"Damn it, Clare! He's got no business here. I know he's your father, but he's never taken care of you or Barty. And what he did to Miggie—." Here his voice faltered, as if he were either overcome with emotion or not sure that Clare knew what Ravi had done.

"Dan, I know why Ravi didn't want to be part of Barty's life earlier. He told me last week." She wasn't sure how Dan would feel about Miggie telling her first.

"How could a man do that to his children? How could he do that to the mother of his children?" It was a cry from the soul from a man who put Miggie and his family at the top of his list every day. There was no way she could explain—she didn't understand it herself.

"Ravi hasn't been a father," Clare said slowly. "He didn't take care of us; he didn't even try. He left Miggie to do it all—that's something he has to live with. And I think he's starting to realize it, finally." She peered into Dan's face, watching his eyes, waiting for the anger in them to dissipate. She leaned over and put her hand on his arm. "I know for sure that Barty thinks of you as his dad, his real dad. He loves you and he wants to be like you. I think, though, he's curious about where he comes from. What kind of people made him—because he's probably trying to figure out who he is. And he's been sneaking around because he doesn't want to hurt you. He might even be embarrassed that he wants to know."

Dan looked away. His shoulders went up and then down abruptly as he blew air out of his lips. Then, he nodded and patted her hand, which was still on his arm. He lay back down on the creeper and scooted under the Impala.

Clare walked slowly back to the house, wondering if a meeting between Ravi and Miggie was worth all the heartache.

Chapter Forty-Three

Donna and I did our Whozit communication every Tuesday and Thursday. I talked her through relaxing and she put the phone on speaker next to where Whozit was positioned. Donna practiced her own contact on the nights we didn't do Team Whozit and she said she was getting better at it.

One night, after we'd talked about the upcoming baby shower, we settled into our baby sensing routine, beginning with me walking Donna through a relaxation exercise. "You're very comfortable. Relax your forehead, your eyes . . ." I talked her through relaxing each part of her body.

"OK," she said after a few minutes. "I'm so relaxed, I might fall asleep again. So, tonight, why don't you ask her if she likes Brussels sprouts."

Brussels sprouts? "OK, put your hand on Whozit, see if you can sense her." While Donna relaxed, I waited for the Voice. I could hear Whozit's baby song clearly. It seemed to check for a second like it usually did when she sensed me. Or maybe she was sensing her mama. But the Voice did not come to me and Whozit went back to her song. I hadn't heard the Voice, my twin, for over a week and it worried me.

Mindful of Donna's request, I pictured Brussels sprouts—boiled, broiled with bacon, on stalks, in a bowl—and sent the images out into the universe. Whozit's song of contentment didn't change and I didn't sense any images from her.

After minutes of trying to communicate with Whozit about Brussels sprouts, it seemed that without my twin, the Voice, I was only a receiver. I could hear Whozit's song and sense her contentment, just as I had with Jacob and Taylor, but I couldn't send anything. Without the Voice, I wasn't talking with Whozit anymore; I was simply sensing her. It was as if I had returned to the kind of baby channeling I had always done before the Voice appeared.

Where was she, now? Would she ever come back? My heart felt torn, as if a piece of it had been ripped away. How could I miss someone I'd never known, so much?

"I hear something," Donna's voice said in my ear. "Like music, only without music."

I caught my breath, holding the phone closer. "I think you might be hearing Whozit's baby song. They all have one. Move your hand around, like you're giving her a little massage." I waited, hearing the baby song pick up volume and intensity.

"I hear the music—it's louder, now." Donna sounded thrilled. "This is so cool!"

It was beyond cool, that my friend and her baby now had a little more communication going on between themselves. I wished the Voice was there to round out our Team Whozit, but maybe she would come back. I hoped so.

I decided not to tell Donna about the missing Voice. It might make her worry and she was already doing enough of that. Besides, I could still sense Whozit and now, with our practice, so could Donna.

"Sorry, Donna, Whozit seems to just want to relax and sing. She isn't responding to Brussels sprouts one way or another."

Donna's sleepy voice floated into my ear. "Hearing her—you called it her baby song—is pretty awesome. I'll just tell Mom that Brussels sprouts make me burp, or give me heartburn. Anything, so I don't have to keep eating them." There was an audible yawn and then, "Goodnight, Clare Bear."

"Goodnight, Donna Madonna."

I hung up, glad for Donna and Whozit, but miserably missing the Voice.

Chapter Forty-Four

The bell over the door jingled merrily as my mother walked into the ice cream shop. Miggie had taken pains with her appearance, but in a subtle way. Her long, honey blond hair was shiny and it rolled in gentle waves over her shoulders. She wore no makeup, but her outfit was the one she wore when going out to a casual dinner—a white peasant blouse embroidered with red flowers and improbable blue leaves tucked into a slim pair of jeans with a beaded belt. Instead of the ever-present Birkenstocks, she wore a pair of soft red leather loafers that I had never seen. The only jewelry she wore was of her own creation—a pair of dangly silver earrings and a silver and copper bangle with four Wedgewood blue beads on it—one each for Dan, Barty, Jacob and myself. She looked beautiful and nowhere near her chronological age of thirty-eight.

I fixed cones for a pair of teenagers. Miggie waited at the far end of the counter until they left before coming up to me.

"You look great," I told her. "I reserved a table for you and Ravi over there. Do you want some ice cream?" The two-person table in the back corner was small, but I had moved the other tables away to give them more privacy

Miggie shook her head. "Just some ice tea, please." She walked to the table and sat with her back to the wall, facing the front of the shop. Ravi would have to sit with his back to the shop. My mother knew her feng–shui and was powering up its support by positioning her back to the wall and facing the front door.

As I brought her the ice tea, the bell above the door jingled again. Ravi held the door open for a woman wearing a maternity smock and gripping the hand of a toddler. It looked as if Ravi had also dressed for the occasion—his jeans and blue tunic shirt were clean and the shirt looked as if it might have been pressed. His cowboy boots were unshined, but they were free of mud and debris and his cowboy hat looked newer than his usual one. Even the sapphire feather that curled along one side looked spruce.

"Do you have a restroom we can use?" the woman asked.

"Uh, sure." I pointed out the restroom and she strode determinedly toward it, the captive toddler trailing in her wake as he wailed, "But I don't havta go."

"Well, I do," was the terse response as they disappeared into the restroom.

Ravi stood at the counter, waiting. I'd seen him flick a glance toward Miggie, but he stayed at the counter gazing at the tubs of ice cream as if they were putting on a performance.

"Did you want some ice cream?" I asked. His reluctance to move made me want to laugh.

Ravi kept his eyes on the fascinating tubs and muttered, "Just the usual."

I'd only served him ice cream once, but apparently that was the usual. I plopped a scoop of vanilla into a cup and handed him a spoon. He took a bite, looked at me and said, "Thanks for setting this up."

He didn't look as if he was truly glad about it. With his ice cream in hand, he sauntered over to the table and took his seat, moving his chair diagonally so he could sit with his back to the big window on the side of the building instead of the dining area. Guess Ravi knew about feng-shui too.

I was proud of Miggie for doing this. Dan had offered to come with her, but she told him she needed to meet Ravi on her own, first. If she decided it was OK, there would be another meeting, this time with Dan, Barty, and me. I was proud of Dan too. He had stayed out in the workshop after our talk, but when I came back into the syrup-smeared kitchen, I found Miggie cuddling Jacob. Her eyes were red and she looked at me inquiringly. I remembered Dan's pat on my hand.

"He'll be OK," I said. "How about you?"

Miggie shrugged, arms full of my little brother. "I couldn't tell Dan about Ravi wanting to connect with Barty without telling him why he hadn't done it before."

Jacob, now full of French toast and soothed with cuddling, was ready for action and he squirmed out of her arms. "I'm going to help Daddy," he announced.

"Put your shorts on first," Miggie told him. He sped out of the room. After he left, she said, "Dan was so . . . angry. He was mad at Ravi; he was mad at me for not telling him sooner and for even thinking about talking to Ravi." Her eyes welled up again. "I felt so bad for hurting him."

Out of the corner of my eye I saw Jacob fly through the kitchen and out the screen door. Halfway across the yard, he met Dan who was coming in from the barn. Dan scooped him up in a giant hug and then the two of them walked back to the house, Jacob hopping on alternate feet while holding Dan's hand.

"He'll be all right, "I repeated. "Jacob is some pretty good medicine."

Miggie smiled, seeing the two of them. As I turned to get my things for work, I saw Dan's face through the screen door. His eyes were no longer angry.

Later, Miggie told me that they had gone for a walk with Einstein while Jacob rode his bike in circles around them. Both of them had apologized. Dan told her that he would support whatever she decided about Barty and Ravi, but he wasn't going to let her be hurt by that man again. They had talked about how important this might be for Barty. Miggie said that first she needed to feel that Ravi was sincere and that Barty could benefit from getting to know his birth father.

I knew Miggie would be relying on her intuition at this meeting rather than fact. She'd always made decisions that way. While her intuition allowed her to pick out the right color beads without looking at them, it was more fallible with other situations. When she'd told me about the meeting, I'd called her on it, wanting her to really pay attention. I wanted Barty to know his father, but would Ravi be a positive influence on my brother?

"Well, I'm usually right," she'd said. I stared at her, my face set in a frown. She saw it and shrugged. "OK—except for men." She scrunched her face up before adding, "That's only because I get caught up in my feelings and I don't pay attention to what my intuition is telling me."

Dan was a keeper, but she had brought plenty of non-keepers home, including Ravi.

Chapter Forty-Five

The little boy and his mother emerged from the bathroom just as Ravi seated himself at the table.

"I want a *lot* of ice cream," the toddler announced. His little blond head bobbed impatiently just below the glass of the display case. He held up his arms, "Want to *see*."

His mother picked him up, saying, "OK, we'll look at the ice cream." To me she said, "But he'll still want a scoop of strawberry with gummies on top."

I snuck a look at Ravi and Miggie, wishing I could hear what they were saying. Ravi appeared to be explaining something, but Miggie's face was blank, as if she was blocking his words.

My attention shifted back to the counter when the mom said in a disappointed tone, "Oh, you don't have plain strawberry."

The toddler immediately set up a howl. "I want strawberry! I want strawberry!" At least that's what I think he said as his mangled pronunciation of strawberry sounded more like Klingon.

I threw another look at Miggie and Ravi who each appeared to be staring at the table in front of them. Miggie looked up and said something to Ravi. At another howl from the little boy, Ravi shot a look toward me. I could swear he was begging for help. I hoped Miggie was lighting into him, but the little howler and his mother were my first priority.

"We do have strawberry, but it's vanilla cream with frozen strawberries in it. Maybe not very safe for young eaters," I said to the mother, remembering choking episodes with Jacob. The howl escalated. I had to get him out of the shop if I wanted to eavesdrop on Ravi and Miggie.

Peering over the counter at the toddler, I made my eyes big, and dropped my voice dramatically. "Do you know the Grinch?"

The howling paused. I was a little surprised that he could hear me. I lowered my voice to a whisper. "Did you know that he loves ice cream?" Round blue eyes were fixed on me, waiting. "Well, the Grinch especially loves strawberry ice cream, but one day, guess what?" This time, I waited. He shook his head slowly.

"One day, there was no strawberry ice cream in Whoville! Not anywhere! The Grinch was so mad!" I opened my eyes wider and shook with terror. The kid's eyes were as big as saucers. "Right then and there, he decided to make his own ice cream so he could have it whenever he wanted. And, because he is a friend of ours," I looked around as if to make sure no one was watching us, "he brought us this tub of his special Grinch ice cream."

I walked down to the end of the front display case. The mom followed me, the kid leaning out of her arms, trying to see. I pointed to the tub of neon green ice cream with my forefinger, still looking around as if to make sure we weren't being watched. "It's got secret stuff in it." Leaning toward him, I whispered, "I'll tell you if you don't tell anyone else."

He nodded and leaned toward me.

"Strawberry jam," I stage-whispered. "It has bright red strawberry jam inside. Look!" I scooped a bit from the top and, sure enough, there was a swirl of red popping out against the neon green. "Would you like to try a little bit?"

He nodded and I slid a wooden spoon along the top of the ice cream, making sure that he got a taste of the jam. He looked at it doubtfully, but with his mother's encouragement, a tiny tongue flicked out.

All three of us waited for the verdict. He rolled the ice cream around in his mouth like a professional wine taster. At last I asked, "Would you like a scoop of the Grinch's special ice cream—with gummies on top?" He nodded. His mom decided on a scoop of Mocha Pretzel Twist and after I'd settled them at a table with their ice cream, she leaned back toward me, one hand on her baby bump.

"Thank you so much. You're really good with kids," she said as she touched my arm. A powerful wave of baby radar shot through me. I hoped the mom had an endless store of patience and Grinch ice cream because her new baby was another boy and he was kicking up a fuss.

I flicked a look toward my parents before walking back behind the counter. Should I sidle over and pretend to wipe down the tables near them? What were they saying? Miggie's face was smooth and blank, giving nothing away; Ravi's face was half turned away from me, but I could see the tightness of his jaw.

As I picked up the cleaning rag from behind the counter,

Ravi and Miggie stood up. Ravi put on his hat, nodded to Miggie and then to me before sauntering outside, the feather in his hatband drooping. Miggie stayed in her corner, sipping her ice tea. I'd missed everything.

Chapter Forty-Six

"There are a few conditions," said Dan. All of us: Dan, Miggie, Barty, Ravi, Jacob and me, were sitting around the big round table at the ice cream shop. It was a Tuesday, our slowest day, a week after Ravi and Miggie's big meeting. Norm had come in early to man the fort, leaving me free to sit in on our neutral ground family meeting.

Ravi, kicked back in his chair, cowboy hat tilted low over his eyes, nodded once. Barty, seated next to Dan and across from Ravi, looked apprehensive, while Miggie seated on the other side of Dan, smiled at her husband serenely. Jacob, between Miggie and me, was slurping up a bowl of ice cream at breakneck speed. With Ravi on the other side of me, I waited to hear the conditions of Ravi and Barty's bonding and prepared to hose Jacob off before he could touch anything.

"For now, any meetings will be in Minden and nowhere else," Miggie continued Dan's words as if they had choreographed this between the two of them. Ravi frowned before nodding. Miggie and Dan had thought this out—Ravi was going to have to make an effort, have to drive down from Virginia City.

Dan picked up the next line. "No casinos, clubs or bars." He glanced at Barty who caught his eye and then looked quickly away.

"No alcohol, drugs or cigarettes," added Miggie.

Ravi gave a tiny shrug as if to say "of course." Then he added his own condition. "Clare can come if she wants to."

All heads swiveled to me. I did the family shrug and gave a secret wink to Barty. I could be available to act as a buffer if needed, but only for a couple of weeks before I went back to college. Still, it felt good to be included.

Seemingly out of nowhere, Miggie leaned forward with a question, "Are your parents still alive?"

Ravi shrugged. "Maybe. I haven't talked to my father since you and I ran off." Ravi and Miggie—a duo that seemed almost impossible for me to imagine.

"Grammie said they were," interposed Barty. Both Miggie and Ravi's heads turned toward him. "They still live in El Dorado Hills."

He'd talked to Grammie about this? Out of the three parents present, Ravi looked the most shocked.

"Do they know about you?" Miggie asked Barty.

He shrugged, looked at Ravi. "I dunno, Grammie didn't say. She hasn't, like, talked to them . . . she just knows they still live in the area because they use the El Dorado Hills branch of the bank."

Ravi quirked up an eyebrow and looked at Miggie. "As I said, I wouldn't know what they know—unless, of course, you reached out to them, which I guess, you didn't."

Miggie shook her head and shrugged. "They didn't like me, remember?"

Ravi chuckled. "Nope, they didn't. Not anymore than your mother liked me."

Incredibly, they both grinned. This was getting creepy. I slid eyes toward Dan. He looked like his usual calm and easy-going self, but under the table I could feel a vibration as if he were bouncing his knee.

"So, not only do we have another grandma, we have a grandpa too!" Barty looked thrilled.

The rest of us, except for ice-cream eating Jacob, wore identical expressions of surprise. Who knew Barty had wanted a grandfather? We had never had one –Dan's parents were both deceased and Grammie never talked about Miggie and Nita's father. According to Ravi, our only grandfather was no prize. Still, the thought of having new grandparents was interesting, even though Grammie had always been enough for me.

Ravi looked bored, as if news about his parents was the last thing he ever wanted to hear. Maybe it was.

Miggie looked at Dan, her green eyes soft. She said nothing, but Dan picked up the ball and said, "Barty, are you willing to obey these conditions in order to spend some time getting to know your father?"

Barty squared his shoulders and sat up straighter. After an apologetic glance at Dan, he said, "Yeah, all right." It sounded like he thought it was a dirty job but someone had to do it. "Maybe he can tell me something about my . . ." another apologetic glance, this time directed to me, "our . . . grandparents." He shot a look of challenge at Ravi, who winced and looked away. If Ravi thought that hanging out with Barty was going to be like Andy and Opie on that old TV program, he was going to have to think again. I could tell that my brother was going to make him pay for years of neglect because Barty had already found one thing that seemed to get under Ravi's skin.

Jacob finished his treat. The pile of frozen gummy bears he had fished out of his ice cream lay on a napkin next to him. "Can we go? What's a grandfather? Can I have my gummy bears now?"

Dan scooped up the bears, napkin and all, before Jacob could start on them. "How about one at a time, this time?" Dan asked. The last gummy/ice cream experience had almost ended in disaster as Jacob had swiped ten of them into his mouth at one shot and we'd had to pound them out of him.

With a damp white cloth in hand, I wiped down my squirming brother. He gazed imploringly at Dan who stood up, saying "How about one gummy per mile?"

I smiled, knowing Dan would make a game out of gummy eating all the way home. Dan reached around and took Miggie's hand, helping her out of her chair. He and Miggie nodded to Ravi as they left, Miggie calling back to Barty and me, "See you at home, you two."

No hugs, no handshaking. No one was ready for any of that yet, if ever. Ravi stood up and looked at Barty. "Want to take a walk?"

Barty nodded and the two of them headed for the door as I put my ball cap back on and walked behind the counter. Barty walked outside, but Ravi turned back to me and said, "Tell your mother, and Dan, thanks."

I nodded, too full of relief at the outcome of the family meeting to speak. Miggie and Ravi's initial meeting at the ice cream shop had been brief and relatively calm, but it had been frustrating. The apology I hoped Ravi would issue never materialized.

Miggie had scrunched up her face when she told me

about the meeting. "He said that you had told him he needed to talk to me, about . . . you know."

"And did he?"

"Not exactly, he just said something like it was a different time and we were young and he wasn't the same person."

He had sounded like the same person to me, weaseling out of a long-due apology and using me as the reason he said anything at all. Miggie deserved more than an apology. I had been angry all over again, until she said, "This is about Barty, not me. I'm working on myself, but I'm hoping that Ravi will talk to Barty about why he ignored him all these years, try to make amends in some way. Has he apologized to you, yet?"

When she'd asked that, I realized that while expectations for how Barty and Ravi interacted were going to be set, I had never set any of my own for my relationship with Ravi. I had simply allowed him to come back into my life, thinking it was too late for another dad or for an apology. Now, at Miggie's question, I felt an unwanted vein of hurt and anger trickle through me. Why *wasn't* I included in Ravi's remorse? He'd left me too. Was everyone more important than me?

I took a breath, reminding myself that this outcome with Ravi and Barty getting to know each other was what I wanted for my brother. I was an adult. I didn't need Ravi. "Guess it skipped his mind," was all I said.

Now, as Ravi went outside to join Barty, I wondered if Miggie had also felt it was too late for apologies. Despite Ravi's abandonment and betrayal, she had found the strength to keep a door open for Barty without cluttering it with her own anger. Her calm had kept the family meeting from possible disaster. Technically I was an adult, but maybe I wasn't grownup enough to admit my own anger, much less let it go.

Chapter Forty-Seven

My final day at the ice cream shop was literally a dark and stormy night—a summer thunderstorm had blown up and, although there was no rain, there was plenty of thunder and lightning. Myron, the shop owner, had blown in as well, looking perky and eager to get back to work.

"I got some great ideas for tie dye after seeing your Bug," he said. Whipping open a duffle bag, Myron pulled out some tie-dyed clothing. With a magician's flourish he snapped open a tie- dyed T-shirt. A long wavy green curve, splashed with red and yellow, covered the front of the shirt and wrapped around the back, ending in a point on the front of the shoulder.

"I call it 'The Lizard'," Myron said proudly. It did look a bit like a lizard, with the red and yellow parts reminiscent of a tongue and eyes. Then he began pulling out dozens of other shirts. "I was inspired to create a whole line of nature-oriented shirts—I've got praying mantis, owls, butterflies—and this is for you!" He revealed a white shirt with a huge circular patch of red. Breaking up the expanse of scarlet were a few wavy black dots. "It's the Ladybug," Myron announced. "For you to wear when you're driving."

He looked so pleased with himself that I didn't have the heart to tell him I would look like the survivor of a massacre or maybe even the perpetrator if I wore it while driving. With Coachinella's top down, I might even get pulled over. Instead, I thanked him—not hard to do since he had also given me a bonus on my final paycheck.

I wasn't too sad at leaving Groovy's until next summer, but I was already thinking about how much I would miss my family. Ravi and Barty had gotten together a few times and they were still speaking, which was encouraging. Miggie and Dan were more outwardly affectionate than usual and they seemed less tense each time Ravi met up with Barty. Jacob was Jacob. I was looking forward to Donna's shower and then spending some time with Grammie before going back to UNR. The only bumps in my road were a lack of appetite and energy, which I attributed to a summer cold, a crick in my neck, and a nagging sorrow that the Voice hadn't resurfaced. Donna was doing well with her baby communication, but my twin had disappeared.

Just before closing, Ravi came into the shop. I introduced him to Myron and Norm (who had seen him before). As I served him his cup of vanilla, he said, "Do you have enough room in the Bug for a passenger?"

With my college paraphernalia and clothes, there was barely going to be room for me. And who would this passenger be? If Ravi was behind this, it could be anyone, or anything, at all.

"Not really," I hedged.

"How about for one skinny potter?" He grinned at me. "I need to get to California City and my van isn't feeling up to it. Can I bum a ride?"

Crapadoodie. Ravi squished up next to me in a Volkswagen Beetle for hundreds of miles? According to the route that Dan and I had mapped out, California City was way down by Lancaster, almost two thirds of the way to Huntington Beach. A loonnnng way from Minden.

"You know, I'm not coming back to Minden," I told him. "I'll be driving up to Grammie's after the baby shower. How will you get home?"

"Oh, I'll figure out something—a buddy of mine down there wants to come up and see the studio, check out the tourist traps in Virginia City. I'm buying an amp from him."

I didn't know how to say no. I didn't even know if I should. Ravi must have seen the indecision on my face, because he said, "Don't worry about the gas, I'll pay half and I know all the good places to stop. And I can drive if you get tired."

It was to have been my big adventure, the first long road trip all by myself. Still, it might be good to have another driver in the car in case there were problems. What with missing the Voice for the past week and trying to spend as much time as possible with my family, I hadn't been getting a lot of sleep. I couldn't muster up the energy to think of a reason why Ravi shouldn't accompany me. Besides, the trip from Donna's house in Huntington Beach to Grammie's house in Placerville would be almost the same mileage, so I would still get my Big Girl Adventure.

"OK. I'll be leaving around five on Friday morning—and the Bug will be stuffed so there won't be much room for extras."

If he heard the lack of enthusiasm in my voice, Ravi

didn't show it. "Sounds good—going early, we'll miss some of the heat and traffic. I'll meet you here." He tipped his cowboy hat to me and sauntered out the door, leaving me to wonder what else I might have to leave behind for Miggie and Dan to bring when they came to UNR for my birthday weekend.

Driving home that night with the display of heat lightning emblazoning the sky, I thought about the summer, of Miggie and Ravi's revelations, of finding the Voice as a part of me—a part I missed—of Barty building a relationship with our father, of feeling connected to them all and of all the changes, so many good ones, now part of our lives. Who knew there were more revelations to come?

Chapter Forty-Eight

We packed the car on Thursday night—cramming in suitcases of clothes; books; my laptop; bedding; towels; a bag of cheese bites, granola bars, and veggies from Miggie to which Dan had added blueberry Pop Tarts and Oreos. Jacob contributed his three favorite rocks to keep me company, and Norm, the ice cream shop part-timer, had made me a mix tape CD of "guaranteed to keep you awake" music.

While Dan finished checking and rechecking Coachinella's fluids, Miggie carried out a box of warm clothing to deposit onto my passenger seat. I stopped her, saying, "I have to leave the passenger seat open, so can you bring that box with the other stuff when you guys come up for my birthday weekend?"

Miggie put the box down, frowning. "You have a passenger?"

I took a breath. "Ravi needs a ride to California City, so I'm picking him up at the ice cream shop at five tomorrow morning."

Dan peered around the rear of the Beetle, a scowl furrowing his forehead. Miggie pursed her lips. Barty, tucking Doritos, Red Vines and a six pack of Pepsi—his favorites—behind the driver's seat, looked up, a smile on his face.

I knew Dan didn't trust Ravi, but before I could say anything, Barty spoke up. "Well, that'll work out, right? You'll have someone with you for most of the trip." He looked around at us like a cheerful little chipmunk.

After a minute, Dan wiped his hands on a towel and gave a nod. "Might be a good idea." He was worried about me driving alone through the mountains and desert—hence our route rehearsals and the "what if" scenarios, such as "What do you do if you get a flat?" or "What should you do if the car overheats?" or "How do you safely stop for gas or a bathroom break?" Having another adult in the car with me, even if it was Ravi, probably made Dan feel a little better about the whole thing.

"If he shows up," muttered Miggie.

We finished the packing in silence. I had already said my goodbye to Jacob, who had interrupted my reading of the next chapter of *Charlie and the Chocolate Factory* with strangling hugs.

I said goodbye to Barty after we finished the packing, knowing he would still be asleep when I left in the morning. He was on his way out the door to play *EverQuest* at a friend's house when I stopped him for a hug. Bigger than me, his arms wrapped all the way around me—like being hugged by an adult. He grinned and said, "You'll be safe, Ravi came through."

With that mysterious pronouncement, he left to battle foes and survive quests.

· · ·

At four-thirty the next morning I was rinsing out my cereal bowl in the sink when Dan and Miggie, still in their pajamas, came into the kitchen.

"Have you got everything you need?" Dan asked as he gave me a quick hug. I nodded, hugging back.

Miggie, yawning behind a hand, said, "Have fun." She squeezed my shoulder and turned as if to go back to bed. Then she leaned toward me while Dan busied himself with the coffee machine, and in a low voice said, "If Ravi doesn't show up on time, don't wait around for him."

I don't know if Dan heard, but as I gathered up my backpack and took a last look around to make sure I hadn't left anything behind, I thought about their different approaches to my departure: Dan, worried and affectionate; Miggie, casual, concerned more that I might get stuck waiting for a known offender than lost in the mountains. But after this summer, I felt I understood Miggie better. Both Dan's hug and Miggie's shoulder squeeze said the same thing.

Ravi was not late. When I arrived at the deserted ice cream shop at five, he was waiting in the parking lot with a backpack and a thermos. Greeting me with a casual wave, he inserted himself into the narrow space we had left for him in Coachinella's passenger seat.

"Whoa, I might need a shoehorn to get all the way in," he joked, sliding his legs under the dash. Ravi wasn't a tall guy, only about 5' 8", but it was still a squeeze.

As I headed out to US 395, Ravi offered me a cup of coffee from his Thermos. I shook my head and pointed to the can of Pepsi precariously perched between my knees. No cup holders in a 1978 Beetle.

Ravi grimaced. "That stuff will kill you."

I gave him a look. This might be a very short trip for Ravi . . . or a super long trip for me.

Ravi looked abashed. "At least it's not diet," he mumbled. He looked out his window.

To cover the silence, I put in Norm's mix tape CD. Dan hadn't put in cup holders but he had updated Coachinella's original radio with a radio/CD/ cassette player in the glovebox. "*I'm too sexy for my love, too sexy for my love*" rolled out of the speakers. Another wince from Ravi, but he recovered quickly. The song romped along to its big finish about being too sexy for this song and was followed by "*Who let the dogs out? Who? Who? Who? Who? Who?*"

I slid a look over at Ravi's appalled face and started giggling. Ravi held up a finger as I turned down the volume on the second verse which was the same as the first. In a skeptical voice he asked, "Is this your CD?"

I wanted to mess with him, but it was a long trip. "It's something a friend made me so that I would stay awake."

"Would you consider listening to something else?" Ravi pulled a CD jewel case out of his backpack and popped it in after ejecting the mix CD.

"OK, but if I don't like it, we pick something else," I warned him.

He smiled and nodded. Music floated out of the speakers —a quiet, mellow tune that became a ballad about where to find rain in the desert. Ravi's baritone voice was sweet and smooth. It was a good song.

Ravi caught my eye and I nodded in approval. "I like it," I said. "But it might be too mellow to keep a driver awake."

"That's OK," he said with a smile. "I've got more rousing songs, but this is something new. Besides, there's all kinds of stories I can tell you about US 395."

. . .

Ravi was a surprisingly good traveling companion. He knew all the cool places to visit along 395 like Devil's Postpile, Grover Hot Springs, Bodie, Mono Lake, and Manzanar. We didn't have time on this trip to visit them, but I planned to make time in the future.

Ravi knew a lot of trivia, too, including all the names of the movies that were filmed in Lone Pine under the shadow of Mt. Whitney—and there were a lot of them. His recitation of them took us all the way to our first pit stop in Bishop.

When we stopped there for gas, Ravi hopped out, paid for the gas, and filled the tank, while I wiped down the windshield and then used the restroom. Before getting back into Coachinella, I spent a few seconds trying to work out the kinks in my neck and left shoulder.

Watching my gyrations, Ravi said, "Are you OK? Want me to drive?"

"No, I'm fine. I've had a little twinge in my neck and shoulder for a few days. It will work itself out." There was no way I was going to give up driving and being in control. With Ravi behind the wheel, who knew what side trips we would end up taking?

Back in the car, Ravi said, "As long as we're in Bishop, we have to stop at Schat's."

He wouldn't tell me what Schat's was or why we had to stop. Our new destination turned out to be only a few hundred feet down from the gas station and it was a bakery. With its own traffic intersection and light.

"I've got blueberry Pop Tarts and Oreos," I protested, as I drove into the bakery parking lot.

Ravi rolled his eyes and said, "What bakery do you know that has its own traffic light? Believe me, you don't want to pass this up."

Pastry-filled display cases covered three walls of one large room, so much deliciousness that the world-famous Sheep-herder's Bread was housed in a whole different room. Completely overwhelmed, I stared into each delightfully packed display case. How could I ever choose? Would this be the end of my road trip, captured by endless pastries? While I agonized over the turtles, the cinnamon rolls, and the strudel, Ravi went to the other side of the bakery and bought a round of Sheepherder's Bread. When he returned, I still hadn't decided.

"There's only one thing to do," he announced. "We'll take two cannoli," he told the bakery clerk.

Piqued at having my choice pre-empted, I was about to tell Ravi what he could do with his cannoli, but all that fresh cream and flaky pastry undid me. Since I couldn't drive a stick shift while eating a cannoli and I was salivating too much to focus properly, we ate them as soon as we got back to the car. The cream was cold and sweet, rich and delicious; it coated the ends of Ravi's moustache, making him look like a skinny walrus. Perfect.

Back on the road and full of cannoli, I asked the questions I had been storing up for the past few weeks. "So, what are my grandparents like?"

Ravi blinked, yanked out of his sugar high. He shook his head before saying, "My father is an asshole; my mother is frustrated. What else do you want to know?"

I looked over at him and rolled my eyes. "Please?"

His shoulders went up and down in a huge sigh, but he said, "I haven't talked to them in years, so I don't know how they are now."

"Well, tell me about when you were growing up."

"I think I'm still growing up." His smile was wry. He stretched his legs as best he could under the dash before saying, "My dad wasn't into music, but my mom was a classical pianist. When he was home, the television was always on. When he wasn't home, the radio or the stereo was always on. It was only when they entertained that my father thought music was OK; he would trot my brother and me out to play a few classical pieces and my mom would finish up with a few more."

"Wait, you have a brother?"

"Yeah, Peter—Pete. Two years younger."

"Have you kept in touch with him?"

"Not for a while—he's a big-time lawyer in San Francisco."

It was a good thing that this stretch of 395 was long and straight. I had an uncle and a musical grandmother—my head was spinning. But I wanted Ravi to keep talking so I kept the millions of questions to myself.

"Mom wanted us to be able to play something, so I had piano lessons. When Pete was four, he started learning the violin. For my dad, only classical music was a worthwhile use of his money and only until we reached high school. Then we had to give up the 'artsy-fartsy' stuff and concentrate on sports.

"My piano teacher came to the house, and as I got older, I wanted to explore all kinds of music—not just classical. My teacher was cool, so we agreed that we'd spend the first half of the lesson on classical pieces and for the second half, she'd teach me jazz tunes, current pop music, ragtime, stuff like that. My mom listened from the kitchen and when Mrs. Rasmussen left, Mom would make me show her the new music. We had a lot of fun playing those forbidden tunes." Ravi looked out the side window for a moment and then continued. "When I was eleven, I really wanted a bass guitar so I could play what I heard on the radio. My dad said no way was he going to put out more money for an instrument that wasn't going to take you anywhere but Drug City. Mom bought me an acoustic guitar; she told Dad it had belonged to the son of a friend and he didn't play it anymore, so she got it free. He wasn't happy, but he told me I could play it after piano practice and homework—in the house, in my bedroom with the door closed.

"I didn't care—I just wanted to play guitar. It was hell learning to play those steel strings, but, man, I loved that thing. Still have it."

There was a silence—Ravi remembering, me trying to process. I changed lanes to pass a heavily laden pickup—only possible now that I was going downhill. "Tell me about Pete."

Ravi shrugged. "Pete wanted to be all the things that Dad thought were important—the All American quarterback, the honor student, the music prodigy, the prestigious and successful lawyer—and he did it—all of it."

"Were you jealous of him?"

"Sometimes, but . . . we were so different. I never wanted to do or be any of those things. Pete was good at whatever he tried—he was just that kind of guy. Always driven to be the best. I just wanted to be left alone to play my music, make my art." He smiled, but then I saw the ends of his moustache droop. "Pete's a great guy, but I don't know how happy he is."

My eyebrows lifted in inquiry.

"The last time I talked to my brother, he was working for a big law firm in San Francisco. He told me it was too hard to come home for visits because Dad always hassled him about not being married."

"He didn't want to get married?"

"Pete's gay."

"Do your parents know?"

"Maybe they do now, but the last time I talked to him, no. And it was getting harder and harder for Pete to be one person in his life in San Francisco, and another person with my parents. When we were growing up, being gay, especially in a small town, wasn't cool. It definitely wouldn't have been cool with my father. He was very proud of Pete, but James Robert Ingersoll did not tolerate any departure from the plans he'd made for our lives—his sons were supposed to be athletes and scholars who went to prestigious colleges, hopefully on scholarships. We were to earn degrees in something impressive and build successful careers being something even more impressive—like brain surgeons or Supreme Court justices. We would marry well (women only), have sons to carry on the name and make a lot of money. The end. Anything else was not acceptable." Ravi's voice sounded bitter . . . and sad. "When I left, not planning to fulfill any of Dad's dreams, Pete was still in high school. We'd talk whenever I was in a place with a phone, but, even though he was living my father's dream and everybody liked him, he always sounded miserable."

Ravi looked pretty miserable himself. I decided to change the direction of the conversation a bit. "Your father might not approve of me."

Ravi looked at me in surprise. "Are you gay?"

"No, but I do something that's sort of . . . different." It was Ravi's turn to raise eyebrows. I didn't know what he might think of my baby channeling, but if he was going to be in my life, I wanted to put it all out there. Like my Uncle Pete, I was tired of secrets, of only being part of myself. I'd changed my name, but part of me was still in hiding. I still hadn't officially told Dan or Barty about my baby channeling. I told myself that it was because the subject never came up, but I knew that I could have brought it up.

After a moment, I said, "I can communicate with babies . . . when they are in the womb. I can hear them. I can sense what they need, what they want." Ravi looked at me and nodded as if in approval, so I went on. "And, this past semester, when my roommate got pregnant and I sensed her baby, my twin began to talk to me and help me communicate with Whozit. Whozit is what we nicknamed the baby."

Ravi looked at me, shock written on his face. I couldn't tell whether the shock was because I had admitted my baby channeling and talking with my twin, the casual mention of Donna's unwed pregnancy, or the nickname. After a glance at him, I returned my eyes to the road and kept them there, focusing on the long stretch of black pavement and the sage-brush-dotted desert on either side of it

"Your mom told you about being a twin?" Ravi's voice was quiet, thoughtful sounding.

Wow, not freaked about baby channeling or Donna? Just the twin? Interesting.

I said, "I kept hearing someone calling me '*sister*,' when I was communicating with Whozit and it frightened me that I might be going crazy. When I told Miggie, she said she had been pregnant with twins and lost one of them." There was a catch in my voice as I spoke, surprising me. How could I feel so strongly about someone who was never even born? Even just talking to Ravi about her brought a feeling of sorrow and longing. Where was she?

Pushing back the sorrow, I said, "Miggie thinks the voice I hear might be my twin . . . and . . . now I know it is." There —if that made Ravi think I was crazy, then so be it. If he wanted to know how I knew, that would be harder to explain. I just knew.

His next words caught me off guard. "That was a sad day —the saddest day I've ever had."

I looked over at Ravi who was staring out the side window.

"After Miggie graduated from high school, we split from El Dorado County to find fame and fortune as artists," Ravi began. It sounded as if he was making fun of those long-ago dreams, but in a sad way. "About six months later, Miggie turned up pregnant. She was excited—wanted to call the baby 'Fresno' if it was a girl, 'Bakersfield' if it was a boy." He shook his head and gave me a side smile.

"A few weeks later, she started bleeding. We didn't have any money for a hospital visit and the clinic was closed, so our friends helped us." He shook his head, "It was so bad. Miggie was devastated.

"I thought I would feel relieved since I hadn't wanted any kids, but I didn't. I felt . . . bereft. Like something I should have held close had slipped away. Later, when we found out Miggie was still pregnant—with you—I felt like I'd been given another chance."

My heart squeezed at the sorrow in his voice, but then I remembered that later, he'd thrown his chances away when he found out that Barty was coming.

"Did you ever tell your parents?"

"Not about the twin, and not later about Barty—hell, I didn't even know whether Barty was going to be a boy or a girl when I left." He shrugged apologetically. "But, yeah, I called my mom and told her when you were born. My dad and I weren't speaking, so I don't know what Mom told him, but she came to a craft festival where Miggie and I had a booth when you were about two months old. Pete told her where we were.

"Miggie split as soon as my mom showed up—they didn't like each other—but she left you with me, and my mom held you the whole time she was there. She'd always wanted a little girl." He smiled, his face softening.

Then a huge grin burst over his face. "Well, maybe you

did inherit something from me besides my curly hair. Your uh . . . grandmother always knew when a lady was pregnant, even sometimes before they knew. And, if there was one baby in a roomful of people, she would be the person holding it. If it had been wailing away before she got it, it would mellow out as soon as she touched it. There were times when you were little that I wished she was around to chill you out." His half smile was both wry and wistful.

A chord of warmth thrummed through me. Like me. There was someone else like me. I had inherited a family gift from both sides of my family. Caught up in the relief and wonder of it, I almost missed Ravi's next words.

"Those shoes," Ravi nodded down toward the red Converse high tops on my feet. "Mom brought a pair of little red Converse High Tops in a tiny drawstring bag for you. They were too big for you then, so I stowed them in my guitar case. I never even told Miggie about them. They became a kind of secret connection to my mother, one that I saw every time I opened the case. Finally, when you were big enough, I gave them to you."

When I was big enough—when Barty was on the way, when Ravi left. My lucky red shoes weren't just a fashion choice; they were a little girl's last connection to her daddy, the only connection to a grandmother she didn't remember. I wondered what Ravi would say if he knew I still had that first pair, faded and worn, but wrapped in tissue paper, tucked into my suitcase inside their drawstring bag.

Chapter Forty-Nine

It was 165 miles to California City from Schat's Bakery. Ravi said I was to drop him off at the McDonald's in California City and he would call his friend to pick him up. I offered to drive him to his friend's house, but he said he didn't know where it was.

We passed Lone Pine, the portal to Mt. Whitney, and Ravi pointed out the peak and the Lone Pine Film Museum. I really wished we had time to stop, but there were some four hours left on my journey and I had told Donna I would be there before dark.

We listened to music and I found that I enjoyed the eclectic mix of mellow ballads and original rock of Ravi's CD —songs that spoke of rain in the desert, loss, finding wonder in the everyday world, and even a rousing one about tax evasion. He flipped through my CD case and pulled out Destiny's Child. Green Day got some play as did Bon Jovi. Then Ravi found my Fleetwood Mac *Rumors*, CD. It was an oldie, but one of my favorites and apparently one of Ravi's too.

During "Gold Dust Woman," Ravi turned to me and said, "We've been talking a lot about my family, but you're my family too and I don't know very much about you."

His words, "You're my family too," softened something in me.

"Now it's my turn to ask questions," he said.

I tensed a bit, wondering how personal this might get, but since Ravi already knew my major secret, I kept my face forward and said, "Fire away."

"What's your favorite color?"

"Green."

"Any particular shade?"

"I like them all, but especially blue-green."

He laughed. "When you were little, your favorite colors were purple and red. Always two colors, never just one."

This was interesting. Miggie never talked much about what Barty and I did or said when we were toddlers.

Ravi's next question was predictable. "What's your favorite food?"

"Sausage pizza with mushrooms and olives . . . and lobster."

"Lobster *on* the pizza, or lobster in that you have two favorite foods?"

I made a face. Lobster on pizza would be nasty. "Two favorites."

"Ok, so you're either a cheap date or a pricey one. Good to know." We both laughed this time. I was feeling more relaxed because his questions were so easy. Then he said, "So, what does your mother think of your ability to talk with babies? Does your grandmother know?"

I felt the heaviness return at his questions. When Ravi had been talking about his family—my family too—and enumerating the movies to be found in the Lone Pine Film

Museum, I hadn't been thinking about the Voice and not being able to connect with her, except for the few minutes that I told Ravi about her. Worry and confusion filled me—Where was she? Why did she stay away? And Grammie—surely Ravi had to know how Grammie felt about paranormal abilities. Miggie would have shared that with him, wouldn't she?

I tried to answer Ravi. "Miggie seems to think it's OK, but Grammie doesn't want to talk about it."

Ravi nodded. "Guess some things never change. She was pretty tough on Miggie about any demonstration of her thing with colors—that was one of the things we had in common—a parent who didn't want us to be who we were."

It was the first thing about their relationship that made sense to me. "I don't know why she acts like it isn't real—I was with Grammie when Barty got stuck being born." At this, Ravi winced. "And we were together when Miggie had trouble with Jacob, so it doesn't make sense that she won't talk about it." I gave him a brief synopsis of my involvement with Jacob's birth.

Ravi stroked his bushy moustache. "Wow, that's amazing. I don't remember you talking to babies, but the twin thing . . . It was weird, but you always asked for two cookies, two Popsicles, two of any special thing. We didn't always give you two things, like Popsicles, but if we didn't, you would break off a part of your treat and put it on a doll plate for 'Sissy.' Your mother thought it was strange, but I thought it was just an imaginary friend, like the one I'd had as a kid."

I still couldn't remember the imaginary friend, but somehow it eased my mind just a little. Miggie and Ravi had known I was a twin and both of them seemed to accept that she was still in my life. If they had been "normal" parents, would they have been so accepting?

We had been seeing signs for miles and miles about Gus' Fresh Jerky. Ravi said there was an ancient gas station in Olancha, about halfway between Bishop and California City, where the sweet and spicy jerky was the best in the world. "It's pricey, but good stuff," he said. "We can get out and stretch our legs."

My short legs didn't need much stretching, but Ravi was shoehorned into the passenger seat. It seemed only minutes before the fresh jerky signs became almost constant and then, a tiny white gas station appeared. There were no gas pumps, but the number of cars in the parking lot indicated that Ravi's claims about the jerky might be true.

Ten minutes later, laden with bags of the "best jerky in the world," we continued our journey. It felt as if we had talked enough about family and our conversation was now about the sights along the road, Ravi's upcoming gigs and what I was studying in college. I told Ravi that I couldn't decide what career I wanted to pursue. "I like to write and I've gotten some awards and a scholarship for things I wrote for class and for my high school newspaper, but I also want to help people, so maybe I should do something like be a social worker, the way Grammie suggested."

"Why can't you do both?" he asked. "Can't you be a writer who is also a social worker or be a social worker who writes?"

He was right, of course, but I hadn't thought of it in that way before. Still, being a social working writer or a writer who did social work didn't ring any bells with me. I would have to pick a major soon, even if I did end up doing both things.

Out of nowhere, Ravi said, "I've been around . . . you know?"

I nodded—not that I actually knew all the places Ravi

had been in his life—just showing understanding and wondering where this was going.

"I've learned some things and one of them is that the world rolls in a lot of different ways, not just one. That's why it's round. "

It sounded like a bumper sticker or a caption for a motivational poster, but when I looked at his face, I could see that Ravi was sincere about this. Who would have thought that my long-absent father could sound like a dad? While I considered this turn-about, I made another realization.

"Do you really have a friend in California City?" I asked.

Ravi's eyes danced with mischief. "Course I do. And he has an amp."

"Does he know that you're coming?"

"He's always home."

Barty. My brother and my weird uncle father had colluded to keep me safe, to make sure I was comfortable with this long trip. Hugs, shoulder squeezes, favorite rocks and protection—it seemed that there were more ways of showing love than I had realized. I looked out the side window so Ravi wouldn't see the sudden moisture in my eyes.

As we came into California City, Ravi guided me to the McDonald's on California City Boulevard. After I parked, he went to the phone booth on the corner and I went inside to use the bathroom.

When I came back outside, Ravi was waiting for me. He gave me a thumbs up and said, "Wes will be here in a few minutes to pick me up."

I wavered, wanting to make sure he had a ride, but also not wanting to make it seem like I didn't think he was adult enough to take care of himself. I handed him the burger and fries I'd bought for him and gave him a hug—the first hug I had given, or received, from my father since I was two.

"Thank you," I whispered into his ear. As I stepped back, Ravi cleared his throat and nodded at me.

"You remember how I told you to get back on the route?"

Now he was sounding like Dan. I repeated the directions back to him. He nodded again and I slid behind Coachinella's wheel. As I pulled out of the parking lot and onto the boulevard, I looked back. Ravi, standing under the eaves of the building, waved. He looked like an older, hairier version of Barty. I waved back.

During the few miles to Lancaster, I pondered my conversation with Ravi. It was strange, what he had said about me always wanting two treats, having two favorite colors. Even now, I had two possible career paths, favorite colors and favorite foods. I had always agonized over making decisions, having to choose between one thing or the other. Maybe that was why I only wore red Converse—no decision to be made—only one option. Did my dual nature come from being a twin? It felt like I was always battling between the practical, logical side of my nature and wanting to fly off into my imagination. I was waiting for a life purpose to reveal itself to me, but so far, it was, like my major, undeclared.

And baby channeling. How did that fit into things? A family ability that scared other people wasn't something you could build a career on, was it?

Chapter Fifty

Donna and her family lived in a two-story stucco mini-mansion in a Huntington Beach neighborhood filled with such homes. Lawns were green and bordered by palm trees, succulents and spiky cactus. I pulled in front of the house and before I could set the parking brake, Donna flew out of the front door, looking three times bigger than I'd ever seen her. She circled Coachinella, marveling at the bright color and the ladybug dots, before reaching me. We hugged at arm's length—couldn't get any closer with the baby bump.

A lanky boy with floppy blond hair came out of the house and offered to carry my overnight case inside. Donna wiped the look of surprise from her face before introducing him as her little brother, Mark. I knew, from what she had told me, he was a junior in high school and loved to surf. As he preceded us into the house, Donna held back and whispered to me, "Mom must have bribed him with surf wax or something." We giggled our way into the house.

In the stainless steel and granite kitchen, Mrs. Middleton

was setting out snacks on an enormous island. Mr. Middleton was watching sports on TV in the adjoining family room from the cushy confines of a leather recliner. I had met them several times while Donna and I were roomies. Mr. M greeted me with a wave; Mrs. M gave me a hug. She was an older, plumper version of Donna with unnaturally white-blond hair. Donna's dad was tall and slender except for a bit of a tummy pooching out over his khaki shorts. His receding hairline was usually covered with a hat or a visor, but apparently not when he was watching television.

Donna took me to her bedroom where brother Mark had already deposited my bag. The room was very Donna—girly, with pink-and-white checked curtains, white walls and a light pink comforter on the queen-sized bed. A rollaway bed had been set up for me along one wall under white floating shelves filled with stuffed animals, soccer trophies, photos of family and friends and a clear box with bottles of nail polish in it. It was quite the contrast from my leaf-green room in Minden with its varnished wood Mission-style bed and chest of drawers. I have books instead of stuffed animals, and on the wall in front of my bed, there are two framed prints of Van Gogh's sunflower series that I found in a discarded art book. They look like the same print at first glance, but they aren't. The more you look at them, the easier it is to see the differences.

After dinner, which Mr. Middleton barbecued for us in the spacious back yard, Donna and I helped her mother wrap pink tulle and ribbon around sweet-scented candles for the baby shower guests. I was given my assignment for the next day.

"Clare, you'll sit next to Donna and make a list of the gifts and who gave them so she can write thank you cards," said Mrs. M. It wasn't a request, but I didn't mind. I was shy of being around so many people I didn't know and hoped this would keep me occupied.

After we put all the shower favors into a white wicker basket, Mrs. M excused herself to make some food preparations for the shower. Her voice followed us down the hall as we made our way to Donna's room. "Donna, did you take your vitamins? Don't stay up too late, you two—sleep is important for the baby, you know."

Donna said, "Yes, Mom" and rolled her eyes at me before saying, "Can we try to talk to Whozit? Like we used to?"

I hoped so. I hadn't told Donna yet that I hadn't been able to hear the Voice for the past two weeks. As long as I could still hear Whozit, that wouldn't be a problem for Donna, but it was a problem for me. Every time I tried to contact my twin, it was as if a damper had closed down. I couldn't feel her; the atmosphere felt heavy and dense. If I hadn't been able to sense Whozit, it would have freaked me out, but as it was, the lack of contact with my twin made me uneasy and sad. Worry about it had been messing with my sleep.

We got into our pajamas. Donna's stomach pushed out her red pajama top, making her look like the world's biggest strawberry. Laying a hand on Whozit was much simpler than it had been at UNR when Donna's baby bump was smaller and I wasn't sure where Whozit was lying. Now, I couldn't miss—she was everywhere.

We got into our usual Team Whozit positions: Donna lying on her back and me sitting on the bed next to her with my hand on her belly. I sensed a sleepy contentment as I reached out to Whozit. A glimmer of recognition flickered from her, but without the Voice, it was as if I was sensing through a thick syrup. I took Donna's hand, trying to be the conduit through which she could communicate with her daughter, but worry about my missing twin blocked any further sensing I might have been able to do.

Suddenly, Whozit gave a mighty kick right where my hand was resting.

"Holy moly! Kid's got a kick!" I moved my hand down, slightly, and received another kick.

"Tell me about it," Donna said. "I'm trying to decide whether to sign her up for soccer or football." She giggled sleepily.

Despite our great kick-off, I couldn't get any other reads on Whozit and the recognition I'd sensed earlier was gone.

"I think she's too tired to carry on a conversation," I told Donna. "That last kick must have worn her out."

"I'm tired too," she yawned. "I've been taking naps and I didn't get one today."

"I'm ready to crash, myself," I admitted. "But you've been doing this on your own and you said it's been going well."

"It's been fun. I try to tune into her every night." She smiled a mother's smile of love and pride before saying, "It's like our special time together. Last week, it felt like we had a code—two kicks for no, one kick for yes. It seems that she really doesn't like Brussels sprouts after all, but neither do I. Grandma, on the other hand, thinks we should eat lots of them."

We laughed—Mrs. M. had urged extra salad and zucchini on Donna at dinner because "veggies are good for you both." If Donna had been putting up with this much smotherage with such good humor, then she was going to survive the next couple of months.

"I don't think you have to worry any more about being a good mother," I said. Even without my help, she had built a link with Whozit, one beyond sharing space in the same body, one that would last a lifetime.

Donna reached up and hugged me. I hugged back.

Naps, kicks, and veggies—boy had my party-loving friend's life changed. We spent a few minutes gossiping about our former dorm mates before Donna nodded off in the middle of a sentence. I turned off the light and climbed into the rollaway. I was tired too—my first road trip had gone well, even with the confusion and perils of driving on Orange County freeways, but it had been a long and emotional day.

Lying in the darkened room, listening to Donna's familiar purring snore, I was glad for the connection between Donna and Whozit, but it made me realize just how much I missed the Voice. Without her, I felt like an imposter, as if part of me was missing. Months ago, I hadn't even been aware of her existence; now I didn't feel I could live without her.

Chapter Fifty-One

The baby shower was held in a covered patio in Donna's aunt's backyard that was as big as half our entire home in Minden. It was bustling with people in black pants and white shirts arranging food, flowers, and decorations. A semi-circular pool boasting a mountain with a waterfall in the center of it took up most of the rest of the manicured yard. It looked like something you'd see at a resort, not someone's backyard.

An older woman with light blond hair, about my height and shaped like an apple, hovered at the mosaicked edge of the pool. She held a crystal goblet filled with what looked like orange juice. Heavy-looking pendants threaded with crystals hung from her neck and her peach and yellow chiffon caftan fluttered in the light breeze. She saw me and floated over in bejeweled flip-flops, hot pink polished toenails peeking from beneath the caftan.

With all those crystals, she had to be Ria, Donna's psychic aunt and the host of the baby shower. Her round build and facial structure reminded me of Grammie, if Grammie had eyelash extensions like furry caterpillars and a seven-figure divorce settlement.

Donna accepted my baby channeling because of this woman whose predictions included several earthquakes, Mr. M's hernia, and a burst water pipe in the Middleton house. She read palms and Tarot cards and had once identified the loss of a womb twin as the reason for over shopping. I wondered if she would want to read my palm and hoped I didn't have any syrup left on it from breakfast.

Ria's small, square hands with their manicured nails gestured gracefully as the sun glinted off a plethora of silver rings. "Oh, you must be Clare," she trilled before dropping her voice to a whisper, "The baby channeler."

Crapadoodie, did everyone know?

Her blue eyes, framed by the caterpillars, peered into my face as she patted my arm. "Don't worry," she continued, still whispering. "Donna only told me because I have a similar gift. I'm her Aunt Ria."

I didn't know what to say to her. Could she read my mind? If so, then maybe I wouldn't have to say anything at all.

Ria was equal to the occasion. She took a sip of her orange juice and then darted over to a table covered with an artful display of fresh fruit, flowers and crystal goblets. She returned with a goblet full of orange juice which she handed to me saying, "Come over and sit with me a moment. We should talk."

I took a nervous sip of my orange juice and gasped. The color was deceptive—my water goblet was filled with a tiny bit of orange juice and a whole lot of champagne. I liked champagne, but wow. Aunt Ria gave me a conspiratorial smile and lifted her own glass.

"If you must host a baby shower, mimosas will get you

through it," she said, leading the way to a couple of patio chairs near the pool. While caterers set out trays of canapes and arranged chairs, Ria took sips of her mimosa and looked me over. As we settled into our chairs, her eyes widened and she said, "Oh, my. You are carrying a *lot* of energy around with you."

It sounded, from the way she said it, like that wasn't a good thing. The more energy the better, I thought, although I didn't feel energetic—I felt heavy and slow and depressed— the way I'd being feeling for the past couple of weeks. Since I had lost the Voice again. Miggie and Dan, Ravi, Barty and Donna all seemed to be doing better now, but I was feeling worse. Was my lack of energy that obvious?

"It's not *your* energy," Ria continued. "It's emotional energy from other people and it's draining you—keeping you from doing what you want, from being who you are . . . and from hearing her."

Her? Had Donna told Ria about the Voice? My attention sharpened.

"I can help you release all that baggage and show you how to protect yourself from picking up any more." Her eyes were as clear and blue as Lake Tahoe.

Should I set my mimosa down and run? Through Miggie and her friends, I had way too many years of experience with New Age channelers, psychics, wanna be psychics, healers, charlatans and people who claimed to be in communication with extra-terrestrials. A psychic healer once told Miggie that I had a tumor in my stomach and that she could remove it with her fingers. In spite of being around all those people, I'd never been around anyone, besides Miggie, who had any real psychic abilities.

Ria reached over and touched my left shoulder. "Here," she said, "and here." She touched the side of my neck lightly.

"And your stomach—that's where all this energy has settled. Have you been having problems with your shoulder or a stiff neck? Had a stomachache? And you don't seem to have much of an appetite?" She peered at me, waiting for an answer. "And you feel as if you're trying to function in dense fog?"

OK, the shoulder *had* been giving me grief, but that was probably because those ice cream tubs were heavy and the drive from Minden had been long. My stiff neck might be because of the way I slept, and the ever present low pain in my stomach was why I didn't have an appetite—except for cream-filled cannoli. But when Ria talked about trying to function through a dense fog and not being able to hear "her," I was riveted, despite my misgivings about phony psychics.

"She's here, you know. She's always around you." Ria peered at me as if checking my aura. "You have both names."

My twin? As if reading my mind, which was a scary thought, Ria said dreamily, "Your mother chose two names and after your twin died, she gave them both to you." Her eyes were closed. I could see the sparkles in her blue eye shadow. "She's here to help. And you're going to need her very soon." Ria opened her eyes and looked at me as if wanting confirmation.

I took a sip of my drink and looked toward the pool. Ria might look like Grammie, but she lived in my grandmother's Forbidden Zone. Torn between wanting to know more and Grammie-fostered doubts, I said nothing.

A waterfall gurgled down the side of the Matterhorn in the pool. The breeze ruffled the water, splintering shards of brightly reflected sunshine into my eyes. Behind me, I heard a gaggle of voices—Donna, her mother, other women.

Temporarily saved from my doubts about Ria, I got up from my chair, "Well . . . thank you." What did you say to someone who has just given you the benefit of her psychic gift—especially when you don't know whether it is genuine or not? "I better see if I can help Donna—I'm supposed to record the gifts for thank you cards."

I escaped with my mimosa into the knot of women. Mrs. Middleton shepherded guests to chairs and gifts to the display table. Donna waddled over to me. "I see you've met Aunt Ria." She grinned and nodded at my drink.

"What did you tell her?" I hissed.

Donna looked surprised. "Nothing—well, just about our Team Whozit."

"Not about the Voice? Or my real name?"

Mrs. Middleton appeared next to Donna. "I think just about everyone has arrived. Here, honey," she took Donna's arm and guided her over to a comfortable armchair with cushions. "You sit here in the middle and that way everything will happen around you."

Donna widened her eyes at me, but meekly sat down, looking like a plump little queen with adoring subjects gathered at her feet. She jerked her head to the left and I slid into a patio chair at her side just as Mrs. M handed me a notebook and pen. "Just write down each gift and the name of the giver."

Through the next hour, we ate, played some ridiculous baby games like "Guess the Circumference of Donna's Belly," and cooed as Donna opened baby gifts. I had to admit that tiny ruffled hoodies and teensy socks were pretty cute. I had given Donna a handmade IOU card, since my own gift was back-ordered, and had chipped in with some of the girls from our dorm on a baby monitor system. It was either that or a breast pump and none of us wanted to have anything to do with that.

I managed to make my mimosa last for an hour, being too busy fetching for Donna and writing down names and gifts, to drink much of it. Ria drifted past a few times with a bottle of champagne for refills, but I put one of the gift cards over the top of my glass. Other guests weren't quite so circumspect and Ria kept their goblets filled, which made the "Guess What's in the Diaper" game a laff riot. The tiny diapers filled with melted candy bars sent a few of the guests into sloppy hilarity and one of the caterers had to keep rescuing inebriated ladies, including Donna's grandmother, from pitching into the pool. I hope Ria paid the caterers extra.

As the shower wound to a tipsy end, Donna, her mother —who was used to her sister's parties—and I, were about the only sober participants left. Mrs. M phoned relatives to pick up Donna's wobbly aunts, cousins and grandma. She rounded up Donna's high school buddies in order to drive them home, while Ria floated around the pool, picking up escaped gift ribbons and sipping from her goblet.

Donna's dad arrived in his Suburban to load up the baby gifts while her mother began ferrying drunken guests home. I was carrying a Pack and Play out to the Suburban, when Ria suddenly appeared at my side.

She took off one of her pendants. It was a round, quarter-sized piece, chased in silver. The back was silver too, but the front was an enameled circle made from two fish-shaped pieces, one black, one white, flowing in opposite directions and curving into each other. Yin and Yang.

She handed me the pendant and said, "One day soon it will help you remember what to do." At my puzzled look, she continued, "You'll be able to talk to her if you spend some time clearing out other people's energy. Just find a quiet place and relax all your muscles, one at a time. Imagine filling your whole self with white light. Look for any dark spots of other people's energy and when you find them," here she touched my shoulder and neck again, "imagine them vanishing, just disappearing into the sky. When you don't have any more dark places, fill yourself with white light again. Then, open your heart and let her help you. Everyone has a purpose." With those cryptic words, she drifted away again, mimosa in one jeweled hand.

Chapter Fifty-Two

I wasn't able to talk to Donna alone until evening. She looked tired and kept rubbing her belly as we slipped into pajamas. We had planned to do our Team Whozit thing, but again, Donna was too tired and Whozit was too quiet. Instead, we each climbed into bed and talked, the way we had often done during the school year.

"Donna, did you tell your aunt that I heard a Voice? Did you tell her about my twin?" I jumped right into it, the way Ria had jumped into giving me her psychic advice.

"No, it felt like it was too private." Donna sat up and looked over at me. "Besides," she grinned mischievously, "I wanted to see if she would pick up on it. Did she?"

I nodded. "Ria didn't say anything about having a twin at first, but she said 'she' was always near me and I was going to need my twin's help very soon. By the way, did you tell Ria my real name?"

"After you swore me to secrecy and told me that you wouldn't help me with Botany if I ever told?" She laughed. "Of course not. It's lots more fun if you don't tell my psychic auntie anything. C'mon, don't tell me she came up with 'Fresno Bakersfield'?" She leaned forward, eyes wide.

"No, but she said my mom gave me both names after my twin died."

"Wow, that's so cool!" After that statement, Donna slumped back against her pillows and closed her eyes. In a few moments, I heard her purring snore.

It was only about eight o'clock, but since I had to get up early to drive to Placerville in the morning, I plumped my pillow and closed my eyes.

The bed was comfortable and the room was air-conditioned cool, but slumber eluded me. Ria's words kept returning and I kept trying to figure out what they meant. Finally, I decided to give her "white light" thing a try—if nothing else, it might help me fall asleep.

Tensing each muscle group and then relaxing it occupied part of my mind. It was almost like counting sheep. I visualized a waterfall of white light pouring into my body, feeling a little silly as I did so, but it was strangely calming. I cast my mind's eye around looking for dark spots and found a surprising number of them. Probably the power of suggestion, but I was still wide awake, so I occupied myself by imagining myself zapping each one of them with the white light, sort of like Wonder Woman using her bracelets. Some of them had to be zapped several times, but eventually, they were all gone and a feeling of peaceful calm filled me. Just as my thoughts began to lose their focus, I heard her.

"*Sister.*"

Relief and joy flooded me. I struggled to stay awake but my world dissolved into sleep, an image of my laughing twin filling my mind. We were back.

Chapter Fifty-Three

I left for Placerville at six the next morning and despite the early hour, everyone in the Middleton house was up—Mr. M drinking coffee and watching the Sports Channel, Mrs. M making me a healthy version of a Sausage McMuffin to go, Donna taking a shower, and Mark off surfing. In my family, no one except Jacob rolled out of bed before eight on a Sunday.

The journey from Donna's house in Huntington Beach to Placerville was almost a straight shot up Interstate 5, the backbone of California, and then east on Highway 50 to Placerville. Mr. M talked me through the rest stops along the way and the truck stop on the Grapevine at Frazier Mountain Park with good gas prices. I still had plenty of snacks and beverages to keep me going, my neck and shoulder pain had disappeared, and best of all, the Voice was back. Her reappearance had filled me with enough energy to fly to Placerville.

Donna appeared as I was thanking Mr. and Mrs. M for their hospitality. Wet-haired, smelling of freesias and wearing a pink sweatshirt over her very noticeable baby bump, she was like a radiant spring flower on a dew-filled morning. We walked outside together and as I hugged her goodbye, I said, "Eat your veggies, get lots of sleep and have fun in Lamaze class. I'll see you when Whozit is born."

She punched me lightly before hugging back, saying "Yes, Mom. How is it again that I'm supposed to have fun in Lamaze class without alcohol?"

Laughing, I gave Whozit a gentle pat and slid into Coachinella's driver's seat. Buoyed by breakfast and the joy of reconnecting with my twin, I was ready to roll.

Coachinella climbed laboriously up the Grapevine, passed by every car on the planet, or so it seemed. A van full of little kids passed me with arms waving out of every window. A battered 1950s pickup passed me, the ancient driver giving me an encouraging thumbs up. It was a bit annoying, but finally Coachinella reached the summit and began the long glide down the Grapevine into the straight arrow that led to Sacramento and the turnoff to Placerville.

The road trip was just what I needed to clear my head and process the past few months. Ria's white light energy clearing and reconnecting with the Voice had made me feel lighter and energized, but I could feel there was still something heavy lurking inside me. I promised myself to do more energy clearing that night—in my own bed, in my own room at Grammie's house.

As Coachinella trundled her way down the long, straight highway, I fingered the new pendant around my neck, my thoughts drifting to the events of the past few days. According to Donna, Aunt Ria was "almost always" accurate in her predictions. So what had Ria meant about needing a reminder to help me remember what to do? It wasn't a straightforward type of prediction, like "an earthquake will occur tomorrow afternoon" or "don't get on that plane: it's going to crash." It was more of a Nostradamus sort of riddle.

I shifted my attention to what lay at the end of my long drive. Grammie, with her straight-forward approach to life and her practical good sense, had always made me feel safe and cared for. In Minden, as much as I loved all of my family, I felt as if I needed to be the strong one—to take care of every-one, even though, to be fair, none of them had ever asked me to take care of them. Being with Grammie was easier—as long as I stayed out of Grammie's Forbidden Zone .

The last time we talked, the day before I left Minden, Grammie said she had something to tell me. In the rush of packing, driving with Ravi, and Donna's shower, I hadn't given it any thought, although I had tried my best to get her to tell me on the phone that night. Grammie had refused to budge.

"It's a face-to-face kind of thing," she said.

Now I thought, could she have a boyfriend? Maybe plan-ning to marry? Grammie having a steady would be great—not that Placerville had many men her age to choose from. Grammie had dated a few different men during the time I had lived with her, but none of them were keepers.

"I'm at that in between stage," Grammie joked. "The ones my age want girls your age. The older ones are looking for a nurse in case they need one in a few years."

So, maybe a boyfriend. As the miles to Placerville decreased, my curiosity and excitement increased. By the time I reached Stockton, I had listened to Ravi's CD three times and I had Grammie's wedding all planned out.

Chapter Fifty-Four

Clare only had time to drop her suitcase on the bed in her old bedroom before Grammie set her down for "the talk." She'd expected an announcement, the flaunting of a diamond on Grammie's ring finger. Never had she expected a new aunt.

"It was the sixties," Grammie said, as if that explained everything. She shrugged, sort of devil-may-care. She and Clare were sitting at the kitchen table, glasses of ice tea in front of them.

"What does that mean? Were you, like, a hippie?" Clare could not imagine Grammie barefoot with flowers in her long hair, dancing on the green, high on acid or life or both. And pregnant.

"Oh, heck no!" Grammie looked both exasperated and wistful. "I was just stupid. My family was very conservative. I wore my hair in a flip and went to church and Bible study. Until I met Jimmy Borner in eleventh grade, the most wicked thing I'd ever done was to roll the waistband of my skirt up after I left the house so I could show my knees."

Clare grinned, not quite understanding the situation, but laughing at her grandmother's idea of evil behavior.

"Jimmy had a mop of black hair that he wore like the Beatles and if you squinted, he looked a little like George Harrison." Her grandmother sat back in her chair, squinting as if she could see Jimmy/George in front of the kitchen stove.

Clare had heard of the Beatles, like who hadn't, but George Harrison was her seventh grade science teacher's name. And he had been bald. She suspected that he had never been cute.

"He sat in front of me in World History." Grammie said, " and even though I liked history, our teacher was so incredibly boring that we spent the entire period passing notes and giggling over Mr. Faugstead's ability to lecture for an hour without ever moving his lips." She smiled and shook her head.

"My parents wouldn't allow me to date until I was a senior, so Jimmy and I met up at football games, homecoming float building parties, movies during Christmas break. One thing led to another, the way it always does, and by April, I was three months pregnant. My mother didn't find out for another month. By then, Jimmy and his family had moved to Ohio and I'd realized he didn't look that much like George Harrison anyway. I was scared, but not heartbroken."

"What did your parents say?" Clare had no memory of her great-grandparents who had died years before, within two years of each other.

"My dad never knew. My mother worked for a doctor, a general practitioner, and he knew of a couple who were desperate to adopt. So, she helped me hide the pregnancy until school was out in June and then she and I went on a road trip to visit my Aunt Julia in Santa Rosa. Mom went home after a week and told everyone that I was spending the summer helping Aunt Julia. Instead, I went to a maternity home where I lived until my baby was born on October 18, 1963. By the end of that month, I was back in school for my senior year."

"So only you and your mom knew?"

"And the doctor and the couple who adopted Terry."

Terry, the first of Grammie's two, no, three daughters. Grammie said Terry had called her, out of the blue, two weeks earlier. She had gotten Grammie's name from her birth records and looked her up in the Placerville phone book. Since Grammie had gone back to her maiden name after her husband died, Terry had found her, and now she wanted to meet her birth mother in person.

"What did you tell her?" Clare, flabbergasted at Grammie's announcement, fired questions out like bullets. "Do Miggie and Nita know about her? Are you going to meet her? How do you feel about it?"

"I never told them." Her grandmother looked sad. "I never, ever thought it would come up." Her voice trembled as she admitted, "I don't know what to do. I want to meet her, to know who she is, but what about Marjorie and Juanita? How do I tell them? What if they're mad at me for not telling them or think badly of me for having a baby out of wedlock? What if they hate me?" Her voice was growing more and more distressed sounding with each word. Clare had never seen her grandmother so agitated and worried.

"Grammie," Clare made her voice low and soothing as she touched her grandmother's arm. "You told me and I don't hate you. It is weird, thinking about having another aunt, but I'm OK with it. I'm sure that Miggie and Nita will be too, even if it takes them a while to get used to it."

Her grandmother gave her a tremulous smile. "When you

told me about Donna, it all washed over me again and then . . . Terry called."

Clare tried to wrap her head around a whole new way of looking at her family—and her grandmother. Would Terry really become another aunt? Show up at Christmas and family events? Despite her reassurances to Grammie, Clare wondered whether Miggie and Nita would welcome an older sister or snub her. Secrets. Even Grammie had them. Secrets made Clare feel sticky, trapped. She hated them. But it seemed that everyone had at least one, including herself.

And babies—they were everywhere in her life. Wanted babies, unplanned for babies, babies with birth issues, babies who needed help, babies who got stuck, a grandmother with baby calming gifts, a grandmother with a secret baby, a twin baby. Secrets and babies.

Chapter Fifty-Five

The days flew by in a whirl of shopping, lunches with friends and holding Grammie's hand as she called first Terry and then Miggie and Nita. A meeting was set up at the house on Saturday for all of them to get together. Clare thought maybe her grandmother should meet Terry alone, first, but her normally pragmatic grandmother was too fluttery and distracted.

Donna called on the Friday before the big meeting. Her voice was high and quavery as she said, "Whozit is coming feet first and I might have to have a Caesarean! Dr. Gupta said she's just sitting there, like Buddha. Babies are supposed to come out head first. If they come out feet first or butt first, it could cause problems with the birth. The cord could get caught on their arm or leg or even around their neck." Her words were coming faster and faster. "They used to do things to get the baby turned around during the birth, but they don't do that anymore because it's problematic, because of the cord, so if she doesn't move, I'll have to have a C-Section or she could die."

The last few words were wailed out, so they were difficult to understand, but once I processed Donna's wail, I understood her anxiety. When we were reading *What to Expect When You're Expecting*, the chapter on Caesarean birth and labor complications scared us both sleepless.

Before I could say anything, Donna's frightened, warp-speed voice continued, "So I've got these exercises to do to encourage her to move and they scheduled me for an ECV which is short for I-don't-know-what, next Wednesday. My doctor is going to try to flip Whozit by pushing on my belly. If that doesn't work, then I have the exercises and sometimes acupuncture works, so . . ."

"Wow, it sounds like you have a bunch of options," I broke in, trying to apply some brakes to this situation. After a summer of practice with Miggie, Grammie, Barty, and Ravi, I automatically took a breath and spoke calmly as I said, "I'm sure at least one of them will work, plus maybe you can talk to Whozit and get her to move—you've gotten really good at communicating with her. You're not due until September 21 —so you have almost six weeks for Buddha Baby to get with the program."

I heard a sigh over the phone, not quite relief, but the kind of sigh that meant Donna had taken a breath and let it out, along with some of her fear. Then, "Yeah, you're right. Plenty of time. Even my mom said not to worry because lots of babies take their time to get into the birth position. And you know my mom worries about everything."

We laughed and then Donna was calmer. We joked a little about Buddha Baby and Donna promised to let me know when Buddha found enlightenment and moved. I could tell that Donna was starting to think and make plans—always a better place for her to be than in full panic mode.

When I got off the phone, I checked in with myself. The heaviness around my heart had remained despite my nightly energy clearing. Was this where it was coming from? And what about Ria telling me that I would need help remembering what to do? Do what?

Chapter Fifty-Six

I tried not to stare at my new aunt. Seated in my favorite armchair in Grammie's living room, Terry appeared calm and composed, but her fingers, clutched in her lap, were white with tension. She had medium-length dark hair done in a becoming style, blue eyes exactly like Grammie's, and she wore a periwinkle blue sleeveless dress. When she'd come inside the house, I could see that she was taller than Grammie and built leaner, more like Miggie. She'd told us that she was married, with a daughter in college and a son who worked in the tech industry. Her husband was a civil engineer and they all lived in the San Francisco Bay Area, except the daughter who was attending Southern Methodist University in Texas. I had more cousins!

Grammie introduced Aunt Nita, Miggie, seven-year old Taylor and me. We gave Terry thumbnail sketches of who we were and where we lived. Aunt Nita's speech was particularly short and curt, as in "Juanita Brewster, Placerville"—like someone you'd meet at a convention who has no intention of networking with you.

I'd thought Aunt Nita would be welcoming and Miggie would be . . . Miggie, but now, in the living room, Nita stood in a corner clutching Taylor like a life preserver. And Miggie was smiling after hugging her new-found sister. It was a puzzlement.

Terry kept casting anxious glances over at Nita as if expecting to be bitten. Nita hovered in her corner while Miggie and I sat silently on the couch. And no one spoke. I think we were all waiting for Grammie, but she had escaped to the kitchen after the introductions. She brought out food and put it on the table. Then, she took some of it back to the kitchen. She brought out a pitcher of ice tea and then went back into the kitchen for sugar, back for lemons, back for spoons, back for glasses. Still, no one spoke. At last, I left my mother and aunts—thinking of aunt as a plural felt very weird —and cornered Grammie in the kitchen.

"It's pretty quiet out there, Grammie" I spoke to her back as she fussed over a plate of deviled eggs. "Are you all right?"

She turned toward me, put her hands over her face and then took them down. "Juanita hates her, I can tell. Marjorie seems easier with her, but who knows? What do you think?" she pleaded.

"I think Aunt Nita just isn't used to the idea of having another sister yet." I shrugged. "Miggie is enough of a handful for her. Terry seems nice to me. What do you think of her?"

Grammie had talked to Terry on the phone a few times during the week since I'd arrived. Every time she got off the phone she seemed to glow. But now, worried about Nita and Miggie, she wailed, "Oh, I don't know what I think. This is just so . . . unexpected."

That was an understatement. I picked up the plate of deviled eggs and gave Grammie a one-armed hug. Together, we went into the dining area, Grammie calling out in her cheeriest voice, "OK! Who's hungry?"

It appeared that no one was except Taylor who grabbed two deviled eggs and popped them into her mouth at the same time. Who knows why?

Nita and Grammie went into action to rescue Taylor from choking to death, a chore that involved a lot of truly gross maneuvers. A grim-faced, silent Nita then took her tearful, egg-splattered daughter home, leaving the rest of us standing awkwardly around the kitchen table.

Dan picked Miggie up an hour later. In that time, we had managed to exchange pleasantries about Placerville weather (super-hot), the weather in Minden (also super-hot), and the weather in the Bay Area, which was overcast and not so hot. No one had touched the deviled eggs after Taylor's episode and, privately, I decided to never eat another one again. Dan and Jacob were introduced to Terry who told Jacob that her daughter was in college, just like his big sister. Jacob, between alternating bites of a deviled egg and a chocolate cupcake, informed Terry that he didn't care for girls. On that note, Dan, Miggie and Jacob departed for Minden after reminding me that they would see me in Reno on September 11, the day before my nineteenth birthday.

Terry stayed a few minutes more and told me she was looking forward to introducing me to my cousins, especially since her daughter, Lisa, was almost the same age as me. I told her I was looking forward to meeting them and left the room so Terry and Grammie could have some time together.

As I was leaving the room, Grammie said to Terry, "If I can just locate my address book, I can write down your address." She was forever misplacing the old leather book since she carried it all over the house. In addition to addresses, she stuck her shopping lists and notes about anything and everything between the pages.

I heard Terry say, "Oh, it's on the little table in the hall."

There was a silence. Terry had only been in the living room and the kitchen—how would she know there was anything on the table in the hallway? I really wanted to turn around and see Grammie's face, but I kept walking, down the hallway, right past the little table with the address book lying on it.

It was strange, thinking of having cousins a little older than myself. I had always been the oldest, the one in charge. I wondered too, if Terry or my cousins had inherited any of our family's secret abilities.

Chapter Fifty-Seven

Classes started at UNR. I was busy with labs, homework, and my new roommate, a gum-chewing Goth princess. I was sharing a room in a residence hall again because Donna and I had planned to get a campus apartment together, but she was having a baby instead.

The Goth princess was nicer than she looked. She had a boyfriend who lived off campus and since she spent most of her time with him, I usually had our room to myself. I missed the close camaraderie I'd instantly had with Donna. Next semester, I promised myself, I would move into a co-op.

Grammie and Aunt Nita were talking to each other again. After two weeks of the silent treatment from Nita, Grammie had been in despair until Uncle Jeff, Nita's husband, suggested to Nita that maybe Terry's wish to know her birth mother was like that of Nita's own long-held wish to know her dad, the dad she shared with Miggie, but who had died so early in their lives that neither remembered him. So, now Nita and Grammie and Miggie were talking—about Terry and, finally, about Miggie and Nita's father, a subject

Grammie had long avoided. It felt as if things were going to be all right. Maybe even better than all right.

Things weren't going so well with Donna. We talked every Thursday night as that was my short day and she was free of Lamaze class, breast feeding class, parenting class and whatever other class her mom had signed her up for. Whozit/Buddha hadn't budged despite Donna's doctor performing an External Cephalic Version to try to turn the baby, a procedure that Donna found very painful. She'd also had acupuncture and was doing daily exercises and positions to encourage Buddha to move. Each time we talked, Donna sounded more panicked. It didn't help that she had been reading everything she could find on breech births and possible labor complications and that she felt she'd lost her ability to communicate with her baby. I spent most of our conversations trying to reassure her and calm her down. Then I had to calm myself down. Whozit/Buddha's due date, on or about September 21, couldn't come too soon.

Being back in class felt good, exciting, but the syllabus for each class was daunting—filled with quizzes and tests, papers and project deadlines. Getting used to juggling classes and homework and applying for a part-time job was challenging. Sometimes, in class or on the way to class, my heart would race and I couldn't catch my breath. I felt trapped. The student health clinic doctor described this as a panic attack and told me that I was probably feeling overwhelmed. I remembered feeling overwhelmed at the beginning of my freshman year, but this was different. This felt as if I was confined in some way.

During the days I spent with Grammie, I had started a nightly practice to clear my energy using Ria's method, and to try to talk to my twin. Could I connect with her without having a baby involved? With the worry about Donna and the overwhelm from school, it felt as if doing this now was imperative. I tried to do my Twin Connection Practice, TCP, as I had been referring to it in my mind, at night before I went to sleep, but usually all I did was fall asleep. I'd found a few quiet corners on campus where I could tune in and drop out between classes. Sometimes I could feel my twin's quiet presence, like an echo. Other times, I felt nothing but the calm relaxation that this practice seemed to give me. Once when, I heard her call me *"Sister,"* the feeling of wholeness and peace that filled me carried me through a sociology quiz and an interview for a position at the student bookstore. I got both the job and twenty-three out of twenty-five on the quiz.

Buoyed by my TCP success, I had tried to lead Donna through her own clearing exercise, but it was hard for her to get those pervasive thoughts about Buddha Baby out of her head enough to focus. The clearing exercises helped me get to sleep, but twice, I awoke with nightmares. Each time it was like my panic attacks but with added special effects. Not only did I struggle for breath and feel my heart race, but it was dark. I could see nothing and the trapped feeling now included a sense of walls closing in around me and the feeling of something encircling my neck, tightening, then loosening, then tightening again. Every time it tightened, it felt like the blood in my veins stopped moving. I couldn't seem to catch my breath. I woke up sweating and panicked. This was way beyond what I had experienced in my freshman year.

One Friday night in early September, after I'd been back at school for three weeks, our resident assistant knocked on the door and told me I had a phone call. My stomach took a plunge down into my shoes.

"Clare," Donna's voice whisper-shrieked, "The baby won't move into position and Dr. Gupta scheduled a C-section for me on September 18th." I could hear her breathing, trying to calm herself down. In a low voice, scarier to me than her whisper-shriek, she finished with, "I'm OK with the C-section, but I can't feel her move anymore. The doctor says everything is fine, but I know something is wrong. I'm so scared."

She rushed ahead with, "Can you come, Clare? Please, please can you come now? My mom says she will buy a ticket for you on Southwest. Please, I need you."

The selfish part of me reminded me that my family was coming for my birthday on Sunday and that I was starting my part-time job at the bookstore the day after—my actual birthday. The logical part of me wondered what I could do to help. It made more sense for me to be there in nine days for the birth if I was going to have to take any time off work. And how long would she want me to stay? Still, I couldn't resist the desperation in Donna's voice. "Do you need me to come tonight?"

"Mom will get you the ticket tonight if you can be on the first flight tomorrow. Can you?" The relief in her voice was palpable.

After hanging up, I called Miggie and told her about Donna. "I don't know what I can do to help," I said, "but I really feel I need to be there. Are you OK with this?"

Miggie's voice was reassuring. "No problem—we can come next weekend and by then you'll have even more to celebrate. Donna will be OK," she said, confidence lacing her words, "and whatever you do, it will be what she needs."

Miggie didn't usually make predictions, but I hoped her Spidey-senses were on target this time.

The doctor had said things were fine. If Donna was willing to wait overnight, then maybe it wasn't that serious. Miggie had said that things would be OK. Despite my rationalization, I went to bed with my stomach in a knot, the shadow on my heart finally having a focus—Whozit.

I did my clearing exercises and reached out for Whozit. For a few moments, I sensed nothing—not a presence, not hunger or discomfort—nothing. The panic started to rise in me as I remembered Donna saying that she hadn't felt Whozit move.

Then, it was as if my nightmare returned. I wasn't Clare in my dorm room. I was someone else in some dark place. I tried to call out for help but no sound emerged. No one came. I was alone, unable to breathe, unable to move. Just when I felt as if I were going to die, I heard the Voice call me.

"Sister."

I woke up, covered in sweat, my chest vibrating with the pounding of my heart. I reached for the bedside light and turned it on with a shaking hand, revealing the dorm room with its bulletin board, my roommate's sleeping form barely visible under her black sheets, my desk with the laptop on it, pictures of my smiling family above it on the wall. Safe. Familiar.

In my psychology class, we had talked about dreams. The professor had said that you could go back into a nightmare after you woke up and try to re-dream it, changing the parameters and the outcome. I'd tried it with the previous nightmares, but it hadn't worked. This time, all I wanted to do was to walk out of that enclosed room and into a bigger space. Much bigger. Somewhere where I could breathe.

I slid out of bed and threw on my robe as quietly as I could, pulled my flashlight out of the box under my bed and turned off the bedside lamp. Out in the hallway the night lights were on and I padded down to our study room.

I expected the room to be dark, but someone had turned on a few lamps. A girl I didn't know was sitting at one of the round tables, papers spread out in front of her. She looked up when I came in and nodded at me when I settled into one of the armchairs. I was glad she was there—at least I wasn't alone. She went back to her papers and I sat in my chair and breathed. Slowly, my heart began to resume its usual steady beat. I took deep breaths filling my lungs, over and over—just to make sure I could.

I replayed the dream, shying away from the terror that had panicked me, and focusing on what had happened. Somehow, through the fear, I had heard my sister's voice—a clarion call in the dark—and I had come out of the nightmare. Even as I sat in the armchair, I continued to feel the comfort of her presence, as if she were watching over me.

A touch on my shoulder startled me. The girl from the table was standing next to me, a commiserating smile on her face. "It's almost five-thirty. I thought you'd want to go back to your room before the day starts and the dorm chaos begins."

Her words shocked me into wakefulness. I had come into the study room at one o'clock and somehow, despite my anxiety, I had managed to doze off.

"Thanks." Together, the girl and I turned off the lamps and then went our separate ways, gliding through the silent night to the waiting day, her with her papers and me with my guardian twin.

Chapter Fifty-Eight

Back in my dorm room, I packed like the world's most silent whirlwind, throwing things into my backpack in the feeble bit of light coming from the breaking dawn through our blinds. My Goth roomie snuffled in her sleep but didn't wake. I left a note for her on the nightstand.

By the time I boarded the Southwest flight to John Wayne Airport in Orange County, I was jacked up on coffee (which I still disliked), and anxiety. A panic attack set in as I searched for a seat, unease tightening my stomach and tensing my muscles. I was out of breath, couldn't seem to catch it. As I put my bag in the overhead bin and slid into an open middle seat, I was fighting for breath and my heart was racing. I tried to calm myself by taking slow, deep breaths, relaxing my clenched muscles, but it didn't seem to be working. An older lady filled the window seat on my left, a man in a business suit overflowed the aisle seat on my right. As the plane began to taxi down the runway, the feeling of being trapped and squeezed overwhelmed me.

I had flown many times before, jetting my way from Sacramento to Provo when my family lived in Utah. I had never been afraid of flying. I even liked the rear-facing seats up in the front of the plane, loved the swoopy feeling of the takeoff. This panicky feeling wasn't my usual response to flight. This was like my nightmares and I knew it had something to do with Whozit.

Suddenly, I could breathe again. Barriers still pinned me in place—the businessman with his beefy arms and torso and the elbows of the woman in the window seat, industriously crocheting—but at least I could breathe. I began to relax. Whatever was happening to Whozit seemed to come and go. I didn't know when the next cycle would come, but I knew I needed to get to her quickly.

The plane touched down on the runway and I was already standing despite the admonishment of the flight attendant. I slipped past, under, and around people, getting off the plane and out into the terminal as fast as I could. As soon as I stepped out of the terminal building and onto the walkway crowded with people going in and coming out, I spotted Donna's father waiting for me in the family Suburban.

"I sure appreciate you coming, Clare," Mr. M. said as he followed the line of cars out of the airport. "Donna has been pretty worked up." At my sound of commiseration, he said, "She's trying to put a good face on it, but I can tell she's upset. Not good for her. Not good for the baby either, probably."

I didn't know what to say. Mr. M's concern deepened my own. "Thank you for coming to pick me up," I finally said. I didn't know what he knew about Whozit or the Voice, or whether he put any faith in baby channelers, but I knew he was in Donna's corner. I felt welcomed and . . . needed. And scared. It felt as if they were all depending on me for something and I still didn't know what I could do.

When we got to the Middleton home, Donna came outside, moving slowly, as if she were afraid to step on something. Her usual exuberant hug felt more like the grasp of a drowning person. There were dark circles under her eyes, mirroring my own. Guess neither of us had been sleeping.

Clutching one another, we walked inside where Mrs. M hugged me hard and asked if I was hungry. The now familiar feeling of something tightening around my neck pushed my heart into overdrive. I didn't want to eat—I wanted to catch my breath. For a moment, I felt as if I would black out and then, the loosening again. I could breathe.

Before Donna pulled me down the hallway to her room, Mrs. M. took me aside to whisper in my ear. "My sister called a few minutes ago. She said you have something to do and it will take two of you to do it."

As if I weren't already panicking about Whozit and what might be expected of me, now I had Ria's cryptic words to decipher.

"She also said not to worry because you will figure it out." Mrs. M. patted my shoulder. My mouth gave a smile of reassurance as if I knew what she was talking about but my heart picked up speed.

In Donna's room, we both sat on her bed. Through sobs that she tried to control, Donna told me of her fears: that she couldn't feel the baby anymore, that she couldn't communicate with her; that Whozit might be dead; that she might die too. I tried to do more listening than talking—easy because I had some of the same fears—but after Donna's third repetition of her dread, I said, "What can I do to help?"

Donna stopped. Then, looking at me with tear-filled eyes,

she said, "Talk to her—see if she's OK. If she's still alive." She took my hand and squeezed it tightly.

A shiver ran down my spine as if someone had scraped a fingernail on a chalkboard. This talk of death—Whozit's, Donna's—made everything real. Up until the panic attacks and nightmares, our Whozit team had been fun. We had been exploring a new experience together with my twin thrown in as an added bonus. But now, I felt the darkness of reality step up. This wasn't my experience—it was all on Donna. And at the end there would be a real baby, a small human who would come into the light. Or not.

My own doubts took over: There was no magic, no psychic bond. There was just a frightened girl and her baby. I couldn't help her through this, couldn't change the outcome, whatever it might be. I started to pull away, but Donna clutched me tighter, putting her other hand on my arm as if to hold me in place.

Then I heard the voice of my twin. *"Stay. Help."* I felt her reach for me. Usually, I had been the one with the need to contact her, but now, something touched me inside, pulling me back toward Donna, pulling me inside, into black, pulsating warmth. Again, I felt the constriction around my throat and panic surged up in me. But it wasn't my panic or Donna's.

Whozit was trapped. The constriction I had been feeling off and on for days was the umbilical cord, wrapped around her neck. There was little room in her warm dark world in which to move. If something wasn't done right now, Whozit could die.

Mrs. M came into the room and sat down in a chair by the side of the bed. Her face was drawn with worry. I knew I should tell Mrs. M to call for an ambulance, even at the risk of terrifying Donna. But I didn't. Because a wave of peace washed over me and my twin's voice said, *"Now. Together."*

So instead of doing what logic told me I should have done, I smiled at Donna reassuringly and said, "OK, let's see what Whozit has to say."

Chapter Fifty-Nine

I was Clare; I was Whozit. As I focused all my attention on Whozit, willing her to move, we flowed between our two selves: Clare gently giving Whozit mental pushes; Whozit, trapped in an enclosure, no longer a joyful swimmer. The pushes made me anxious because I could not move, the cord around my neck tightening if I tried.

I felt Whozit's resistance—a tensing of her muscles—and stopped pushing. I began to send her calming thoughts, feelings of floating, of flying, of warm water pouring over her tight muscles, relaxing them with its warmth.

As Whozit, I relaxed, enjoying the feelings. The walls of my enclosure expanded slightly and warm liquid seeped through the space. Sliding, slippery, I remembered the joy of movement. The cord loosened.

"Follow, follow," the Voice called to us.

We, Clare/Whozit, yearned toward the Voice, wanted to follow, to be where she was. We wiggled. More liquid flowed around me. Slippery, heaviness gone, rolling. Let go. Follow. Joy to move again.

Tentative movement. There seemed to be less resistance, the cord lifting as we rolled. I sent another gentle mental push with more feelings of floating, flying. I heard Donna, lying next to me on the bed, exclaim something about seeing her belly move, but I had no time for her. All my focus was inside.

"Follow, follow."

My twin called, guided. I pushed; she encouraged and enticed. The little Whozit/Buddha boulder softened, began slowly, slowly to move. The dropping of a no longer bent knee, a push off with a foot. A delicious sense of release.

Then Whozit stopped. As much as she wanted to follow the Voice, Whozit was afraid. She began to tighten up again. I rocked back and forth on the bed, jostling Donna as I tried to send Whozit the sensation of movement, but she balked. With her feet inching up and her head and torso inching downward, she stopped. Tightened again. The cord tautened. Fear-stiffened muscles locked in place.

A wave of warmth and love suddenly washed through me. Muscles relaxed into the enveloping feeling of safety. The feeling receded a bit and I followed it, wanting to stay with it forever. The constriction around Whozit's neck loosened again, lifting.

"Come."

My twin stayed just below Whozit, pulling us down toward her with a blanket of warmth and safety. We moved again, just the slightest bit. Another wave of love washed over us, undercutting the resistance, unwinding the cord another twist.

Gently, gently I pushed; my twin pulled with love and enticement. An image of the Yin and Yang pendant flashed into my mind. My twin and I were like two fishes swimming in a circle with Whozit lovingly cradled between us. Not opposites, but working together from different perspectives.

I felt the slight recession of my twin's blanket of love, safety and warmth and then I pushed when Whozit reached out for her. I filled her movement with joy and, encouraged, Whozit reached further, inching both up and down in that small space, rolling her body. I put every feeling of joy and fun I could dredge up from every corner of my being into her movements, working in concert with my sister.

The cord floated free, spooling away from Whozit as the two of us worked to keep her moving. When she was almost head down and feet up, almost there, she stopped, exhausted.

Dripping with sweat, exhausted beyond anything I'd ever known, I managed to send Whozit a feeling of great satisfaction. Enough for today. I felt a weak sense of approval from my twin. She must have been exhausted too. Before I closed my weary eyes, I sent my sister an image of the pendant. Yin and Yang, two fishes swimming in a circle of love.

Chapter Sixty

Donna peered over at me, a look of wonder and joy on her face. "I felt her, Clare! I felt her move. She's alive!"

I nodded, barely able to keep my head up. "She's almost there. Later, I think we'll be able to help her move the rest of the way. She's too tired now."

On the other side of Donna's bed, Mrs. M stood up from her chair, letting go of Donna's other hand. The look on her face was one of comprehension, as if something she had wondered about was now confirmed. "You need something to eat before you sleep," she said, adding, "Ria always does."

She left the room quickly. Donna whispered, "Are you OK? You were rolling around on the bed with your eyes closed. It was like you were in a trance or something. Did you feel her? Did you hear the Voice?" The panic was gone from her voice. "Did you make her move? Because I felt her, I felt her move!"

Too many questions. I just nodded. Mrs. M came back into the bedroom with a plate and a glass. She put them on the nightstand near me and reached down a hand to help me sit up. "Eat everything you can and then you can have a nice, long sleep."

When Donna started to say something, her mother interrupted. "Don't keep her awake with talking. She worked hard for you today." She squeezed my shoulder and said, "Thank you," before she left the room again.

Donna looked a bit puzzled, but I followed directions, washing down most of a turkey sandwich and a Kitchen Sink cookie with milk before sleep overtook me.

Chapter Sixty-One

Sunlight streaming through Donna's pink- and- white checked curtains woke me in late afternoon. In the light, I realized how crowded the room seemed—a white crib, a white changing table and a white wicker chair with pink cushions had been added to the bedroom. The soccer trophies had been replaced with toys, baby lotion and baby powder. Donna's bed had been tidied and except for furniture and me, the room was empty.

I took a shower in Donna's bathroom and changed into the clothes I had brought. When I walked into the kitchen, Donna and her mom were talking, perched on barstools around the kitchen island. They looked up as I came in, both of their faces mirroring to me the relief and joy I felt. Donna was bright-eyed and seemed refreshed, looking more like the Donna I knew instead of the frightened person who had clutched me only this morning.

"You look good," I said. "How are you feeling?"

Mrs. M smiled at me as she got up from the barstool and

gave my shoulder an affectionate squeeze on her way to the refrigerator.

"I feel great! I took a nap while you slept, "said Donna. "I think Whozit took a snooze too and now she's full of energy. Look!"

Through the thin material of her maternity T-shirt, I could see a protrusion—it looked like a foot. And it was toward the top of her baby bump, just where it should be. If that's what it was, anyway.

"I think Whozit still has a little way to go before she is in the right position," I cautioned. "Maybe we should do one more session tonight to make sure. If you're OK with that?" I included Mrs. M, who was rinsing lettuce at the sink in my questioning look. She looked at Donna.

Donna said, "Whatever you think, Clare. I'm up for it. I still can't believe that you got her to move." She caressed the foot, or whatever it was, with gentle fingers.

"How about after dinner?" Mrs. M asked, her eyes checking with me. I was starving and as I nodded an enthusiastic "yes," I realized that Team Whozit now included Mrs. M and my twin, although both of them had been members of the team all along. It felt so good to be part of this.

While Donna and I were putting the dishes in the dishwasher after dinner, Ria showed up, wafting into the kitchen wearing her usual conglomeration of pendants and rings and a layering of floaty tunics over her leggings. Wrapping her arms around me, she gave me a jasmine-scented hug. Donna got the second hug. Mrs. M got the third hug, but Mr. M escaped into the family room and his television.

"Am I too late?" Ria's expectant look took in all three of us.

Mrs. M. looked apologetically at Donna and I who were wearing the same puzzled expression. "I told Ria about moving the baby and that Clare wasn't quite done, yet. Ria wanted to be part of it."

Ria smiled at us and nodded, her eyes bright. She looked as if she were getting on one of the E-rides at Disneyland.

Donna and Mrs. M. looked at me. I shrugged. "Might as well."

Donna lay down on her bed and the three of us sat around it. Closing my eyes, I practiced Ria's clearing exercise, bringing in white light and filling myself with it, reaching out for my twin. This time, I felt a strong boost of energy, as if something were bolstering me. I caught a flash of Ria in my mind, a halo of white light surrounding her.

My twin was there almost immediately, guiding me into Whozit's warm, dark world. Whozit was wiggling in her cramped environment as if eager to get started. This time, my mental pushes and my twin's guidance were barely needed as Whozit seemed to know exactly what to do. She glided into birth position with tiny jellyfish movements and then, wrapped in our love and approval, she promptly fell asleep.

I got the distinct impression from Whozit before she fell asleep that she could have finished this herself, but she had waited for us. That was kind of her.

A wave of well-being from my twin wafted through me. I sent her a smile, hoping she would understand.

When I opened my eyes, with the smile still on my face, Donna, her mom and Ria were all staring at me. The whole thing had taken only ten minutes.

I couldn't stop smiling. "I think she's done."

Donna said, "I felt her move."

Mrs. M. said, "I saw her move."

Ria leaned across Donna and touched my pendant. "You did good, both of you," she whispered in my ear.

I smiled at her. That bolstering energy—looked like Team Whozit had another member. Maybe that saying about taking a village to raise a child is true. It sure was taking a village to get her ready to be born.

Chapter Sixty-Two

Sunday morning, I walked into the Middleton kitchen to see a cloud of helium-filled ladybug balloons crowding the dining area. Donna catapulted out of the middle of the cloud, shrieking, "Happy birthday!"

Mrs. M. appeared, wrapped in an apron. "We felt bad that you missed your birthday visit with your family to help Donna and the baby, so we're making you an early birthday brunch!"

My birthday was the next day, September 12, which was also the first day of my new job. Today's afternoon flight would get me home just in time to finish homework. Classes and an afternoon moving books at the bookstore weren't my idea of a fun birthday, but a birthday brunch sounded delightful.

Ria arrived, bearing champagne and orange juice. After a huge breakfast with quiche, fruit, blueberry muffins and sausage, Mr. M handed me a small rectangular box and said, "Happy birthday from all of us."

Inside the box was a cell phone. Mr. M told me that he

had added me to their family phone plan. "So Donna can call you every time the baby cries," he joked. "And so you can call for help if you need it on the road," he added more seriously.

No one in my family had a cell phone. I was overwhelmed and tried to give it back, but Ria shook her head and said, "You're going to need it." At the horror-stricken looks on all our faces, she said, laughing, "No, no, not for a catastrophe, just for being a young adult."

The cell phone rang in my hand. After Donna showed me how to answer it, Miggie's voice filled my ear. "Happy early birthday, Fresno Bakersfield Clare Elizabeth Ingersoll. I love you."

It was like magic to hear her on the cell, but Miggie explained that Mr. and Mrs. M had called earlier to ask permission to give me a phone and add me to their plan.

"Amy said you were amazing. She is so grateful," Miggie said.

Amy? Mrs. M had a first name, apparently. Miggie continued, "I am so proud of you, Clare. You have a wonderful gift and I hope you keep using it."

Tomorrow, I would be nineteen, the same age as Miggie had been when I was born. She'd been through so much in those years, and now, it felt as if we were both starting new chapters—Miggie shedding her shame and anger, and me looking toward whatever might come next.

In the background, I could hear Jacob and Barty clamoring for their turn to wish happy birthday, but it was my mother's words that stayed in my mind throughout the day.

Chapter Sixty-Three

Monday morning, Donna called my new cell phone to wish me happy birthday. Monday evening she called to tell me that her obstetrician confirmed that Whozit was definitely in the right position. "She said those exercises and acupuncture must have done the trick," Donna chortled. "I didn't tell her that we had some help."

It was a great birthday present, but the real present arrived on Friday morning, September 16, when Whozit made an uncomplicated slide into her beyond-thrilled grandmother's hands. Five days early and without a Caesarean. Donna called me with the news in the evening, giving me the vitals—nineteen inches long, weighing in at six pounds, nine ounces, with all parts present and accounted for—and then a blow by blow account of the process.

In the midst of what the nurse did, what Donna's doctor said and how Donna felt when Whozit was placed on her chest— "It was amazing. She looked right at me and I just fell in love,"—I ventured a question.

"Uh, does she look like Derrick?"

"Well, it's hard to tell just yet, but her eyes have the same shape and . . . oh, you mean her coloring. Yes, she's Derrick's." This was said in a resigned sort of voice, as if she'd been hoping for a different result, but had accepted the inevitable outcome.

"Did you ever have that talk with your mom and dad?"

"Not, exactly. But I told Aunt Ria and I think she might have said something, because neither my mom nor my dad seemed surprised at her coloring."

A huge weight fell from my shoulders that everything had turned out well, even the big reveal that Whozit was bi-racial. For me, the experience was over; for Donna and Whozit, it was just beginning.

I had been showered with approval and praise from everyone, but even though my part in Whozit's birth was done, it felt like there was unfinished business—mostly in my head. Miggie's words about using my "gift" kept coming back to me. Was this something I could do, should do? Did I even want to? Twice now, once with Jacob and Miggie, and once with Donna and Whozit, I'd felt panic and pain. I'd even felt Barty's fear so long ago. How could I keep doing this, no matter how much it helped? How would I even go about it? And would my twin be there to help?

Chapter Sixty-Four

The second day on my job, I was in the back room trying to open a box of textbooks newly delivered by UPS. As I looked around for a tool to slit the packing tape, the outside door opened and a shaggy-haired guy walked in.

He looked surprised to see me, but recovered quickly, holding out his hand and saying, "Oh, hey. You must be the new girl."

I ignored his hand for the moment, not knowing who he was or why he was slithering into the backroom of the bookstore. "Who are you?" I countered.

His eyes widened and then he grinned, dimples denting each cheek like butterflies on a pillow. "I can tell you who I'm not."

The grin widened and then he drew his face into a scowl and made peace signs with his fingers. Shaking both his peace signs and his jowls (not that he had any), he said, "I am not a crook."

For a minute, I drew a blank. Disappointment began to

fill his eyes and then I remembered something I'd seen in my high school history class. "Tricky Dick?"

His eyes sparkled.

I rolled my eyes at his impersonation of ancient history and stifled my giggle. "So who are you really and what are you doing here?" I hoped I sounded more authoritative than squeaky.

Again the hand and dimples came out. His blue eyes twinkled at me as he said all in a rush. "I'm Liam Oliver, I work here, and I'm late—hence the back entrance."

I gave his hand a brief shake, feeling both warmth and calluses. And something else—a ripple of excitement down my spine.

After Liam showed me where the box cutter was hanging, we opened the box and carried armfuls of the textbooks out to the storefront.

By the end of the day, I'd found out that he was a geology major in his third year, that he lived with his parents in Sparks, just a few miles from UNR, and that we both liked the mochas at the campus coffee bar. By the end of the week, we were spending work breaks together and meeting up at the library to study and whisper.

Liam insisted on driving me to the airport on Saturday after work—the earliest time I could get away to see my new goddaughter. This time when I boarded the plane, there were no feelings of anxiety—no feeling of being trapped or struggling to breathe. Instead, I enjoyed the snacks on my two – and- a- half hour flight, got a little homework done, and exited the plane with no worries at all. No panic attack.

Backpack in hand, I looked around for Mr. M., who was now Rick to me. My cell phone rang. "Hi Clare, this is Ria. I'm here to pick you up. I'm in the red Mercedes."

Did everyone have my number? I looked around and saw

the Mercedes curbside across the terminal roadway. An elegant, be-ringed hand waved out the window. I hurried across the roadway, dodging a bus and two cars with angrily gesticulating drivers.

"Just put your backpack in the back seat," Ria said. I tried to slide into the white leather upholstery without fully opening the door. I was slender, but still feared that anything sticking out might be forcibly removed by impatiently passing vehicles.

Ria pulled out into traffic as soon as my door closed. It's possible that she relied on her psychic ability instead of actually looking first, as a cacophony of horns and swearing followed us. Certainly she did not use a turn signal. I sank down into my comfortable seat, deliberately refusing to look at the surrounding cars and their angry drivers.

"I twisted Rick's arm to let me pick you up," Ria said, grinning. "It wasn't hard—he is gaga over that baby—can barely tear himself away."

It didn't take psychic ability to know that Ria probably had something to say to me. I hoped it wasn't going to be cryptic. Or scary.

"You and your twin did a great job with moving the baby. The doctor seemed to think that it was the result of those exercises Donna was doing." She turned her head, facing me so that I could see her wink. A horn blared next to us.

"Thanks. And thanks again for the pendant—I think it really did help me focus on what we were doing, working together." I sounded so matter of fact to myself—as if I talked about things in the Forbidden Zone all the time.

Ria nodded and steered the Mercedes across three lanes of traffic to the HOV lane as horns flared into sound all around us. "I hardly ever get to use this lane—usually it's just me in the car."

I could understand that. Driving with Ria once would be enough for most people. She sped up and then applied the brakes, then she sped up again. Then more braking. I found out later that this was Ria's usual method of freeway driving so she didn't go too fast in the fast lane.

"So, Mr. and Mrs., uh . . . Rick and Amy seem to be pretty happy about Whozit?" Donna hadn't said much about their reaction to Whozit being bi-racial. I didn't know how Ria felt about it either.

"Whozit?" Ria swerved into the next lane, slicing ahead of a brown BMW. I heard a horn, long and loud. "Oh, you mean the baby. Being of mixed heritage. Yeah, I took care of that after Donna told me about your vision. She was really worried, so I told Amy."

Another swipe back into the fast lane, not quite clipping the fender of a white van with her bumper. I think the driver might have been too shocked to honk; I was too shocked to breathe.

"Little Whozit, as you call her, is going to be good for them, help them make some realizations and changes." Ria glanced over at me and smiled, "It's going to be all right."

Then she asked a question of her own—the reason for this crazy ride. "Have you given a thought to what you are going to do next?"

Next as in with my life? Next as in if I survived the ride to Donna's house? Before I could ask her to be more specific, Ria said, "I mean, are you going to continue to work with your twin? What will you do together? You're not just going to fold up shop, are you?"

Her barrage of questions was exactly what I had been asking myself for a week. I still didn't have an answer. Without waiting for whatever I might say, Ria continued with, "If you choose, you can have a happy, fulfilling life of service and wholeness *with* your twin. Or you can choose to ignore her and have a mostly happy life with a big hole in it."

Not exactly cryptic, but also not very helpful. Service, wholeness and happiness? What would that mean? It wasn't clear to me, but the thought of ignoring the Voice, of pretending my twin wasn't part of my reality, made me sit up in the seat, my heart twisting with pain.

"Ask her." Ria's words were spoken softly but they were firm. And they made sense to me. If I decided to work with mothers and babies, would my twin work with me? Would she always be there? Would this be something that would cause trouble as Grammie thought, or something that could actually help, like with Donna and Miggie?

As if I needed more proof that Ria could read my thoughts, she said, "It wasn't your fault, you know—that girl in high school." At my startled look, she continued, "The boy was mad when she told him that morning. He told her to deal with it, so she did. He still carries that guilt with him."

So maybe Rhoda hadn't overheard me in the locker room. Still, mixed with the relief was a sharp stab of sorrow in my heart at how alone and desperate Kelly must have felt. Maybe Kirk Tracy carried guilt over his treatment of Kelly, but I had felt what she felt and done nothing about it.

Ria's lurching driving rhythm mirrored the conflict in my heart. Then she said, "If you're worried about over-empathizing and feeling everything that the babies and mothers you work with feel, I can show you how to protect yourself." She paused a few seconds before saying, "There will always be people you can't help, no matter how hard you try, but the ones you *can* help will make everything worth it."

In a switch as fast as her lane changing, Ria began to talk about work she was having done in her yard and Amy's reorganization of the Middleton home after Whozit's homecoming—things to which I didn't need to pay attention. It felt like a deliberate change designed to give me some space. So thought-bound was I that I stopped noticing her predilection for talking with her hands while alternating acceleration and braking. When we pulled up in front of the Middleton home, I was surprised at our safe arrival without a cadre of raging drivers behind us. Gratitude at my survival made me think I might have a purpose after all.

Inside the house, the family was standing around the kitchen island—Rick and Amy Middleton; brand-new uncle, Mark, who wasn't surfing for a change; and Donna, cuddling a pink bundle that looked like a heftier version of the little pink bubblegum cigars that new fathers passed out with *It's a Girl!* printed on the plastic wrapper. She gave me a careful one-armed hug. I pulled my long back-ordered baby gift out of the backpack and set it on the kitchen island in front of Donna before turning my attention to Whozit.

She was wearing a soft pink cap on her head and her tiny hands were tucked inside a pink swaddling blanket. Donna slid the little cap off to show me Whozit's head of soft, reddish-brown baby fuzz. She had pouty lips in a round, honey-colored face. I already knew what she was going to look like in two years, but I hadn't expected her to be so beautiful already. Rick and Amy were beaming as if they had never seen anything so amazing. Mark reached out a tender finger and brushed a piece of pink fuzz off Whozit's tiny face. Another, unperceived, stone rolled away from my heart. Whozit was already loved and accepted.

At the sudden coolness on her scalp, the baby opened her eyes and I peered into dark blue mirrors. Then, my reflection disappeared, replaced by a flash of what looked, and felt, like recognition. It was only a flash and my reflection returned as

Donna said, "Clare, meet your god daughter, Emily Fresno Middleton."

Fresno? I glanced over at Donna's parents. Amy was trying to cover a wince with a smile, but not succeeding very well. Rick was shaking his head, but his grin looked real. Ria gave me an impish smile.

"Are you kidding me? Fresno?"

Donna's grin was a replica of her father's as she said, "You saved us both."

That was an exaggeration, but I'd take it if she just changed that awful middle name.

Donna opened the gaily wrapped baby gift and held up the tiny red Converse high tops inside it. Everyone looked from the little red shoes to my feet encased in my own lucky red Converse. Then they laughed.

Chapter Sixty-Five

"*S*ister."
"What can I call you?"
"*Sister.*"
"No, a name."

I want my twin to have a name, like the real person she is in my life. Quickly I mentally review names I think might work: Elizabeth, Bakersfield, (hope she doesn't pick that one), Fresno (or that one either)—running through every girl's name I can think of until I feel something like a firm hand stop me. An image appears against the black curtain of my mind—a softly glowing light, curving slowly around in circles and arabesques. So graceful, and calming, this moving light. Graceful. Grace. As I think the name, a feeling of recognition and joy envelopes me. Grace, my twin, my sister.

I have the normal life I always wanted—a normal name, mostly normal family, friends, a job and maybe even a boyfriend. But would a life without Grace, without my baby channeling, be normal for me? Do I want everyone else's normal or can I build my own?

For nineteen years I have skimmed along the top of life like a water bug, looking at people and events at a surface level because life at depth can be scary. With Grammie's belief that what I did with babies and what Miggie could do with colors was just fantasy, I'd felt as if "knowing" might unhinge me from the world. So, I'd chosen to change my name, to live with my stable grandmother to fit in, to ignore the part of me that kept me from being "normal."

What if I choose differently now? What if I choose to dive deep and explore the murky depths of the world to bring back the wisdom hidden there? With Grace.

My cell phone buzzes and jitterbugs on my dorm desk. I'd turned off the ringer so that I could concentrate without interruption but had forgotten to turn off the vibration mode.

Needing a break from my deep thoughts, I decide to answer it.

"Hi, honey," Grammie's well-loved voice sings in my ear. "I talked to your mother—she told me all about what happened with Donna and how much you helped her."

Despite the cheeriness in her voice, my shoulders tense up. This is teetering on Grammie's Forbidden Zone. How weird is this that she happened to call just when I am thinking about doing something that she would so disapprove?

"I'd rather tell you this in person. . . ." Fingers of doom trail ice down my back. "But this is too important." Grammie's voice sounds breathy, as if she is talking through tears. "Since my secret about Terry came out and I've been talking to your mother and Nita about Terry and your grandfather, it's like I can finally breathe again. Like there's nothing holding me down, anymore." The joy in her voice gladdens my heart, even while I tense for whatever is coming.

Grammie doesn't disappoint. "You know," she continues,

"I've realized how hard secrets can be to hold, how much they take away from you. And, honey, I'm so sorry for all these years of making you hold the secret about your baby sensing. Instead of letting you tell me what you were experiencing, I put my fingers in my ears and pretended not to hear any of it, but I remember . . ." Her voice becomes tremulous. "I remember when Barty was born and you were staying at the motel in Tahoe with me. You thrashed all night, struggling with the covers and crying out that he was stuck." She takes a breath. "And you knew about Nita's first baby."

I am startled. No one ever mentions the baby Nita had miscarried.

"And when Nita was pregnant with Taylor you didn't say anything, but you knew when Nita needed something to drink, a foot rub, a pillow for her back. And I know—I saw— what you went through with Miggie and Jacob and yet I pretended that it was all just a big coincidence. I made you, and your mother too, hold secrets about who you are and now I know how awful that must have been for you. I'm so sorry."

The tightness in my shoulders releases. My held breath whooshes out of me. Has Miggie told her how her shutdown made both of us feel? That's a conversation I would have liked to have heard.

I listen, feeling my whole soul is at stake as Grammie says, "I didn't want you to have a gift, like your mother. I thought if you didn't talk about it, it would go away. Miggie was hard for me to raise—she was so different from me and she had this thing she could do that I didn't understand. And she never quite fit in, probably because I made things harder than they had to be, trying to make her 'normal.' You see, I knew what it was like not to fit in, to be different in some way that others didn't understand.

"After I had Terry, I went back to high school to finish my

senior year. But, while everyone else was buzzing about Senior Pictures, graduation day, Senior Ball and going steady, I had given birth. My friends seemed so young, so inexperienced compared to me. I didn't fit in with them anymore. And even though no one else knew about me having a baby, it felt like everyone knew—that they could all see how different I was. I stopped hanging out with my friends. I got a job after school. One by one, all my friends faded away and then I felt like an outcast. I decided that being different was bad and being normal like everyone else was how I could live my best life. So, I got married right out of high school to a boy who had a good job, and we had two babies and bought a house. Then my daughter started showing everyone in preschool how she could pick the blue crayons out of the crayon box without looking, my husband committed suicide, and I was a single parent at the age of twenty-five." Grammie's voice shudders. "Nothing was normal. The only way I could find normal again was by squashing out every bit of chaos I found and your mother's color sense was the first to go. I didn't want her to feel different and alone."

I can't speak. Grammie's story is so sad, so much like Miggie's. What must it have been like for her to give up a baby and then to become a single parent whose husband had committed suicide?

I ache for my grandmother, but her voice lilts up as she says, "But in spite of me, Miggie has become the person she wants to be and she uses her gift in her art. I am proud of her. And I am proud of you."

Something begins to bloom within me as I stare at the phone in my hand, amazed at the acceptance in Grammie's voice.

"Maybe you'll find a way to use your gift as your mother has—the way you did with Donna—but whether you use it or not, I know that this is real for you. I love every part of you, even the parts I don't understand."

As her voice fades away, part of my own words return to me. "Thank you, Grammie. I really, really needed to hear that." Her acceptance means so much. I can't say more, not yet, not until the dam within me has a chance to spill over.

She seems to understand as she says, "I don't expect that you and Miggie will forgive me for being so stubborn and rigid, but I hope you will help me to understand. I love you."

"I love you, Grammie." It is all I can manage, but it feels like enough. I hear her hang up, knowing that she is probably going through her own spillage. For myself, it feels like a huge flower of space has opened up inside me, pushing all those shutdown and shutout feelings out of my heart and down my cheeks. I let the tears flow and flow, not bothering to wipe them away until I feel only the space, uncluttered, untainted.

Now, it's my turn to accept. Ria told me I had to ask; Judge Potts told me I would need to be patient and determined. They were talking about two different things, but it feels like they are connected. I will need all the patience and determination I can muster to follow the path my twin opened for me—I can change my major to nursing to learn all I can about how the body works, search for teachers like Ria to help me focus my gift, and invite Grace into my life—but will she always be with me? I don't think I can do this without her. Will she want to remain an adjunct to my life without ever having one of her own?

I send Grace an image of the Yin and Yang pendant with the two fish and a question—*work, together?* Will she understand?

I am answered. Two fish, our two fish, swim into my mind's eye. Side by side in a river of light, they swim—and the river stretches on forever.

A Request

Reviews are the lifeblood of independent authors and publishers. If you liked meeting Fresno/Clare following her on her journey, please leave a review on one of the many sites that review books. And be sure to sign up for the Mumblers Press newsletter at https://mumblerspress.com.

Warmest thanks,
Wendy Schultz

Acknowledgments

Writing and publishing a book is a set of Herculean tasks. Writing is the fun part—everything else is a slog. Thank you to all of the brave and hardy souls who helped me survive the slog—reminding me that writing was supposed to be fun and giving me the tools and encouragement to polish the rough edges (both the book's and my own), and to finish what I started.

To my writing group—Mike Karpa, Melinda Maxwell Smith and Jan Stites, authors all, huge thanks for your nurturing advice, excellent catches and amazing comments. Editors Barbara Siessel and Susie Hara, and sister-in-law and fellow author, Lynn Lok Payne, please receive my thanks for your critiques, advice, and ideas.

Thank you to my terrier, Cali Mae, who sat on my lap while writing, made me laugh, and came to fetch me off the chair when she thought we both needed a break.

Thank you, last of all, to my husband, Bob, who has learned not to ask me questions when I'm in the midst of writing a chapter and who makes the best brisket in the world.

About the Author

Wendy Schultz lives in Oceanside, California with her husband and feisty terrier, Cali Mae. As a former reporter and columnist for California's oldest continuously operating newspaper, *Mountain Democrat*, Schultz earned several California Newspaper Publishers Association first and second place awards for her columns. She is also the author of *In the Pockets of Dreams*. Her goals in life are to successfully hula-hoop, spend time on every beach in San Diego County, and publish many more books.

Also by Wendy Schultz

In The Pocket of Dreams

Home of the Dragonfly (forthcoming)